Lily's Ride

Reviews of the Original

Originally published anonymously, the book's publisher had this to say about the press reviews that follow: "The reception accorded to this anonymous book both by press and public has been so unusual and the impression made by the work as been so marked that these facts are worth recording. The press reviews both by their careful preparation and their length many running to one, two and even four columns in daily papers which are always crowded for space have evinced a sense of the peculiar interest and importance of the book."

An awakening book a thrilling book indeed. So powerful and so real a book about the South has not been written before. The style is clear and lively even brilliant, but the only merit the modest author claims is that of absolute truthfulness There is romance in the book to enchain the attention. The characters are depicted with rare skill. —*Cincinnati Commercial*

If this is a first effort a new name in fiction has been created by a single book for the author must soon become known. The book will rank among the famous novels which represent certain epochs of history so faithfully and accurately that once written they must be read by everybody who desires to be well informed.—*Portland Advertiser*

The elements of deep romance are here curiously blended with an intensely realistic view of social life in the South since the close of the war and during the process of reconstruction. It is a work to be read with profound interest for its luminous exposition of historical facts, as well as to be admired for its masterly power of picturesque and pathetic description.—*New York Tribune*

The story throughout exhibits a naturalness a composure a reality a self restraint which belong to the best class of literary work and the more thrilling passages of the book are written with calmness as well as strength.—*Boston Literary World*

The story is brilliant and fascinating evidently a leaf from experience.—*Chicago Evening Journal*

Abounds in sketches not to be matched in the whole range of modern fiction. The author's keen insight into character gives him a power which never relaxes to the end while his skill in dialogue and humorous touches add greatly to the charm of the story.—*Boston Traveller*

There can be no doubt that *A Fool's Errand* will take a nigh rank in fiction a rank like that of *Uncle Tom's Cabin*—*Boston Traveller*

It is a powerfully written work and destined we fear to do as much harm in the world as *Uncle Tom's Cabin*, to which it is indeed a companion piece.—*Raleigh NC Observer*

Ought to be as serviceable in enlightening the North about the startling events of the reconstruction period as *Uncle Tom's Cabin* was in illustrating the phases of an earlier epoch—*Christian Union*

It was a novel which first aroused us from our lethargy to a consciousness of the growing magnitude of the evils of slavery and it is a novel now which calls attention in a clarion voice to the dangers which yet threaten a nation divided against itself. If *Uncle Tom's Cabin* was an electric light revealing in one flash the cursed system of chattelism this more recent account of *A Fool's Errand* is a sledge hammer.—*NY Daily Graphic*

The half fictitious narrative of this book is clothed in words of soberness and truth. Indeed the whole endeavor of the author seems to have been to extenuate nothing nor set down aught in malice. We have not anywhere seen an account of the troubles that beset a Northern family's residence in the South which impressed us as being more truthful more complete or more powerfully written than this.—*Chicago Tribune*

The man paints the South as it is and knows how to paint both land and people with malice toward none with charity to all.—*Der Deutsche Correspondent* Baltimore

With personal knowledge of the evil and the good of both North and South, the author teaches each side much of the other's way of looking at things.—*New Haven Journal and Courier*

The author possesses the ability to put himself in the place of the characters representing the opposing factions and from the stand point of each holding the other to account for the wrong admitted by both to have been done. A book that must be productive of lasting good.—*Philadelphia Times*

Its word pictures are so realistic that one sees hears and feels the very presence of the individuals that crowd its pages. The night ride of young Lily Servosse is one of the finest and most thrilling incidents that has ever been told in history or romance.—*San Francisco Chronicle*

A very conservative but correct glance at the South as it is. It is from the pen of an officer in the Federal army through the late war who became a *bona fide* settler of the South, subsequently with wife, family, and fortune, a keen observer an intelligent thinker and reasoner. The native Southron the poor white, the carpet bagger, the old Unioner the freedman, the Ku Klux, and the social moral and political life of the South are all handled with uncommon power and humor coupled with a relentless satire.—*Washington (DC) National Republican*

Lily's Ride

Rescuing her Father
From the Ku Klux Klan

Cowards die many times before their deaths.
The valiant never taste of death but once.—*Julius Caesar*

Albion Tourgée and Michael W. Perry

Inkling Books   Auburn   2014

Description

Lily's Ride dramatizes the nation's first civil rights movement. It takes place in North Carolina just after the Civil War and tells of those who bravely defied white supremacy and fought for equality. Comfort Servosse is a Union officer who has moved South. John Walters is a poor white who desperately wants his two daughters to get a good education. Jerry Hunt is a black pastor who openly defies the Klan. Lily Servosse is a teen-aged girl whose night ride to warn her father about the Klan lies at the heart of this moving story.

Lily's Ride is adapted from *A Fool's Errand*, a bestselling 1879 novel by Albion Tourgée,. As a North Carolina judge, he clashed with the Klan, founded Bennett College for black women (1873), and argued eloquently against segregation in the crucial U. S. Supreme Court case, *Plessy v. Ferguson* (1896).

The original novel was more complex and assumed a knowledge of Reconstruction era politics that few have today. This book is shorter, focuses on the most memorable people, and includes helpful commentary. The text that's included is the same. Punctuation and paragraph breaks are adjusted to fit today's styles.

Dedication

To all the children of poverty, both black and white, who suffered under racism.

Library Cataloging Data

Title: *Lily's Ride: Rescuing her Father from the Ku Klux Klan*
Authors: Albion W. Tourgée (1838–1905) and Michael W. Perry (1948–).

Description:

206 pages and 29 pictures, including stock photos from Big Stock Photos and public domain images from the Library of Congress.
Size: 6 x 9 x 0.47 inches, 229 x 152 x 12 mm. Weight: 0.68 pounds, 310 grams.
Library of Congress Control Number: 2014907402 (paper edition).

BISAC Subject Headings:

FIC014000   FICTION / Historical
FIC049040   FICTION / African American / Historical
FIC037000   FICTION / Political

ISBN Assignments:

Paperback: 978-1-58742-082-5
Epub: (iBookstore): 978-1-58742-083-2
Kindle: (Amazon): 978-1-58742-084-9
Smashwords: (other digital editions): 978-1-58742-085-6

Publisher Information

Print edition published in the United States of America on acid-free paper.
First edition. First printing, May 2014
Publisher: Inkling Books, Auburn, AL 36830
Internet: http://www.InklingBooks.com/

CONTENTS

1. LILY AS A CHILD

Michael W. Perry

Step with me back into the era when travel by horses and steam locomotives was so common, the central drama in our story is a race between the two, with the death of a father to follow if the train wins by more than a few minutes.

It's the evening meal and your parents seem worried. They look down a lot, as if there were something they want to tell you but can't. Despite your efforts to brighten their mood, their usual sense of humor has deserted them. Even the household servants appear frightened. They have so much to lose. Only a few years earlier, none were free.

You suspect this is linked to a man who rode up on horseback in the late afternoon, talked quietly with your father, and then fled as if a pack of wolves were on his heels. Soon after, your father sent for the men who work in the family's orchards and met with them in his office. They now linger in front of your house, as if waiting for something to happen.

You finish your homework and go to your bedroom, where the window looks out on the road that passes in front of your home. You soon fall asleep, but your dreams are troubled by the clatter of horse hooves, angry voices, and flaming torches.

You awake. Your father's hand is on your shoulder. In his right hand, pointed carefully upward, is the large service revolver he carried in the war. In his left hand is the small pistol you've been taught to use. He puts the latter on your bed, making sure it points away from you.

You know what to do. You get up, put on a robe, and crouch behind your bed, with that pistol pointed at the window. You are your family's last line of defense. If someone tries to break in through that window, you are to start firing and keep firing until your father and

the orchard workers can reach the room to drive off the intruders. Everyone depends on you.

Welcome to North Carolina just a few years after the Civil War. That nightmare about mobs and torches is real. Your kind and gentle father is hated because he believes that everyone, whether black and white, rich and poor, should have the same rights. The Ku Klux Klan hates that and intends to teach him a lesson, perhaps by lynching him and burning down your home. That has happened to people you know and love.

You're Lily Servosse. Your father's name is Comfort and your mother is Metta. You're about ten, and this life, with its many dangers, is all you've known since you were four. You have learned to be brave because you must. This is your story and that of your friends and family.

A Fool's Errand

THE BOOK YOU'RE READING has never been published before. I created it from a longer book—a bestselling 1879 novel called *A Fool's Errand*. That book sold 200,000 copies. Today, a book that popular would sell about 1.2 million copies. The story it tells is that fascinating. In fact, shortly after it was published, the *San Francisco Chronicle* wrote: "The night ride of young Lily Servosse is one of the finest and most thrilling incidents that has ever been told in history or romance."

That book so important, it's still in print for history students. But because it was written in the 1870s, many people today don't understand the background. In fact, much of the history of that era has been distorted or suppressed, perhaps deliberately. That's where I'll help you. As you read, you'll find notes I've added to help you understand what's happening. That matters, because to fully enter into this incredible story, you must know what Lily herself knew. Then you'll understand why she undertakes, without a moment's hesitation, her brave ride through a night ruled by the Klan.

Now for some background. The author of *A Fool's Errand* is Albion Tourgée, and he's well worth knowing. He was born in Ohio, trained as a lawyer, and fought for the Union in the Civil War. After the war, he moved to North Carolina, where he became a judge whose fairness and skill was respected even by his opponents. Although this is a novel, there are similarities between the him and the Comfort Servosse of this tale. Both even had a daughter, with the long-haired Lily of this tale being matched by Tourgée's own daughter, nicknamed Lodie.

The 'fool's errand' of the title describes how Tourgée felt about his brave efforts to get the South to see the folly of racism. Later he would put a lasting mark on our nation's history by challenging legalized segregation. He fought an 1890 Louisiana law that required trains to provide separate cars for black and white people and took his fight all the way to the U.S. Supreme Court. To their credit, the railroad companies hated the trouble the law caused and helped him to sue.

Unfortunately, his bold legal challenge also proved a fool's errand. By the 1890s, indifference to the rights of black people wasn't just a Southern problem. It was everywhere. In a U.S. Supreme Court decision called *Plessy v. Ferguson* (1896), Tourgée lost his Louisiana case seven votes to one. That decision put the legal principle of 'separate but equal' into our law, where it would remain for some six decades. A madness about race had infected the entire nation—educated Northern judges as well as illiterate Southern farmers.

Only in 1954 with *Brown v. Board of Education* did the U.S. Supreme Court began to unravel the vile mess it had created with *Plessy*. While Tourgée lived, good people like him were a minority in both the North and the South. In this book we'll meet some of those people and see the brave sacrifices they made. Remember, wherever you are and at whatever time in history you live, that there are always good people and bad people. Learn to distinguish between the two and join the good. Don't retreat into ignorance and indifference. Be brave like Lily and fight.

Stoop Labor

MONEY LIES BEHIND so many evils, so we now turn to the economics behind this evil. In that day, the South did not harpoon whales, make tools, or transport goods in ships like the Northeastern states. It was agricultural like the Midwest, but its crops were more labor-intensive. Growing cotton and tobacco required many hours of hard labor under a hot sun. Few people would choose to chop or pick cotton—dull, repetitive stoop labor—if they could do anything else. Even scrapping out a bare living from the poor soil of a tiny farm was better. With your own farm you were your own boss.

To understand just what that meant, look at the picture I put at the start of this chapter. It was taken in 1913 near McKinney, Texas by a once well-known photographer named Lewis Hein (1874–1940). It's a picture of a family of white migrant workers. You can see why they call it 'stoop labor.' It's a hard life.

Now imagine you're one of the little girls or boys in that photo. On the day that picture was taken, your father wakes you up while it's still dark. A single flickering candle lights the one room in the unpainted, tin-roofed shack where you live. Soon the sun will be blazing down, so it's best to start early.

Your mother has made breakfast. It's just a watery bowl of grits and a little piece of dried cornbread. Your diet is mostly corn because that's the cheapest. No one knew at the time, but that puts you at risk for a vitamin deficiency called pellagra, which leaves its victims with red blotches on their skin and feeling weak, disoriented, and confused. That might be why your older brothers have trouble in school. People with healthier diets think your brothers are lazy. You know better. They work very hard.

Once breakfast is over, to get protection from the sun your mother makes sure that every one of her much-loved children wears long sleeves, with bonnets for the girls and caps for the boys. You see that in the picture. You feel sad for her. She's often up late, working by candlelight to hand-sew the family's clothing from old flour sacks.

You hurry into the fields just as the sun rises. Time can't be wasted. Your family is paid not by how long it works, but by how much cotton gets picked. Being just seven and with tiny hands, you can pick only about a hundred-and-fifty pounds in the long hours between sunrise and sunset. It's dull and exhausting work to put the white cotton bolls into a sack you pull along the ground behind you, always making sure no leaves are included. You are penalized for leaves. Your older brothers can pick two or three times as much as you. But no matter how much your family picks, it's always poor and hungry.

You hate the work with the peculiar anger of a child who has never know anything else. The blazing sun means you're always hot and thirsty. The constant stooping makes your back ache, and the picking leaves your tiny hands bleeding. When it does, your mother washes each hand carefully, often crying as she does so. You know she loves you and hates this unending, grinding poverty, especially what it means for her children and their future.

That's what this book is about. The suffering we've just described was precisely the reality that some in the South wanted to retain after the Civil War. In fact, if we take into account those in the North who wanted to keep the price of raw cotton as low as possible, it was a horror that many in the North and South knowingly supported. (New England engaged in a similar exploitation, mostly of young, single women in cotton mills.) They wanted that even though it meant the evils we find in this book—slandering good people, killing anyone who didn't conform to their dictates, and terrorizing a entire population.

Yes, there were brave people who refused to go along with all that evil. We'll meet some in this book. They hoped to banish that suffering in a single generation. They believed in equal rights for all and wanted good schools to give their children, both black and white, a better life than the one they knew.

That's why newly freed slaves were so eager to place their children in school. It's why brave, religious women came from the North to teach them, many sent by the American Missionary Society or the Quakers. It's why John Walters, a poor white farmer, will risk his life to give his two young daughters a future better than chopping and picking cotton. Remember, in the end the clash we'll see here isn't about race. It's about giving all children, whatever their race, a decent future.

The Southern Economy

THIS IS WHERE PRACTICAL economics enters our picture. At that time, there were almost no machines to grow or harvest cotton. Under slavery, black people had been forced to do that terrible work. When slavery ended, plantation owners still needed workers for their crops. They knew some blacks would leave the South or become independent farmers. They needed replacement workers, and to get them they also needed poor whites. That's the key to almost all that follows.

Their field workers were to be the newly freed slaves *and* the South's many almost landless whites. As you read history or watch political debates today, remember that things often happen for reasons that are never publicly said. **What we are discussing here is the hidden why behind the racist words and laws. Planters wanted blacks and whites kept poor, so they'd work for low wages. They wanted them kept uneducated, so they could not find better work elsewhere.**

Their obsession with keeping farm labor cheap also meant that both poor blacks and poor whites had to be kept from uniting and demanding better treatment, particularly a better education for their children. United, they'd form a majority across much of the South. Deceived into hating each another, both could be brutally exploited. Understand that and you'll understand almost everything that happens in the South for the next century. Alter a few details, and you'll understand much of the evil that today's politicians do. They use race, class, sex or whatever to stir up anger and fear in order to deceive and exploit. Keep your eyes open for that.

One reason racism in the South began to collapse in the 1950s was that after World War II farm mechanization eliminated many reasons for keeping poor blacks and whites down. Why pay people to do what machines can do cheaper? With no economic motive, all that remained was the Democratic party's desperate need to keep poor whites as a compliant voting block. In the end, that was not enough. White supremacy collapsed.

Populists Alliances

As YOU MIGHT EXPECT, some blacks and whites were wise enough to see that and brave enough to speak out. We'll meet them in this book. From the perspective of the planters and their party, these people—usually called 'Radicals'—were dangerous subversives. When they united, they created movements that was later called *populism*.

When these people were black, they were subjected to horrible violence, including beatings, shootings, burnings and lynchings. All that had been common under slavery, so its continuance raised few objections among whites. If anything, the situation grew worse. A slave owner who beat a slave lost a worker until he recovered, and one who killed a slave lost a major investment. That financial restrain on violence ended with the elimination of slavery.

Unfortunately for those who intended to use violence, the new freedoms these blacks had been given meant that they could accuse those who attacked them in court. That's why we'll hear a debate over whether blacks should be able to testify against whites. Remember, what happens always has reasons. When this story describes the death of brave and godly black man named Uncle Jerry, the black people who knew who murdered him had to be kept from testifying.

Silencing white people was more difficult. Violence directed against them would upset many fellow whites, who might think, "That could be me." Their right to testify in court also complicated matters. It was one thing to keep a former slave from testifying against whites. It was far harder to block testimony from a white, particularly one who'd fought for the Confederacy. That we will also see.

The Black Belt Region

AT THIS POINT, THERE'S an important fact we should never forget. Support for slavery was not uniform across the South. In a region called the Black Belt, slave-owning was popular among some whites because it made them rich. That region slashes across the South from Virginia in the NE to Louisiana in the SW and extends up the Mississippi river valley. The rich black soil that gave the region its name was perfect for growing cotton, so this was where wealthy cotton planters lived. They had the money, the education, and the time to shape a state's politics to their liking. It was they who pushed the South into rebellion and war. Given the worldwide demand for cotton, these were extraordinarily wealthy people. David Davis's *Inhuman Bondage*, says that in 1860, "two-thirds of the wealthiest Americans lived in the South."

Of course, most Southern whites were not rich planters, but they could be manipulated or deceived. Some followed the planters into the war because they were weak and compliant. Some followed because they believed they might become wealthy enough to own slaves. Others obeyed from sheer fear. A poor farmer had reason to fear a wealthy neighbor who might refuse to hire him at harvest time. A pastor whose church lay on land owned by a planter might fear eviction.

Fortunately, not every white Southerner was in the thrall of the planter class. Some hated slavery for religious and moral reasons. We'll meet several of them. Others rejected slavery for economic reasons. They saw that slave labor pushed down the value of all labor, black and white, and that it particularly hurt the poor. Even before Lincoln became President, he voiced their concerns. We meet them in this story.

These people, typically called Unionists, often loved the nation as a whole and fiercely valued their independence—an attitude often derived from a Scot-Irish ancestry. Many were good, religious people who did not want to profit from the suffering of others. The singer Johnny Cash expressed their attitudes in his ballad, "The Man in Black."

Well, you wonder why I always dress in black,
Why you never see bright colors on my back,
And why does my appearance seem to have a somber tone.
Well, there's a reason for the things that I have on.
I wear the black for the poor and the beaten down,
Livin' in the hopeless, hungry side of town,
I wear it for the prisoner who has long paid for his crime,

But is there because he's a victim of the times.
I wear the black for those who never read,
Or listened to the words that Jesus said,
About the road to happiness through love and charity,
Why, you'd think He's talking straight to you and me.

These people often settled in a belt of their own in hillier regions where the climate and soil were ill-suited to cotton. They lived in western North Carolina, western Virgina, eastern Tennessee, northwestern Georgia and northern Alabama. In the aftermath of Lincoln's election, they voted *against* succession. Unfortunately, at the state level, the powerful planter class rode roughshod over them and began the war.

My Rebellious Ancestors

THE RESULT WAS REBELLION against the rebellion. During the Civil War, the people in western Virginia broke away from Virginia and formed West Virginia. Those in western North Carolina, eastern Tennessee, northern Alabama, and a slice of northwest Georgia talked of forming a new state to be called Nickajack, after an Indian word.

In northwest Alabama, the county of Winston went a step further. On July 4, 1861, it proclaimed itself the Free State of Winston. Its feelings were shared by many in the adjacent counties of Fayette, Marion and Walker. The new Confederacy did not take kindly to that and began to brutally arrest and conscript its men.

Memories of Winston county would survive for many decades. Almost a century later, Harper Lee would write about it. In *To Kill a Mockingbird*, her classic tale of life in Alabama during the 1930s, she has Scout say this about her first grade teacher.

Miss Caroline printed her name on the blackboard and said, "This says I am Miss Caroline Fisher. I am from North Alabama, from Winston County." The class murmured apprehensively, should she prove to harbor her share of the peculiarities indigenous to that region. (When Alabama seceded from the Union on January 11, 1861, Winston County seceded from Alabama, and every child in Maycomb County knew it.) North Alabama was full of Liquor Interests, Big Mules, steel companies, Republicans, professors, and other persons of no background.

No, those "Big Mules" weren't farm animals. They were powerful special interests such as factories, railroads, and textile mills. Generally, they worked together with the large planters, but sometimes the interests of the two collided.

Those "persons of no background" that Harper Lee described include my ancestors. Six miles from where my father grew up in rebellious Fayette County was the brutal Hartsook Prison, built to house those who refused to support the Confederacy. They were often brought there by the Home Guard, a precursor to the Ku Klux Klan.

After he retired, my father wrote a family history that included his mother's family, the Hallmark's. The George mentioned in what follows is my great-great-great grandfather, and his son Hopwood is my great-great-grandfather. Both were opposed to what they described as a "rich man's war, a poor man's fight"—meaning poor farming people forced to fight and die for the slave-owning interests of the rich.

"George Hallmark," my father wrote, "now sixty years old was living in Marion County, near Rock City during the war. He owned and operated a small farm on marginal land as he tried to make a living for his family. Hopwood probably lived nearby with his family. One of his granddaughters indicated that he hid-out part of the time to escape the Home Guard."

My father continues, "One night in 1863 a group of ruffians (Home Guard) came to the George Hallmark house, probably looking for money and revenge since four of George's sons had gone north to fight. An argument ensued and they shot and killed George's daughter Ann, who was living there at the time. Old timers [my father knew] say that you could still see the bloody imprint of her hand on the door-facing many years after. The Bible tells us that evil men love darkness to cover their deeds.

"The ruffians returned in 1864 and killed George on this occasion. Three of his sons had already died during the war—so the Hallmark family suffered something awful during the war."

Here I might add that those three sons died serving with the First Alabama Calvary, USV. The last three letters matter because they stand for United States Volunteers. It was a *Union* cavalry that drew volunteers from northern Alabama and Tennessee—Southerners fighting *for* the union and *against* slave owners. That was one of the "pecularities" that Harper Lee wrote about. They were rebels against a rebellion—rebels who fought for their convictions. Those are great ancestors to have.

My father then turns to what happened to my great-great grandfather after the war. "Hopwood left Fayette and all his children shortly after his wife Susan died in 1869. He moved to Morgan County and married Mary Jeffries who bore him two more sons. He died in 1874 near Moulton, Alabama. His death is shrouded in mystery, but it seems to be related to the recent Civil War in some way. None of our parents or grandparents would talk about it. Some people think he was hung or lynched by former Confederates."

For "former Confederates," think of the Ku Klux Klan. The year of his death, 1874, matters. That year the Democratic party vowed to retake the South for white supremacy "by ballots or bullets." If it wasn't a rope, he may have been stabbed or shot.

I sometimes wonder if that rope, knife, or bullet came as he was coming home along a rapidly darkening dirt road in the evening after a hard day working in the fields. Perhaps it was one of the dirt roads I walked down as a child. He might have even been going to a log cabin I found decaying deep in the woods. That would explain why the cabin had been left untouched rather than turned into firewood over the years. As the scene of a murder, it was almost sacred.

You might wonder why those older relatives were afraid to talk about Hopwood's death. There's a reason. My father grew up in the 1920s South while the Klan was undergoing a resurgence. At that time, having a relative killed by the Klan meant danger. Better to remain silent about your family's history and live.

Those murders cast a dark shadow over my family. What I remember most about my grandmother, Eva Hallmark Perry, was that she was sad, one of the saddest people I've ever known. Although we visited her almost every year while I was growing up, I also have trouble recalling her saying anything. She was that sad and silent.

So be warned. This book has stories as sad as hers. The years after the Civil War were mean, and the meanness lingered for generations. Worst of all, that did not have to be. Evil exists because evil people are allowed to do as they want. Oppose them and evil can be defeated.

This Book

Now FOR A FEW details about this book before you begin to read.

- First, this book has long-forgotten words. I give you their meanings inside [square brackets] and also use those brackets to clarify things that may be confusing. The book's text is unchanged, but some punctuation and paragraph breaks have been modernized

- Second, the pictures at the start of chapters are from the entire period of white supremacy, with some being taken as late as the 1930s. That matters little. The cruelty and misery of rural poverty changed little in the century after the Civil War. I saw that same poverty as a child when I attend in a 4-H camp in the 1950s. Even as a fourth-grader I could see my fellow camp mates were terribly malnourished. There was something about their skin that was wrong.

- Third, the story doesn't end with this book. I've almost completed a sequel (perhaps to be called *Not Just the Klan*) that brings events up to modern times. In it, I explain why something this bad could endure for so long. I planned to combine the two, but decided that closing a novel with many chapters of history might be confusing.

- There's likely to be another book you might want to read. I quote in this book from Harper Lee's *To Kill a Mockingbird*. I grew up in a little south Alabama town only forty miles from where she grew up, and my mother was born just a few month before Lee. That means I'm exactly a generation removed from her. She wrote about what racism was like in the 1930s, when it seemed like it might last forever. I'm writing about what segregation was like as it collapsed a generation later in the 1950s and 1960s. At the moment, I'm not sure what the title will be, but you can look for it under my name.

Starting Our Story

WE TURN NOW TO Tourgée's marvelous story, which begins in my retelling just after the Civil War. Comfort Servosse has decided to move to the South. He will chose about as wisely as any Union officer moving there could chose. He settles in the hills of western North Carolina. It's an area that is culturally and politically much like the part of Alabama where my Hallmark ancestors lived. Unionists live there, and the power of the cotton planters is weaker than it is in the more prosperous Black Belt region to the east.

Unfortunately, the presence of white unionists dissenters means that those who want to restore white supremacy are even more willing to resort to violence to get and retain their hold on power. Their hatred will create the need for Lily's brave ride through the North Carolina night.

2. Moving South

The South Just After the War

Michael W. Perry

Here's some true-to-life history that'll help you understand the troubles that Comfort Servosse, his patient wife Metta, and his lively daughter Lily will face when they move to the South.

First, the Civil War left the South impoverished, with its political and legal system in a mess. Many Northerners came South to take advantage of those troubles. They were called *carpetbaggers* because of their cheap luggage, which was sometimes made out of carpet. To his neighbors, Comfort will look like a carpetbagger intending to make quick money from Southern misfortune and return home rich. That's why he keeps telling them he intends to stay.

Second, Comfort was not only a former Union officer, which would have been bad enough after the South lost the war. In this chapter he refers to himself as one of those who "went to the sea with Sherman." He's referring to the most hated Union deed of the entire war, General William T. Sherman's infamous March to the Sea. That march began with the burning of Atlanta, which you may have seen dramatized at the end of the movie, *Gone with the Wind*. The army marched from Atlanta to Savannah, which is on Georgia's Atlantic coast, and then trooped northward through Confederate states, burning and pillaging all the way. No one takes kindly to their home being destroyed and the food they need to feed their children through the winter taken by soldiers. Sherman's march and whether it shortened the war as Sherman claimed is still fiercely debated among historians. What is certain is that it left behind many bad feelings.

That's the South to which Comfort now proposes to return, a South that has no love for Union officers, much less one who is an opponent of slavery and who fought with the hated General Sherman.

The South's Future

WHY DOES COMFORT TAKE such a risk? In part, it's because he believed the South could have a great future. What he hoped for the South has come true over a century later—a healthy economy with vigorous waves of immigration from other regions and countries. But it came in my lifetime and yours rather than his. But never forget that the future he saw for the South was possible even then. Slavery did not *have* to be replaced by white supremacy. The economy of the South did not *have* to continue to depend on one primary crop—cotton—with all the problems that created. Even more important, there were Southerners who wanted what Comfort wanted, as we will see.

Unfortunately, white supremacy was established and the dominance of a cotton economy (often called "King Cotton") continued because *some* people wanted that to happen, believing they benefited from it. Even worse, there was a political party that eagerly championed their cause in the North as well as the South. Those imposed their will by violence. They're the ones who made the South what it was for all too long after the war. Don't blame everyone for the actions of some. Blame those responsible.

As Tourgée will stress over and over, not everyone in the South supported that hate-filled agenda. There were good people who believed we should live from the fruits our own labor rather than exploit others—both black and white. In rough numbers, these people formed some ten percent of the South's population. Generally, they were tradesmen in towns or those who owned small farms, much like my northwest Alabama ancestors. They often called themselves Unionists, and just after the war most would vote Republican. Their critics called them "radicals." Sometimes the radicals are right.

Because many of these good people did not exploit the labor of others, in an era of farming without machines most had to work long hours under the hot Southern sun, laboring with their own hands to feed their families. That left them with little chance to get a good education and little time for politics.

As Tourgée repeatedly stressed, almost nothing in their experience prepared them to be leaders. They ran their small farms with little or no outside assistance. They had no slaves or day laborers to boss. Even the fact that many had resolutely refused to fight for slavery meant that they lost an opportunity to learn to command in the Confederate army. That's why in this story some of the most able leaders for good are actually those who had owned slaves or fought for the Confederacy, but had a change of heart after the war. They were people with a conscience. Unfortunately, there were too few of them to make a difference.

On the other side, the champions of white supremacy also made up about ten percent of the Southern population. This group included the large plantation owners whose wealth, built on slavery, had been devastated by the war. It also included those who'd been closely linked economically with them, such as bankers, lawyers, and especially politicians. They also included those who're always eager to please anyone with money, such as the slippery Ezekiel Vaughn we'll soon meet.

Because this group was well-off and well-educated, they had the time and resources for politics. For them, that meant supporting the Democratic party above all else. Some had acquired their large tracts of land after the Democratic party's founder, Andrew Jackson, forcibly took millions of acres of land in the southeastern U.S. from the Indians. That set the stage for the continuation of another evil after much of the world—represented by the British and French colonial empires—banned slavery in the 1830s. The support of these people waxed even warmer when the Democratic party became the champion of slavery and later white supremacy. They and their party are the real villains of Southern history.

As I mentioned earlier, this second group dominated the Black Belt. The name came from the black soil, but it soon acquired a double meaning. Plantations meant slaves, sometimes a hundred or more on one plantation. As a result, there were counties where the slave population was larger than the white population. This concentration of planter bigotry and political power in the same regions as a large and impoverished black populations created a foul brew. We'll see that vividly in the three chapters that take place in the Black Belt.

Most important all, to understand how the South developed politically after the war, realize that what happened, as terrible as it was, was not all that different from what had gone on before. Slave owners and those who worked for them had always used violence. They ruled their slaves by the whip and branding iron. They continued that after the war, when they reestablished their rule by fire, rope, and gun. Because ordinary people had grown accustomed to that violence under slavery, they had trouble objecting when it continued after the war.

Of course, these planters were careful to let others do the actual killing. Under slavery, they called on slave overseers, some of them black, along with slave drivers with whips, who were almost always black. In the aftermath of the war, these planters duped poor whites into joining the Ku Klux Klan, often loaning them horses and guns for their night raids. After the Klan succeeded in silencing those who dared to disagree, these 'respectable' men could step in, loudly deploring the violence but quietly ensuring that no evil-doers were punished. We'll read about that at the end of this book.

I've thought about these people quite a bit, trying to understand them as best I can. I've come to the conclusion that perhaps their chief failing was that they lack a conscience. Whatever they did was right in their eyes simply because *they* benefited from it. Think of the difference in two meanings of the word good. Good can mean right rather than wrong. Good can also mean 'good for me.' These people chose the second meaning—in fact, some seem aware of no other. Those who had a conscience often left their ranks. We'll meet them too.

Sadly, we all know how this ends. When the South let the second group win, it chose badly. But keep in mind that this was never a fair struggle. One side not only had a disproportionate share of the wealth, education and power, it also readily resorted to violence, both verbal and physical. In this struggle, good people not only rarely resorted to violence, they often failed to speak up or defend themselves well. Sadly, all too often good people preferred silence to action.

As often happens, the majority, belonging to neither group, took the path of least resistance. Over time, that would impose a heavy burden on the South, economically and culturally. In an era when homes were typically heated with wood burned in fireplaces, people in the North often admired the South's milder climate and shorter winters. The Comfort Servosse of this tale certainly did and believed that living there would be good for his health. But the South's racial bigotry kept industry and immigrants away. Racism, imposed from the top down, meant the South remained an impoverished, economic backwater for generations. Those unnecessary events shape the world that Comfort Servosse is considering entering and explain why, on reflection, he calls himself a fool.

Now we turn to the novel at the point where Comfort has just returned from fighting in the Civil War.

Four years have elapsed, and our Fool is lying on the greensward, under the clustering maples, in front of the little cottage from which he marched away in stoical disregard of his young wife's tears.

A rollicking witch [a charming and lively girl], whom he calls "Lil," is fighting a sham battle with the soldier-papa whom she has never seen until a week before, but whom she now tramples and punches and pelts with that sublime disregard for the feelings of the assaulted party which shows the confidence she has in his capacity to "endure hardness like a good soldier" [II Timothy 2:3].

Resting with her back against the tree-trunk, with a mass of fluffy white cloth overspreading the light dotted muslin which rises about her in cool profusion as she sits among the long grass, is Metta, the brave young wife, whose tears ceased to flow when she found they were powerless to detain the Fool away from war's alarms and were all turned into smiles and treasured up to await his return and restoration to his right mind.

Ah! Many a thousand times her heart has stood still with fear for him. And now, as she playfully watches the struggle going on, we can see that there is an older look upon her brow than we had marked there before. The gray eyes have a soberer light, though brimming over with joy. The lips, a trick of closing sharply, as if they would shut back the sob of fear, and the hand wanders often to the side, as if it would hush by its presence the wild beatings of a sad heart.

No wonder, for the Shadow that sat at their table four years before had breakfasted, dined, and supped with her ever since, until the Fool came back a week ago. She knows that she has grown old—lived many a decade in those four years. But she has quite forgiven the unconscious cause of all her woe and is busily engaged in preparing garments which shall carry no hint of his unfortunate malady.

Indeed, it may be said that she has some pardonable pride in the *éclat* [fame or renown] with which he returns. He has been promoted and gazetted [mentioned in the press] for gallant conduct, and general orders and reports have contained his name, while the newspapers have teemed with glowing accounts of his gallantry. He is colonel now, has been breveted [promised a position as] a brigadier-general, but despises the honor which comes as a thing of course, instead of being won by hard knocks. He is over thirty. And, as he romps with their first-born, she looks forward to how many ages of ecstasy in the sweet seclusion of their pretty home.

"There, there, Lily! Go and play with Pedro," she says at length. "You will tire papa. He is not used to having such a sturdy little girl to romp with him."

She is half jealous of the child, who shares her husband's attention, which she has hungered for so long. The child goes over to the old Newfoundland [dog] who is stretched at ease on the other side of the tree. And, when the parents look again, her golden curls are spread upon his shaggy coat and both are asleep. The wife draws her husband's hand upon her knee, lets fall her needle, and forgets the world in the joy of his presence and of communion with him.

Returning to the South

"Do you know, Metta," he said after a long silence, "that I have half a mind to go back?"

"Back! Where?" she asked in surprise.

"Why, back to the South, whence I have just come," he answered.

"What! To live?" she asked, with wide, wondering eyes.

"Certainly, at least I hope so," he responded gayly.

"But you are not in earnest Comfort, surely," with an undertone of pain in her voice.

"Indeed I am, dear!," he replied. "You see, this is the way I look at it. I have been gone four years. These other fellows, Gobard and Clarke, have come in and got my practice all away. It could not be otherwise. If not they, it must have been some others. People must have lawyers as well as doctors. So I must start anew, even if I remain here."

"But it will not be difficult," she interrupted. "You do not know how many of your old clients have asked about you and were only waiting for your return to give you their business again."

"Of course, but it will be slow work, and I have lost four years. Remember, I am over thirty now, and we have only our house and the surplus of my savings in the army—not anything like the competency I hoped to have secured by this time," he said somewhat gloomily.

"But surely there is no haste. We are yet young and have only Lily. We can live very snugly, and you will soon have a much better business than ever before. I am sure of that," she hastened to say.

"But, darling, do you know I am half afraid to stay here? It is true I look brown and rugged from exposure—who that went to the sea with Sherman does not? And my beard, which has grown long and full, no doubt gives me a look of sturdiness and strength.

"But for several months, I have been far from well. I weigh much less than when I left here, and this old wound in my lungs has been troubling me a deal of late. Dr. Burns told me that my only chance for length of days was a long rest in a genial climate. He says I am worn out, and of course it shows at the weak point, just like a chain. I am afraid I shall never practice my profession again. It hardly seems as if I could stand it to sit at the desk or address a jury."

"Is it so, darling?," she asked with trembling lips, while the happiness fled out of her face and left the dull gray which had come to be its accustomed look during those long years of waiting.

"Yes," he answered tenderly, "but do not be alarmed. It is nothing serious—at least not now. I was thinking, as we had to begin over after a fashion, whether, considering every thing, it would not be best to go

South. We could buy a plantation and settle down to country life for a few years, and I may get over all traces of this difficulty in that climate. This is what the doctor advises."

"But will it be safe there? Can we live there among the rebels?" she inquired anxiously.

"Oh," he responded promptly, "I have no fear of that! The war is over, and we who have been fighting each other are now the best of friends. I do not think there will be a particle of danger. For a few months there may be disorders in some sections, but they will be very rare and will not last any time."

"Well, dear," she said thoughtfully, "you know that I will always say as Ruth did, and most cheerfully too, 'Whither thou goest, I will go.' You know better than I, and, if your health demands it, no consideration can be put beside that. Yet I must own that I have serious apprehensions in regard to it."

"Oh," he replied, "there must be great changes, of course! Slavery has been broken up, and things must turn into new grooves. But I think the country will settle up rapidly, now that slavery is out of the way. Manufactures will spring up, immigration will pour in, and it will be just the pleasantest part of the country. I believe one-fifth of our soldiers—and that the very best part of them too—will find homes in the South in less than two years, just as soon as they can clear out their old places and find new ones there to their mind."

So he talked, forgetful of the fact that the social conditions of three hundred years are not to be overthrown in a moment, and that differences which have outlasted generations and finally ripened into war, are never healed by simple victory—that the broken link can not be securely joined by mere juxtaposition of the fragments, but must be fused and hammered before its fibers will really unite.

Ch. 4, "From Bad to Worse," in *A Fool's Errand* by Albion Tourgée.

3. A NORTH CAROLINA HOME

Portions Left Out

Michael W. Perry

The three serious-looking kids above offer me a reason to mention that, almost as soon as the real-life Albion Tourgée and his wife moved to North Carolina, they opened and taught in a school for black children. In 1973, they went on to found a school for black men and women who wanted to become teachers. Today it is Bennett College, one of only two historically black colleges exclusively for women.

Nothing could have enraged their critics more than that. Racist *rhetoric* claimed that black people could not learn. Racist *behavior* showed a fear that they would learn well. A good education threatens those who want to keep poor blacks as pliable farm laborers. Today it threatens those who would keep poor black people trapped on welfare and exploited as pliable voters.

At this point, I should bring up portions of *A Fool's Errand* that I'm leaving out. Chapter 7 of *A Fool's Errand* described Warrington, the North Carolina plantation that Comfort would buy with money he'd saved during the war. The land included a large but decaying brick home in an ancient oak grove, which had been built by a once-prominent family who founded the estate. The land also included a smaller lodge built by an eccentric Frenchman, Mr. Noyotte, who'd bought Warrington some ten years earlier to plant orchards.

Comfort bought the land for the orchard. Later, he discovered that he paid more than it was worth, but it was beautiful land. Its hundreds of acres would support his family even after he sold some land to freed slaves.

In this chapter we see hints at just how difficult life in the South was just after the war. Much of the war's destruction took place in the bitterly contested border regions of the South. On the other hand, there are also the "delights of that first winter," one much milder than was common in the North. Remember, keeping warm in winter was much harder then than now. With no gas or electric heat, you had to go out into the cold, bring logs in, and put them on a fire that had to be kept constantly burning. Also, fireplaces provide uneven heat. You roast on one side and freeze on the other.

Now put yourself in the place of little Lily, who's about five years old. She must be wide-eyed with amazement at what has changed. The climate is different. Her home is different. People talk and act differently. Even her father and mother behave differently here, whispering and looking worried from time to time. Over time, this new home will be almost all she can remember.

Southerners and Yankee Teachers

IN THIS CHAPTER, NOTICE the two groups of Southerners mentioned in Metta's letter. Fearful that the North might deal harshly with them, in the immediate aftermath of the war those who'd owned slaves were careful about how they treated those from the North, particularly former Union officers. They kept their distance but weren't openly threatening. That would change. Compare their cautious attitude to the open friendliness of the often impoverished 'Unionist' Southerners who had wanted to remain in the Union and were delighted that the war was over and lost. Even Lily, as young as she was, must have noticed that some people were friendlier to her family than others.

In her letter, Metta also mentions a wonderful group that has received far too little attention despite the great good they did—the brave and often deeply religious young Yankee women who came to the South after the war to teach black children. A few years ago, I looked for what historians might have written about them. I was unable to find a single comprehensive book, just an occasional passing mention. They deserve far more attention than that. Someone needs to write their history and give them first place in historical novels.

W hy attempt to paint the delights of that first winter at Warrington? Upon examining the place, it was found that the Frenchman's lodge had been used for purposes which prevented its present occupation as a dwelling, and they were forced to go into the old brick mansion. It needed much repairing, and at the best was worth more to look at than to occupy. Yet there was a certain charm about the great rooms, with their yawning fireplaces and dingy ceilings. Transportation was yet defective, and it was long before their furniture could arrive over railroads, worn and old, which had been the object of attack by both armies at different periods of the war.

It was the middle of October when they entered upon their new possession, and all was so new and so lovely to Metta and the little Lily, that no lack of creature-comforts could have checked their enthusiasm. The balmy air, the unfamiliar landscape, the strange sense of isolation which always marks the Southern plantation life, and, above all, the presence of the husband and father who had been absent so long, all united to make them superlatively happy.

Metta rode with her husband all over the country, whose strange irregularity became every day more pleasing to them—through the thick woods along the bridle-path, where the ground was covered with autumn foliage which had fallen from ripeness rather than from the effects of frost, past the little country farm-houses and the seats of wealthy planters, fording rivers and crossing rude ferries. Everyone whom they met, whether of high or low degree or of whatever race, having something about him which was new and strange to one of Northern birth and education.

A letter which Metta wrote to her sister shortly after they arrived will show the feelings of the young wife.

My Dear Julia,

I do not know how I can better employ a few hours of Thanksgiving Day than in writing you the promised letter of our new home and our journey here. While you are shivering with cold, perhaps looking out upon ice and snow, I am sitting upon a little veranda, over which clambers a rose-vine still wreathed with buds and blossoms. There has been a slight frost, and those on the outside are withered, but those within are yet as fresh as if it were but June. The sun shines warmly in, and everything without is touched with that delicious haziness which characterizes the few peculiar autumn days of the North that we call Indian summer. There is the same soft, dreamy languor, and the same sense of infinite distance around us.

Everybody and everything is new to us, that is, to Lily and me. Comfort's four years of soldier life made him very familiar with similar scenes, and, I doubt not, a large part of our enjoyment comes from having him to explain all these wonders to us.

It did seem terribly lonely and desolate when we first arrived. You know Comfort had come before and completed the purchase and made some preparations for our reception—that is, he had engaged somebody to make the preparations, and then returned for us. We had a fearful journey—rough seas and rickety boats, a rough country, and railroads which seemed to lack all that we have considered the essentials of such structures.

The rails were worn and broken, the cross-ties sunken and decayed; while every now and then we would see where some raiding party had heated the rails, and twisted them around trees, and their places had been supplied with old rusty pieces taken from some less important track. Comfort said he believed they would run the train on the 'right of way' alone pretty soon.

All through the country were the marks of war—forts and earthworks and stockades. Army wagons, ambulances, and mules are scattered everywhere and seem to be about all the means of transportation that are left. The poor Confederacy must have been on its last legs when it gave up.

The last twelve hours of the trip it rained—rained as you never saw it, as I think it never can rain except in this climate. To say that it poured, would give you but a faint idea of it. It did not beat or blow. There was not a particle of *storm*, or any thing like excitement or exertion about it. It only *fell*—steadily, quietly, and uninterruptedly. It seemed as if the dull, heavy atmosphere were shut in by an impenetrable canopy of clouds, and laden with an *exhaustless* amount of water, just sufficiently condensed to fall. There was no patter, but one ceaseless sound of falling water, almost like the sheet of a cascade in its weight and monotony, on the roof of the old leaky car.

In the midst of this rain, at midnight, we reached the station nearest to Warrington. It is, in fact, a pretty little town two thousand or so inhabitants. But it was as dark as the catacombs, and as quiet, save for the rain falling, falling everywhere, without intermission. The conductor said there was a good hotel, if we could get to it. But there was no vehicle of any kind, and no light at the station except the conductor's lantern, and a tallow candle flickering in the little station-house.

Comfort got our baggage off and stored in the station-house, after a deal of trouble. And with bags and boxes on our arms and muffled up to the chin to keep out the rain (which seemed to come through an umbrella as if it scorned such an attempt to divert it from its course), we started for the hotel under the pilotage of the conductor with his lantern. Such a walk! As Comfort helped me out of the car, he said, "It's fearfully muddy." He need not have said it. Already I was sinking, sinking, into the soft, tenacious mass. Rubbers were of no avail, nor yet the high shoes I had put on in order to be expressly prepared for whatever might await me. I began to fear quicksand. And, if you had seen my clothing the next morning, you would not have wondered. Luckily it was dark, and no one can ever more than guess what a drabbled [wet and muddy] procession we made that night.

And then the hotel, but I spare you that! Lily cried herself to sleep, and I came very near it.

The next morning the earth was as bright and smiling as if a deluge had not passed over it a few hours before. Comfort was all impatience to get out to Warrington, and we were as anxious to leave that horrible hotel. So he got an ambulance, and we started. He said he had no doubt our goods were already there, as they had been sent on three weeks before, and he had arranged with a party to take them out to the plantation. At least, he said, we could not be worse off than we were at that wretched hotel, in which I fully agreed with him. But he did not know what was in store for us!

Warrington is only six miles from the station. But we were two mortal hours in getting there with our trunks and the boxes we had brought with us. Think of riding through mud almost as red as blood, as sticky as pitch, and "deeper than plummet ever told," for two hours, after an almost sleepless night and a weary journey of seven days, and you may faintly guess with what feelings I came to Warrington.

As we drove up the avenue under the grand old oaks, just ripening into a staid and sober brown, interspersed with hickories which were one blaze of gold from the lowest to the topmost branch and saw the gray squirrels (which the former owner would not allow to be killed, and no one had had time to kill since) playing about, and the great brick house standing in silent grandeur amid this mimic forest, I could have kissed the trees, the squirrels, the weather-beaten porch, the muddy earth itself, with joy. It was home—rest.

Comfort saw the tears in my eyes, the first which I had shed in it all, and said tenderly—"There, there! It's almost over!," as if I had been a tired baby.

Lily was in rapture over the beauties of the old place, as indeed she had good right to be. But I was tired. I wanted rest. We drove to the house and found it empty—desolate. The doors were open, the water had run across the hall, and everything was so barren, that I could only sit down and cry. After some trouble, Comfort found the man who was to have made the repairs and brought out the goods. He said the goods had not come, and he 'llowed there wa'n't no use fixin' things till they come.

Comfort sent the ambulance which brought us out to go back and get some provisions, a few cooking utensils, and some other absolute necessities. A colored woman was found, who came in, and, with the many willing hands which she soon summoned to her aid, made the old house (or one room of it) quite cozy. Our things have been coming by piecemeal ever since, and we are now quite comfortable.

Comfort has bought me a riding-horse—a beautiful blooded bay mare—and he has his old war-horse, Lollard, which he had left in this vicinity with an old man named Jehu Brown—who, by the way, is a 'character'—having an impression that we might come here. So we ride a great deal. The roads are so rough that it is difficult to get about in any other way, and it is just delightful riding through the wood-paths, and the curious crooked country roads, by day or at night.

The people here seem very kind and attentive. A good many gentlemen have called to see Comfort. They are all colonels or squires, and very agreeable, pleasant men. A few ladies have called on me—always with their husbands though, and I think they are inclined to be less gracious in their manner and not so cordial in their welcome as the gentlemen. I notice that none of them have been very pressing in their invitations for us to return their courtesy. Comfort says it is not at all to be wondered at, but that we ought rather to be surprised and pleased that they came at all, and I do not know but he is right.

Two or three countrymen came to see Comfort a few days after our arrival. They were all 'misters,' not 'colonels' and 'squires.' They said they were Union men, and it was wonderfully interesting to hear them tell, in their quaint provincialisms, what happened to them during the war.

We rode out to see one of them afterwards, and found him a thrifty farmer, with four or five hundred acres of good land, living in a log house, with a strange mixture of plainness and plenty about him. Somehow I think I shall like this class of people better than the other—though they are rough and plain—they seem so very good-hearted and honest.

We are going to have the teachers from the colored school at Verdenton here to dinner today to keep Thanksgiving. There are some half-dozen of them—all Northern girls. I have not met them; but Comfort says they are very pleasant ladies. Of course they have no society except a few Northern people, and he has gone to bring them out to give them a treat as well as ourselves, I suppose.

Yours ever, with love to all,

Metta

Ch. 9, "The New Kingdom," in *A Fool's Errand* by Albion Tourgée.

4. AN EARLY DEBATE

What is Reconstruction?

Michael W. Perry

Since so much of our story focuses on the suffering that poor black and white families in the Old South had in common, for this chapter I've included a picture of three white children from 1930s Alabama, barefoot and malnourished. Notice the marks on the face and leg of the little girl on the right and how conscious she seems of them. That's a sign of pellagra, even then known as a nutritional deficiency (niacin) that comes from eating a diet that's almost all corn. Look carefully, and you'll see that her sister and brother probably have it too. This is only the start of the disease. It can get far worse, leading to sores, depression, exhaustion, and even death.

The Reconstruction Era

ALL OF OUR TALE is set during the Reconstruction Era, which was the thirteen-year period after the Civil War (1865–1877) during which the North tried, often half-heartedly and ineffectively, to *reconstruct* the South and make it more like the rest of the country, particularly in its treatment of black people.

This isn't to say that the North didn't have its own problems, particularly in how it treated recent immigrants such as the Irish. A sick joke from that era claimed, "There is nothing wrong with the country that couldn't be solved if every Irishman killed a n__r and was hanged for it." And for many decades, the plight of workers in New England cotton mills was only a little better than those working in Southern cotton fields. The cotton clothing that was so popular then and now came with a lot of suffering attached. Even today, we wrestle to end sweatshops that make clothing in impoverished countries, often clothing sold with prestigious labels by companies that pay their executives large salaries.

But there was a major difference. In the North, blacks and the Irish could vote and, while they were often forced into low-paying jobs, little was done to keep them from improving their circumstances. If they worked hard, they could buy homes, businesses, and farms as well as get a good education—in the case of the Irish through their own Catholic schools and colleges. Immigration was one reason why Northern bigotry was different. Those who wanted to exploit cheap immigrant labor in mines and factories or as household servants didn't need to keep an immigrant's children down. There were always new waves of immigrants arriving. As a result, the exploitation didn't have to be as brutal and the bigotry that was used to justify it did not have to be as nasty.

Or at least it was until the early decades of the twentieth century, when the large families of immigrants began to alarm 'Old Stock' New Englanders who had low birthrates. That resulted in efforts to reduce their numbers with immigration restrictions, eugenic sterilization laws, and birth control clinics. If you are interested, I describe that bigotry in a book I edited, *The Pivot of Civilization in Historical Perspective*.

Those later efforts to reduce the population of unwanted groups had little impact on the South, where plentiful supply of poor blacks and whites were seen as necessary for agriculture. There is a historical reason. The slave trade was abolished in 1808. Only a few slaves were smuggled in after that. For large planters, the existing supply of slaves—with their children and grandchildren—had to be kept up to ensure a steady supply of cheap laborers. Cruel as slavery was, it did mean that slaves had value to their owners. That gave them some protection, however dreadful the racist rhetoric used to justify slavery was.

Cotton also shaped Southern racism. There were no weed-killing chemicals and little farm machinery. Growing cotton meant hours of grueling manual labor under a blazing sun. No one would do that if there was an alternative.

That's why Comfort's planter neighbors were furious when he sold small farms to freed slaves and helped them get a horse or mule for plowing. His efforts to make black people independent made it more difficult for these planters to hire workers and pay them poorly. It's also why they hated schools for black children. Learning to read meant they could find other jobs. Evil has its reasons.

Just after the war, good deeds like Comfort's would go unpunished. Evil took time to organize. But the former slave owners and their supporters quickly realized what their primary goal had to be—keeping freed slaves from becoming educated, independent, self-supporting, allowed to vote, permitted to testify in court, and able to defend themselves. Although little is said about it today, they had similar goals for their other cheap labor source—poor whites.

Keep in mind that in an agricultural society, freedom flows from owning your own land, having farm animals, and learning the old fashioned three-Rs—Reading, wRiting and aRithmetic. If you have those, you might not have to work for someone else, least of all for the pittance large planters often paid. When you work for yourself, you also don't have to be politically silent. That matters.

Freedom also meant being able to defend yourself from those who intend you harm. Even today, help from law enforcement may not arrive quickly enough. In an era without telephones or electric lights, people needed their own protection, especially in the rural areas of counties where the sheriff might have close ties with the Ku Klux Klan.

That's why one of the Klan's first goals was to disarm blacks and Unionist whites like my Hallmark ancestors. Unable to defend themselves, they faced a stark choice. Make trouble and die or remain silent and live, however miserably. That's why gun control often isn't about controlling guns or criminals. It's about controlling law-abiding people. That's why our Constitution has a Second Amendment alongside the First. Without the ability to defend yourself, your right to speak freely is more easily be taken away.

Political History

THERE ARE SOME LONG forgotten events that I should explain so you understand what Tourgée says in this chapter. In the 1864 election, Abraham Lincoln attempted to unite a North divided by the war by selecting Andrew Johnson, a pro-slavery but Unionist Democrat from Tennessee as his running mate. After Lincoln was assassinated, Johnson became President. As "the Executive" mentioned below, Johnson quickly made major concessions to pro-slavery Southern leaders. Though rarely mentioned today, perhaps the greatest tragedy of Lincoln's death was that he was replaced by someone as vile as Andrew Johnson.

As you might expect, Johnson met strong opposition in a Congress led by anti-slavery Republicans. The Howard Amendment was sponsored by Senator Jacob M. Howard, a Michigan Republican. It required that Southern states remove from office those who had participated in the rebellion as a condition for readmission. That's what is meant by the remark below about "our best men have been placed under a ban."

If that long-ago speaker had any sense, he would have realized that those "best men" were the incompetents who had just led the South into a bloody war followed by a costly defeat. Many of those same "best men" would also be responsible for establishing racist policies that would leave the South an economic backwater for generations. I know that all too well. Their political heirs were still around with I was growing up in the 1950s, to my childish disgust.

Notice the fuss at this open-air meeting over allowing "a nigger to testify" in court. Many whites believed that black people could not gain something without the loss of "your rights and mine." That's often called a 'zero sum game' but it makes no sense. Suppose you're a white falsely accused of a crime by a fellow white. Wouldn't you want the testimony of a black man in your defense to be allowed in court? Also, notice that at this time there were some Southern whites who are willing to defend a black man's right to testify against a white in court. They will have to be silenced. We'll soon learn a lot about them.

Finally, remember that the meeting which follows was open to all locals. Even some "colored" attend. But also notice that we begin to hear bits and pieces of the evil ideas our of which the white supremacist, post-Civil-War Democratic party will emerge. In just a few years the party's meetings will be open only to those who agree with its racist agenda. *Giving* something to blacks, the party will claim, means *taking* something from whites, particularly poor whites. If you'd like to acquire a modern feel for what that felt like, when a speaker refers to the rights of 'n____rs,' substitute 'fetus' and for whites substitute women. In fact, Southern racists often claimed to be great protectors of white womanhood. Sadly, little has changed.

Notice Comfort's good business sense. He intends to grow fruit in this warm climate to be sold for a premium in Northern markets during the winter. That matters because many whose minds were shackled by racism seemed to lack that same good sense. Obsessed with getting rich by exploiting the labors of slaves and, after the end of slavery, of poor people in general, they failed to realize that there were better ways to make a living, including growing crops other than cotton. Their folly—in morals and in business matters—will keep the South mired in poverty for over a century.

Servosse was very busy during the winter and spring which followed in building the houses referred to by Metta, and laying out and selling a large part of his plantation. He found the colored men of the best character and thrifty habits, anxious to buy lands, and no one else was willing to sell to them. He purchased some Confederate buildings which were sold by the government, tore them down, and, out of the materials, constructed a number of neat and substantial little houses on the lots which he sold. He also assisted many of them to buy horses, in some instances buying for them and agreeing to take his pay in grain and forage out of the crops they were to raise.

In the mean time, he gave a great deal of attention to the improve-ment of Warrington, expecting to reap his reward from the thousands of fruit-trees which Mr. Noyotte had planted and which had grown to be full-bearing, in spite of neglect since his death. These trees and vines were all carefully pruned and worked, and Warrington assumed the ap-pearance of thrift and tidiness, instead of the neglect and decay which had before been its distinguishing features.

There was some fault found with the sales which he made to colored men, on the ground that it had a tendency to promote "nigger equality." But he was so good-natured and straight-forward in the matter that but little was said, and nothing done about it at that time, though he heard of organizations in some parts of the State instituted to prevent the col-ored people from buying land or owning horses.

Attending a Political Meeting

THE SUCCEEDING SUMMER WAS well advanced when he went one day to attend a political meeting which was held in a little grove some seven miles from Warrington. It was a meeting purporting to be called for consultation in regard to the general interests of the county. Eminent speakers were advertised to attend, and Servosse felt no little curiosity, both to see such a gathering and to hear what the speakers might have to say. He had never been anything of a politician and had no desire or expectation of being one.

He rode to the meeting, which he found to be far greater than he ex-pected, not less than a thousand people having assembled. Almost every man came on his horse or on foot and the horses stood about, tied to the lower limbs of the trees in the grove where the meeting was held. There were many speeches of the kind peculiar to the Southern stump, full of strong, hard hits, overflowing with wit and humor, and strongly sea-soned with bombast. Stories of questionable propriety were abundant, and personalities of the broadest kind were indulged in.

Servosse sat among the crowd, enjoying to the utmost this new expe-rience, and wondering how people could relish contending so hotly over each other's records during and before the war. It all seemed to him very amusing. But, when they came to address themselves to the future, he became interested for another reason.

It will be noted by the reader who cares to trace back a few years of memory, or consult the records which have not yet become history, that this was in the primary period of what has since become memorable as the era of "reconstruction." The plan which was then sought to be put into operation by the Executive [President Andrew Johnson] was what has since been known as the "presidential plan," supplemented by the "Howard amendment," and dependent on the adoption of that by the different States recently in rebellion. The abolition of slavery by constitutional provision, the abjuration [take back] of the right of secession, and the repudiation of the Confederate state-debts were the conditions precedent. Of course the future status of the freedmen was a question of overwhelming interest, though that was left entirely to the decision of the various States.

It was for the discussion of questions thus arising that the meeting we have now in hand was called. The great subject of contention between the opposing factions was as to whether the recently freed people ought to be allowed to testify in courts of justice.

"What!" said one of the speakers, "Allow a nigger to testify! Allow him to swear away your rights and mine! Never! We have been outraged and insulted! Our best men have been put under a ban, but we have not got so low as to submit to that yet. Our rights are too sacred to be put at the mercy of nigger perjurers!"

This sentiment seemed to meet with very general endorsement from the assembled suffragans [voters], and more than one burst of applause greeted the speech of which it was a part.

Servosse Singled Out

WHEN THE MEETING SEEMED to be drawing to a close, and Servosse was considering the question of going home, he was surprised at hearing from the rude stand the voice of this same orator addressing the assemblage for a second time and evidently making allusion to himself.

"Mr. Chairman," he said, "I see there is a man on the ground who has lately come among us from one of the Northern States, who has been here all day listening to what we have said, whether as a spy or a citizen I do not know. It is currently reported that he has been sent down here by some body of men at the North to assist in overturning our institutions and putting the bottom rail on top.

I understand that he is in favor of social equality, nigger witnesses, nigger juries, and nigger voters. I don't know these things, but just hear them; and it may be that I am doing him injustice. I hope I am, and, if so, that an opportunity will now be given for him to come forward and deny them. If he has come among us as a *bona-fide* citizen, having the interest of our people at heart, now is a good time for him to let it be known. If he has come to degrade and oppress us, we would like to know what reason he has for such a course. In any event we would all like to hear from Colonel Servosse, and I move that he be invited to address this meeting."

Had a bombshell fallen at the Fool's feet, it could not have amazed him more. He saw the purpose at once. Vaughn and several others, whom he had reason to suppose had no kindly feelings for him, were evidently the instigators of this speech. They were gathering around the orator, and no sooner had he had ceased speaking than they began to shout, "Servosse! Servosse! Servosse!"

The chairman rose and said something amid the din. Only a few words reached the ears of Servosse:

"Moved 'nd sec'n'd—Servosse—'dress—meeting. Those in favor—aye." There was a storm of ayes. "Opposed—no." Dead silence, and then a period of quiet, with only an occasional yell for "Servosse" from the party of malignants on the right of the stand.

Servosse shook his head to the chairman, but the shouts were redoubled, and there was a closing in of the crowd, who were evidently very curious as to the result of this call.

"Bring him on!" shouted Vaughn to those who stood around. "Bring him on! Let's hear from him! We haven't heard a speech from a Yankee in a long time."

"Servosse! Servosse! Servosse!," shouted the crowd. Those who stood about him began to crowd him towards the platform in spite of his protests. They were perfectly respectful and good-humored, but they were evidently determined to have a speech from their new neighbor or else some fun at his expense.

"Oh, bring him along!," cried Vaughn from the stand. "Don't keep him all to yourselves, gentlemen. We can't hear a word here. Give us a chance!"

This sally was greeted with a shout, and Servosse, still expostulating and excusing himself, was picked up by a dozen strong arms, carried along between the rows of seats—rough pine boards laid upon logs—and hoisted upon the platform, amid a roar of laughter.

"We've got him now," he heard Vaughn say to his clique. "He's got to make a speech, and then Colonel Johnson can just give him hell"

There was another cry of "Speech! Speech! Speech!"

Then the chairman called for order; and there was silence, save here and there a dropping word of encouragement real or mock—"Speech! Go on! Give it to 'em, Yank!," and so forth.

Servosse had noticed that the crowd were not all of one mind. It was true that there was an apparent unanimity, because those who dissented from the views which had been expressed were silent, and did not show their dissent by any remarks or clamor. He knew the county was one which had been termed a "Union county" when the war began; and there was still a considerable element whose inclinations were against the Rebellion, and who only looked back at it as an unmitigated evil. They had suffered severely in one form and another by its continuance and results, and smarted over the sort of compulsive trickery by which the nation was forced into the conflict. He had marked all these things as the meeting had progressed, and now that those whom he recognized as his enemies had succeeded in putting him in this position, he determined to face the music, and not allow them to gain any advantage if he could help it.

He shook himself together, therefore, and said good-naturedly. "Well, gentlemen, I have heard that—

'One man may lead the pony to the brink,
But twenty thousand can not make him drink!'

So, while you have shown yourselves able to pick me up and put me on the platform, I defy you to elicit a speech, unless you'll make one for me. However, I am very much obliged to you for putting me up here, as those rough boards without backs were getting very hard, and I shall no doubt be much more comfortable in this chair."

Whereupon he took a seat which stood by the table near the chairman, and coolly sat down. The self-possession displayed by this movement struck the crowd favorably and was greeted by cheers, laughter, and cries of "Good!," "That's so!," and other tokens of admiration. If it had been the purpose of those who had started the cry to press him to an impromptu speech before a crowd already excited by a discussion they knew to have been in direct conflict with the views he must reasonably entertain, in order that he might meet a rebuff, he was in a fair way to disappoint them. Instead of making an exasperating speech or an enjoyable failure, he had simply refused to be drawn into the net spread for him by coolly asserting his right to speak or keep silence as he chose. And the crowd unmistakably approved.

The chairman, an old gentleman of courtly manner, whose very appearance was a guaranty of his character, urbanity, and moderation, evidently felt that the new-comer had been treated with rudeness, and that he had been made the unwilling instrument of a malicious insult. It was apparent that the stranger so regarded it, and the chairman could not rest under the imputation of such impropriety. So he rose, and, addressing himself to the occupant of the other chair, said courteously—

"I have not the honor of your acquaintance, sir; but I presume you are the gentleman who has been called Colonel Servosse."

The latter bowed affirmatively.

"I assure you, sir, I am happy to know you, having heard so much to your credit that I have promised myself great pleasure in your acquaintance."

Servosse blushed like a boy, for there is no class whose flattery is so overwhelming as that to which the chairman belonged, it being united in them with a dignity of manner which gives peculiar force to the lightest remark.

"I am sure, sir," the chairman continued, "nothing could afford me greater happiness than to hear your views in regard to our duty as citizens of a common country at this peculiarly trying period in our history. I am confident that such is the earnest wish of this assemblage. (Cries of "Yes, yes!") The manner in which you have been invited may seem to you somewhat rude and was certainly inexcusable, considering the fact that you are a stranger. I hope, however, that it will not have the effect of preventing us from hearing your views. Seen from your stand-point, it is to be expected that present events will bear a different interpretation to what they have when viewed from ours. But we have met as neighbors, and it is to be hoped that an interchange of views will do us good. I hope, therefore, that you will permit me to introduce you to this audience, and that you will make some remarks, if for nothing else, to show that you bear no ill will for our unintended rudeness."

Cries of "Servosse! Servosse! Colonel Servosse!"

There was no possible answer to an apology and a request so deftly framed as this, except compliance. Servosse perceived this, and, rising, gave his hand to the chairman and was by him formally introduced to the audience. The crowd gathered around the stand in expectant curiosity.

A little group of colored men who had hung on the outskirts of the audience all day, as if doubtful of their right to be present, edged one by one nearer to the speaker's platform. The short terse sentences of the newcomer were in very marked contrast to the florid and somewhat labored style of those who had preceded him. It was the earnest practicality and abundant vitality of the North-West, compared with the impracticality and disputatious dogmatism of the South.

Ch. 11, "A Cat in a Strange Garret," in *A Fool's Errand* by Albion Tourgée.

5. Servosse Must Speak

The Logic of a Lost War
Michael W. Perry

Yes, another sad picture of poor children, although at least these two little girls have shoes. That's not a barn. That's where this family lives, although as sharecroppers they have no home of their own. Notice the thin layer of boards with mud spread over them to keep out the wind. Imagine how cold it gets in the winter. That misery has only slowly disappeared. When I was the age of those little girls, poor people often lived in what were called "tar-paper shacks." Thick paper soaked in tar replaced the mud to keep out the howling wind. Remember, children just like these are why the adults in our story risk their lives to give them a better future.

Ezekiel Vaugh, who was mentioned in the last chapter, becomes more important in this one. Comfort first met him while serving in a Union army headquarters mere days after the end of the war. Vaughn appeared before him and rather pompously announced that, "Colonel Ezekiel Vaughn desired to surrender and take the oath of allegiance."

At that first meeting, Vaugh was wearing a patched-together uniform that seemed to indicate the rank of colonel, but he couldn't name the regiment to which he was assigned. He had obviously taken care to ensure that his former commitment to the rebellion never put him in harm's way.

His new oath to the Union and his seeming friendship with Comfort would prove equally shallow. It was he who sold Warrington to Comfort at an inflated price. By this chapter, he's flipped sides yet again, rightly sensing that power and money lies in the hands of those championing white supremacy.

Note Vaugh well. I'll write more about his sort later. You'll find many like him in politics. At the national or state level, Vaughn-like politicians can often get away with their slippery ways since our only knowledge of them comes through often news coverage and, as strange as it may sound, journalists tend to fall for such people. In small towns they're usually less successful with their deceptions. There people know each another. That's why there are peals of laughter when Comfort asks Vaughn to "lend me your crutches." Most of those at this meeting knew Vaughn was no disabled war hero.

The chapter opens with Comfort making a speech he did not want to make and at the same time denying any interest in politics. Becoming political opened him up to charges of being a carpetbagger who'd come South to get rich through crooked politics. Notice especially two ideas.

First, at this time Comfort assumes that the Republican party will stand firm on protecting the rights of black people. His entire argument hinges on that firmness. "Resistance is futile" he is saying. But what if the Republican party isn't steadfast? What if some Republicans prefer to be more like the Democrats, looking out for themselves rather than being responsible for others? Then things will go badly.

Second, Comfort tries to persuade his listeners that the South will benefit if it respects the rights of some blacks—those who are literate and property-owning—allowing them to vote and depending on their success to encourage other blacks to improve. But even if that's true, will whites be willing to give up the advantages they get from keeping *all* blacks down? To put it bluntly, will the South as a whole stay poor so that the minority of Southerners who exploit the cheap labor of poor blacks and whites remain rich? Unfortunately, the answer will be yes.

Also, at this time Comfort isn't aware of just how deeply his opponents are committed to white supremacy. The more rabid among them don't want *any* black people succeeding, much less seeing the entire population of newly freed slaves improving themselves generation after generation. Most wealthy landowners want to keep blacks as the same cheap and placid agricultural labor supply they were under slavery. They don't want talented, responsible blacks to get ahead, since their good example is, from their perspective, a bad example. These are the people who will implant in the minds of some blacks that learning to read and studying hard is "acting white," and that it is best to remain poor and dependent. That's still with us, although the goal is now blacks as placid and compliant voters.

Here something vile enters the picture. To keep poor blacks down, poor whites must be duped into blaming black people for their misfortunes. The planters were helped by the fact that the minds of some poor whites had already become so twisted that they would rather be poor themselves than to see some black people ride about on horseback. Envy is for fools, and these particular poor whites were certainly fools.

All that explains why the South would remain an economic backwater for over a century. No society can suppress the abilities of a third of its people without suffering consequences. Hatred diverts human energy along destructive paths. It also silences good people, who're perhaps a bit too nice and unwilling to speak up. That's mentioned in this chapter as: "A few seemed to regard him not unkindly, but made no manifestation of approval." Showing an approval of equal rights for all was risky. Think of today's abortion debate.

Finally, although Lily, who's now about six, is not mentioned in this chapter, you can imagine her overhearing, with her eyes open wide, what her father said to her mother at the dinner table after he returned home from this meeting. The boldness she later displays on her brave ride is much like the boldness he displays here. Like father, like daughter.

"Gentlemen," said he, "I did not come here to make a speech. I am neither a speech-maker nor a politician. Never made a political speech in my life, and certainly am not prepared to make a beginning today. I have bought a home among you, and cast my lot in with you in good faith, for good or for ill. Whether I have acted wisely, or have run on a fool's errand in so doing, is for the future to reveal. I must say, from what I have heard, and heard applauded to the echo, here today, I am inclined to think the latter will prove the true hypothesis Your chairman has intimated that my opinions may differ from yours. And, as this fact seems to be apparent to all, it is probably best, in order that we should part good friends, that I should not tell you what my views are."

Cries of "Yes, Yes! Go on!"

"Well, then, if you don't like my notions, remember that you would insist on my giving them. As I said, I am no politician, and never expect to be. I hope I have common sense, though, And I shall try to know something of what is going on in the world while I am in it. I don't want to discuss what has been done, nor who did it. I want to say one thing, however, about the immediate future.

I have heard a good deal today about what the South wants, and must have, what you will do, and what you will not do. I think you have two simple questions to answer: First, What *can* you do? And, second What *will* you do?

There has been much discussion here today in regard to freedmen being allowed to testify in courts, the repudiation of the war-debt of these States, and one or two other kindred questions. Allow me to say that I think you are wasting your time in considering such matters. They are decided already. There may seem injustice in it, but the war-debt of these States can never be paid. Neither can the freedman be left without the privilege of testifying in his own right. It makes no difference whether you accept the terms now offered or not, in this respect—yes, it may make this difference: it is usually better to meet an unpleasant necessity half way, than wait till it forces itself on you.

"The logic of events has settled these things. The war-debt became worthless as paper when Lee surrendered, and nothing can revive it. The taint of illegal consideration attaches to it, and always will. So, too, in regard to the colored man being allowed to testify. This is settled. He was allowed to testify on the battlefield, and will be allowed to testify in courts of justice. When he took the oath of service, he acquired the right to take the oath of the witness. These, I say, are already *facts*.

"The practical question for you to consider is, How far and how fast shall the freedmen be enfranchised? You have today assented to the assertion repeatedly made, that the South would never submit to 'nigger suffrage.' But again I say, the South has nothing to do with that question either. The war settled that also."

"We will have another four years of it before we will submit," interrupted Vaughn in great excitement. There was an approving murmur from a good portion of the audience at this interruption. The speaker did not seem at all disconcerted, but, turning to Vaughn, said—

"I hope not, Colonel. *I've* had enough; but, if *you* will have it, lend me your crutches and let me join the cripple brigade this time, won't you?"

The roar of laughter which followed interrupted the speaker for several minutes, and left Vaughn the picture of amazement. That the stranger should venture upon such a retort as that to a Southern gentleman was quite beyond his comprehension.

"As I said," continued the Fool, "with the general question of colored suffrage you have nothing to do. It is a fact accomplished. It is not yet recorded in the statute-books; but it is in the book of fate. *This* question, however, you have still in your hands: Shall negro suffrage be established all at once, or gradually? If you of your own volition will enfranchise a part of them, marked by some definite classification—of intelligence, property, or what not—and the others as they reach that development, it will suffice at this time. Wait, hesitate, refuse, and all will be enfranchised at the same time by the General Government.

You say it will be a great evil. Then you ought to lighten it as much as possible. If you will give the elective franchise to every colored man who owns a hundred dollars' worth of real estate, and every one who can read and write, the nation will be satisfied. Refuse, and all will be enfranchised without regard to your wishes or your fears.

"I have told you, not what I think ought to be, but what I believe is, the fact of the present situation. I can see that you do not all agree with me, perhaps none of you, but it will stand thinking over. Don't forget what I tell you, and, if you dislike my remarks, remember that you forced me to say what I have said, as well by your own urgent importunity as by the kindly compulsion of your chairman."

There was a dull, surprised silence when he had concluded. The very audacity of his speech seemed to have taken away all power, if not all inclination, to reply. Some of his audience regarded him with sullen, scowling amazement, and others just with dull wonder that any one should have the hardihood to make such a statement. A few seemed to regard him not unkindly, but made no manifestation of approval.

The chairman rose, and stated that the views of the speaker were somewhat startling and entirely new, he presumed, to the audience, as they were to him. As Colonel Servosse said, they would stand thinking about, and on behalf of the audience he returned to Colonel Servosse their thanks for an exceedingly frank and clear statement of his views. If there was no farther business, the meeting would stand adjourned.

Thereupon the crowd separated, and, after a few moments' conversation with the chairman and one or two others, the Fool mounted his horse and took his way homeward.

Ch. 12, "Compelled to Volunteer," in *A Fool's Errand* by Albion Tourgée.

6. HOSPITALITY REFUSED

Threats and Attacks

Michael W. Perry

The speech in the last chapter had the result Comfort Servosse feared—it set many in the community against him. Those who knew him well, meaning his closest neighbors, still saw him for the decent person he was. Those who drew their opinions from public sources, particularly newspapers, began to look on him with suspicion or even hatred. The press does that. There seems to be something about journalism that attracts those with prejudices and encourages them to indulge their hates. Here their target was Servosse.

Worse still, the burden of this hostility fell particularly hard on Comfort's wife Metta and his daughter Lily. Money is why. Comfort was a large farmer. He bought agricultural supplies and hired laborers. Money creates relationships that, if not friendly, are at least civil. People are nice to get money.

I saw that. In the segregated South, where money mattered, say at a store, there was little discrimination. The color of a person's money mattered more than their skin. In high school, I worked at a supermarket. If I had treated our black customers with any less courtesy than our white ones, I'd have been fired.

In contrast, where social relations mattered more, such as with restaurants and clubs, segregation was more strongly held. That struck me as odd. I remember as a kid wondering why a "White Only" sign in a restaurant window meant no black person would be seated next to you at a table, but black cooks were often preparing the very food you ate. Bigotry can be maddeningly inconsistent. I suspect that was because Southern racism was modeled on cotton plantations, where black people prepared meals but never ate with whites.

Finally, in politics—voting, the schools and courts—white supremacy reigned supreme. In the second grade I realized that was because those were controlled by the Democratic party—the most bigoted of the bigoted and the most hateful of the hateful. Well-to-do white mothers would trust black women to care for their children. White businessmen would let both races into their stores and treat them well. But Democratic politicians would not allow a black mother to send her child to a white school or blacks into voting booths. They made sure schools for black children were substandard. In many big cities today, the party still does.

Since Comfort's wife and daughter depended on social rather than business contacts, they had few friends outside their black neighbors and servants, the small, independent farmers and tradesmen who voted Republican, the brave young Yankee women who taught in black schools, and the few other Yankees who lived in their community. Sadly, when racism reared its ugly head, Southern hospitality came up lacking.

Notice something important—that, while racist rhetoric claimed blacks were so uncivilized and inferior they could only survive by serving white people in menial positions, the deeds of racists showed they believed the opposite. They feared black success more than anything else and reacted violently against it. The early Klan-like group he mentions here as "The Regulators" wanted to make sure black people could not own farms and horses. That fear only makes sense if they believed black people could farm well, so well they might end up "a ridin hossback when white folks is walkin." Envy, fear, bigotry and hatred are closely linked.

Notice also how bravely Comfort responds to the crudely written note. Threats intend to make us afraid, so the best response is often bold defiance. Publishing the letter exactly as it was written did poke fun at this almost illiterate "capting." But notice that Comfort also prepares to defend himself and his black tenants from attack. Readying to fight injects fear into the hearts of those who want to fill *your* heart with fear. When someone intends to come after you, it's often wise put them on the defensive. Just do so carefully.

One final note. Today, many of you—wherever you live—may have trouble grasping just how all-pervasive this hostility toward "Yankee power" was. I can give a telling example. When I was in the fourth grade, my teacher, attempting to explain to us just how common hostility to the North had been during her childhood, told us that she was twelve years old before she realized that "damn Yankee" wasn't one word. In the conversations she overheard growing up, she almost never heard "Yankee" without a curse word attached. That's how much hatred existed. The only good Yankee back then was one who lived far away and kept his nose out of Southern business. Comfort's problem is that he doesn't live far away and no one believes he wants to stay out of Southern politics.

From the day of his speech in the grove, the new proprietor of Warrington was a marked man in the community. He was regarded as an "abolitionist" and an incendiary. While his neighbors did not seem to have towards him any especial distrust in their personal intercourse, and generally met him with affability, yet he gradually became aware that a current of wonderful strength was setting against him.

He became an object of remark at public assemblies; the newspaper at Verdenton had every now and then slighting allusions to him, and the idea was industriously circulated that he was somehow connected—identified—with "Yankee power" and had been sent to the South for some sinister motive. He was not one of them. He represented another civilization, another development, of which they were naturally suspicious, and especially so on account of the peculiar restrictions which slavery had put around them, and which had acted as an embargo on immigration for so many years before the war.

The intercourse between his family and those who constitute what was termed 'good society' gradually dwindled, without actual rudeness or tangible neglect, until the few country-people who "neighbored with them," as it is termed there, comprised their only society, if we except the teachers of the colored school and the few Northern families in the town.

Now and then this feeling of hereditary aversion for the Yankee manifested itself unpleasantly. But it was usually only an undemonstrative, latent feeling, which was felt rather than seen in those with whom he associated in business or otherwise, until the first year had passed away, and the crops had been gathered.

Little attention had been paid to the manner in which he had chosen to build houses and sell lands to the colored people—it being perhaps regarded as merely a visionary idea of the Yankee abolitionist. When, however, the crops were harvested and some of these men became owners of horses and houses in their own right, it seemed all at once to awaken general attention. One night a gang of disguised ruffians burst upon the little settlement of colored men, beat and cruelly outraged some, took the horses of two, and cut and mangled those belonging to others.

When the Fool arose the next morning, he found the following attached to his door-knob, wrapped in a piece of black cloth on which was traced in white paint a death's head and cross-bones above the picture of a coffin.

Colonel Comfort Servosse

Sir,

You hev got to leeve this country, and the quicker you do it the better; fer you ain't safe here, nor enny other miserable Yankee! You come here to put niggers over white folks, sayin ez how they should vote and set on juries and sware away white folkes rites as much as they damm please. You are backin up this notion by a sellin of em land and hosses and mules, till they are gittin so big in ther boots they cant rest. You've bin warned that sech things wont be born; but you jes go on ez if ther want nobody else on arth. Now, we've jes made up our minds not to stan it enny longer. We've been and larned yer damm niggers better manners than to be a ridin hossback when white folks is walkin. The Regulators hez met, and decided thet no nigger shant be allowed to own no hoss nor run no crop on his own account herearter. And no nigger-worshipin Yankee spy thet encourages them in their insolense shel live in the county. Now, sir, we gives you three days to git away. Ef your here when that time's over, the buzzards wil hev a bait thats been right scarce since the war was over. You may think wes foolin. Other people hez made thet mistake to ther sorrer. Ef you don't want to size a coffin jest yit you better git a ticket that will take you towards the North Star jes ez far ez the roads been cut out.

By order of
The Capting of the Regulators

The Fool at once published this letter in *The Verdenton Gazette*, with a short, sturdy answer, saying that he was minding his own business, and expected other people to mind theirs. He paid for it as an advertisement—the only terms on which the editor would admit it to his columns.

This proceeding, which in the North or in any other State of society would have awakened the liveliest indignation towards those who thus attempted to drive him away from his home as well as a strong sympathy for him had no such effect upon this community. Many openly approved the course of the mob. Others faintly condemned, and no one took any steps to prevent the consummation of the outrage threatened.

No one seemed to think that the Fool was entitled to any support or sympathy. That he should sell land to colored men and assist them to purchase stock was considered by nearly the entire community as an offense deserving the worst punishment. And that he should go farther, and publicly favor their enfranchisement was such a gross outrage upon the feelings and prejudices of the whites, that many seemed much surprised that any warning at all had been given by the "Regulators."

The one most interested, however, was not idle. He procured arms and ammunition, and prepared for the defense of his life and property, and the protection of his tenants and those to whom he had sold. A stockade was built for the horses in a favorable position, a guard provided, and signals agreed on in case of an attack. The commandant of the troops at a neighboring station sent a small detachment, which remained for a few days, and was then withdrawn. They had not been required by the owner of Warrington, but the rumor went out that he had called for troops to protect him, and the feeling grew day by day more hostile towards him.

Ch. 16, "The Edge of Hospitality Dulled," in *A Fool's Errand* by Albion Tourgée.

7. Jerry Hunt's Church

Dissimilar Peoples

Michael W. Perry

I included the picture above because we're about to visit a black church. This particular snapshot (from Georgia) must have been taken during a quieter portion of the service since, although everyone else is intent on the sermon, the young woman is the middle is nodding off. Then again, maybe she's praying.

This chapter describes how Comfort's wife Metta felt about the isolation her family was forced to endure. Notice the praise she as a Yankee felt for the milder climate in the hills of North Carolina, something the South could have used to attract industry and immigration—that is if it had not been so obsessed with race. That's the biggest change in the South since I was a kid. Now the region does its best to attract businesses and newcomers.

Notice also the friendship that's developing between Comfort and his young daughter. The fact that she is a "strangely willful child" will serve her well in about seven years when she must act boldly to save her father. Her powers of observation will also help as she makes that long night journey over a route she has traveled only once before.

The family does have friends. The Tom Savage that Metta mentions in her letter is the friendly "Mr. Savage" who appeared earlier in Chapters 13 and 14 of *A Fool's Errand*. There something important happens I must mention. As Comfort was traveling home after his forced speech two chapters back, he is warned by two poor white farmers—Unionist and Republican—that he may be attacked on the way. Further on, a black man named Jerry Hunt, so crippled he is bent almost horizontal at the waist, draws him into the bushes and describes a conversation he overheard about how the attack will occur. This Jerry Hunt is the religious "Uncle

Jerry" much loved by the black community. Metta will write about him in the last part of her letter, and we will find more about him later.

Forewarned, Comfort is able to turn the tables on his attackers, leaving Tom Savage, badly injured. In kindness, he takes Savage home and nurses him back to health, turning an enemy into the faithful friend he has become in this chapter. For a time, Savage's lingering influence over the Klan-like Regulators protects Comfort from attack.

Notice the strong influence that black preachers have on their community. We also see that during the civil rights era of the 1960s. Martin Luther King was a black Baptist preacher, as were many of those involved in the Southern Christian Leadership Conference. That gave them some independence from the pressures applied on other black leaders not make trouble.

With their second Christmas, Metta again wrote her sister. Notice too that Lily was being homeschooled.

Dear Julia,

It is more than a year since I wrote you my first letter from our Southern home. Alas! Except for the improvements we have made in Warrington, and the increased sense of homeliness which we feel in our inanimate surroundings, it is hardly any more like home than it was then. Comfort has been very busy. He has put quite a new face on Warrington, which is more delightful than any description could convey to you. Almost every day he is out superintending and directing the work, and, Yankee-like, 'doing right smart of it' himself, as they say here. This, with the delightful climate and my care—for I must have some of the credit—has transformed my invalid husband into a cheerful, stalwart man, who seems to be in constant enjoyment of life.

Most of my time is occupied with teaching our little daughter, or rather coaxing her to learn, for she is the most strangely willful child in this respect you ever saw. I am taking much pains with her, and she is making wonderful progress in a peculiar sort of a way. She is out with her father on the plantation a great deal, and, as a result, knows the name of every tree and flower, wild or cultivated, which grows about Warrington. She has either inherited or acquired that wonderful power of observation which Comfort has and is already better versed in some branches of knowledge than I am likely ever to be.

This, with my few household cares, and the enjoyment of rides, walks, and all sorts of excursions, makes up my life. Mere existence here is a constant joy. The sunshine is brighter, the moonlight softer, the sky fairer, the earth more seductive, than in the old home. There is a sort of intoxication in it all—the flowers, coming at odd times and with unwonted richness and profusion, the trees, of a strangely charming outline and foliage, making forest and grove, which have always some sort of weird charm, so different from what we ever knew at the North, and over all the balmy air.

And yet we miss our friends—ah! sadly enough—for we have none here, and somehow can not make any. I am sure no one ever came to a new home with kindlier feelings for all who might surround us than we did. You know Comfort would not hear a word about trouble with the people here. He would insist that they were a brave, genial people, that the war was over, and that everybody would be better friends hereafter from its having occurred.

He has found out his mistake. I am afraid we shall have no *real* friends here. There are some, perhaps, who think well of us, and, no doubt, wish us well in the main, but they are not friends. Somehow it seems that the old distrust and dislike of Northern people will not let them be friendly and confiding with us, or perhaps the fault may be with us. We are so different, have been reared under such different influences, and have such different thoughts, that it does not seem as if we should ever get nearer to them.

You heard about our trouble with the 'Regulators.' Comfort got a lot of guns and ammunition for the colored men, and made preparations to fight in good earnest, but they have not disturbed us since. Mr. Savage sent them word that they could not hurt us until they had killed him and came over and staid with us some weeks. I think it was his influence which saved us from further attack.

The feeling is terribly bitter against Comfort on account of his course towards the colored people. There is quite a village of them on the lower end of the plantation. They have a church, a sabbath school, and are to have next year a school. You can not imagine how kind they have been to us, and how much they are attached to Comfort. They are having a 'tracted meeting,' as they call it, now. I got Comfort to go with me to one of their prayer-meetings a few nights ago. I had heard a great deal about them but had never attended one before.

It was strangely weird. There were, perhaps, fifty present, mostly middle-aged men and women. They were singing, in a soft, low monotone, interspersed with prolonged exclamatory notes, a sort of rude hymn, which I was surprised to know was one of their old songs in slave times. How the chorus came to be endured in those days I can not imagine. It was—

'Free! free! free, my Lord, free!

An' we walks de hebben-ly way!'

A few looked around as we came in and seated ourselves, and Uncle Jerry, the saint of the settlement, came forward on his staves, and said, in his soft voice—"Ev'nin', Kunnel! Sarvant, Missus! Will you walk up an' hev seats in front?"

We told him we had just looked in, and might go in a short time, so we would stay in the back part of the audience.

Uncle Jerry can not read nor write, but he is a man of strange intelligence and power. Unable to do work of any account, he is the faithful friend, monitor, and director of others. He has a house and piece of land, all paid for, a good horse and cow, and, with the aid of his wife and two boys, made a fine crop this season. He is one of the most promising colored men in the settlement, so Comfort says, at least. Everybody seems to have great respect for his character. I don't know how many people I have heard speak of his religion. Mr. Savage used to say he had rather hear him pray than any other man on earth. He was much prized by his master, even after he was disabled, on account of his faithfulness and character.

The meeting was led that night by a mulatto man named Robert, who was what is now called an 'old-issue free nigger' (freed before the war). He seemed very anxious to display the fact that he could read, and, with comical pride, blundered through 'de free hunner'n firty-fird hymn,' and a chapter of Scripture. Some of his comments on passages of the latter were ludicrously apt. 'I indeed baptize with water, but he that cometh after me shall baptize with the Holy Ghost and with fire,' he read with difficulty. 'Baptize wid water,' he repeated thoughtfully. 'We all know what dat is, an' baptizin' wid de Holy Ghos', dat's what we's come here arter tonight. ('Amen!' 'Bress God!' 'Dar now!') But baptizin' wid fire!—'clar, brudderin' an' sisters, it allers makes my *har stan' straight* tu think what dat ar *muss* mean! Baptize wid fire! I spec' dat's de tryin' ob de gold in de furnace—de Lord's furnace—dat clars out all de dross, but muss be powerful hot!'

There was nothing special then for some time, until one man began weaving back and forth on his knees, and shouted, in a voice which might have been heard a mile, for fifteen or twenty minutes, only one sentence—'Gather 'em in! O Lor', gather 'em in! Gather 'em in! O Lor', gather 'em in!'—in a strange, singing tone, the effect of which upon the nerves was something terrible.

Men shouted, women screamed. Some sprang from their knees, and danced, shouting, and tossing their arms about in an unconscious manner, reminding me of what I had read of the dancing dervishes of the Orient. One woman fainted, and finally the see-sawing shouter himself fell over. Some water was poured on his head, a slow soothing hymn was sung, and in five minutes the assemblage was as quiet as any country prayer-meeting in Michigan. For me, I found myself clinging to Comfort's arm in almost hysterical fright. I begged him to take me away, but am very glad now that he did not.

After a time Uncle Jerry raised his head, which had all the time been bowed upon his knees since the meeting began, and, lifting his thin hands towards the people, said, in a soft, clear voice—"Let us all kneel down, an' pray—one mo' short pra'r! Short pra'r!"

He knelt with his face towards us. The guttered candle on the rough pine table threw its flickering light over him, as, with upturned face and clasping hands, he 'talked with God.' Oh, how simply and directly! And, as he prayed, a strange light seemed to come over his brown face, set in its white frame of snowy hair and beard. He prayed for all, except himself, and seemed to bring the cares and troubles of all before the throne of grace, as if he had the key to the heart of each.

Then he came to pray for us—"the stranger fren' whom God has raised up an' led, in his myster'ous way, to do us good—bless him, O Lord, in basket an' sto', heart an' home! He don't know what he's got afo' him! Stay his han', an' keep him strong an' brave!" But I can never reproduce the strange tenderness and faith of this prayer.

I leaned my head on Comfort's shoulder, and the tears fell like rain as I listened. All at once there was silence. The voice of prayer had ceased, yet the prayer did not seem ended. I raised my eyes, and looked. Uncle Jerry still knelt at his chair, every worshiper still kneeling in his place, but every head was turned, and every eye was fastened on him. His eyes were fixed—on what? He was looking upward, as if he saw beyond the earth. His face was set in rigid lines, yet lighted up with a look of awful joy. His breath came slow and sobbingly, but, aside from that, not a muscle moved. Not a word was uttered, but every look was fastened on him with hushed and fearful expectancy.

"Hain't bin dat way but once afo' sence de surrender," I heard one of the women whisper, under her breath, to another.

Five minutes—perhaps ten minutes—elapsed, and he had not spoken or moved. It was fearful, the terrible silence, and that fixed, immovable face and stony figure! There was something preternatural about it.

At length there came a quiver about the lips. The eyes lost their fixity. The hands which had rested on the chair were clasped together, and a look of divine rapture swept across the upturned face, as he exclaimed, in a tone fairly burdened with ecstatic joy,—"I *sees* Him! I sees *Him*! Dar He *is*!" And he pointed, with a thin and trembling hand, towards the farther corner of he room. "I sees Him wid de crown of salvation on His head; de keys o' hebben a-hangin' in His girdle—God's keys for de white pearl gates—wid de bress-plate ob Holiness an' de mantle ob Righteousness. Dah He is a-walkin' among de candlesticks *yit*! He's a-comin' nigh us—bress His holy name!—A-lookin' arter His people, and a-gatherin' on 'em in!"

I can not tell you what a strange rhapsody fell from his lips, but it ended as it began—suddenly, and without warning. The glorified look faded from his face. The sentence died midway on his lips. His eyes regained their conscious look, and ran around the hushed circle of attent [attentive] faces, while a knowledge of what had taken place seemed first to flash upon him. He covered his face with his hands, and sank down with a groan, exclaiming, in apologetic tones—"O Lor'! O Lor'! Thou knowest de weakness ob dy sarvant! Spar' him! Spar' him!" The meeting ended, and we went home. Somehow I can not get over the feeling that the little log church is a place where one has indeed seen God.

They told us afterwards that Uncle Jerry often had these 'spells,' as they called them, whenever there was great battle pending or imminent during the war, and they could always tell which way the fight had gone, by what he said in the trances. They say he knows nothing of what he says at such times.

I asked him about it one day. He simply said, "I can't 'splain it, Missus. 'Pears like it's a cross I hez specially to carry. It's made me a heap o' trouble. Bin whipped fer it heaps o' times; an, 'sides dat, I allers feel ez if I'd lived 'bout ten years when I comes out o' one o' dem spells. Can't understan' it, Missus, but Uncle Jerry'll quit in some of dem spells yit!"

We do not often go to [white] church now. There is no positive incivility offered us, but there is a constant coldness, which says, plainer than words can, that we are not wanted. Comfort still has hope that these things will wear away as time passes, but I begin to think that we shall always be strangers in the land in which we dwell. I do not see any chance for it to be otherwise. The North and the South are two peoples, utterly dissimilar in all their characteristics, and I am afraid that more than one generation must pass before they will become one.

Your loving sister,

Meta

Ch. 17, "The Second Mile Post," in *A Fool's Errand* by Albion Tourgée.

8. A Confederate
Soldier Writes

Prosperity and Danger
Michael W. Perry

In case you wonder, this is what chopping cotton looks like. The two are a brother and sister in Georgia, but you can imagine them as newlyweds growing their first cotton crop together and looking forward to starting a family. Unlike corn, which quickly grows tall and overwhelms weeds, cotton plants are scraggly little bushes that need constant weeding. At this point, the cotton plants are just coming up, so that chopping has to be carefully done to kill only the weeds. As you can see, it's tedious, mind-numbing work done under a hot sun.

In the chapters that follow are five letters Comfort received after the publicity surrounding his defiance of the Regulator's threat. It's now 1867, two years after the end of the war. Sensing a weakening Northern resolve, those who want to restore white supremacy are more aggressive. As Edmund Burke put it, "All that is necessary for the triumph of evil is that good men do nothing." Here, good Southern men and women are doing something, but will it be enough, especially if they get little help from the North?

The first letter comes from Exum Davis, a man who—unlike the self-serving Ezekiel Vaugh—had fought for the Confederacy in many of the most important battles from the first at Bull Run in July of 1861 to last near Appomattox Court House in April of 1865. He's not bitter that all his sacrifices have been for nothing. Instead, thankful his health remains strong, he sets about rebuilding his life, taking particular care to treat the former slaves who work for him decently. Remember, not every Southern planter is evil. There are those who treat their black workers kindly. Notice too that his strength of character must have been so obvious that, despite having fought for the Confederacy, Union soldiers were willing to give him two horses.

The threat this former Confederate soldier receives shows that Comfort's being a Yankee has little to do with the Regulators' hatred. Anyone who helps black people get ahead is an enemy, even if he had been a loyal soldier for the South.

Exum's response to these threats illustrates the value of military training and experience. He acts quickly, intelligently, and decisively when faced with danger. Within an hour of receiving the threat, he is constructing a stockade, and that same day he goes to a nearby Union post to get more weapons. Evil is best met with a willingness to fight. Often that means not having to fight.

Davis took other steps to defend himself and his family. Later, Comfort will get another letter from him. Two nights earlier, Davis wrote, while he and his family were praying, the Klan attacked his home, which he had fortified like a blockhouse. Arming his wife and daughter, and "with a prayer for myself and my enemies outside, I put my gun to the port-hole, glanced along it, and pulled the trigger." With their leader dead, his attackers retreated.

Unfortunately, not everyone was as brave and determined as Exum Davis. The harsh treatment the Regulators directed at him, a good and decent white, and at talented, hard-working black farmers illustrates how racism wrecked the Southern economy. Success was punished when it stood in the way of racial hatred and single-party rule. That's true wherever it happens and no matter which race is doing the hating. Black people can be as consumed by hate as whites. Black communities can suffer from the consequences of their foolish prejudices much like white communities do.

Soon after the Fool's publication of the Regulators' warning and his own reply in *The Verdenton Gazette*, he received many letters, some of which may be given as illustrative of the atmosphere in which he lived. The first of these came from a remote portion of the State and from one of whom the Fool had never even heard—

Colonel Comfort Servosse

Dear Sir,

I saw your letter in *The Verdenton Gazette*, and was so struck with the similarity of our positions, that I determined to write to you at once. Some of the worst of our people, as I believe, have formed themselves into a band of Regulators for the sake of attending to everybody's business but their own.

I am a native of this State, and fought through the war in the Confederate army, from Bull Run to Appomattox, never missing a day's duty nor a fight. When it was over, I found myself with only a few hundred acres of land (which had been tramped over and burned and stripped by both armies), and no money, no crop, no stock, a large family, some debts, good health, and a constitution like white hickory.

I made up my mind to go to work at once. I went to the nearest post, told my story, and got two horses. I did some hauling and got some other things—an army wagon and an ambulance. A friend who happened to have saved some cotton sold it and loaned me a little money. I went to work, hired some niggers, told them I would feed them and work with them and, when the crop was sold, we would divide. They turned in and worked with me. We made a splendid crop, and I divided right smart of money with them in the fall.

This year some of them wanted to work crops on shares. I could trust them, as they had worked for me the year before. I knew they had enough to bread themselves and were well able to run a 'one-horse crop.' This would allow me to use my means in putting in more land elsewhere and so be decidedly to my advantage as well as theirs. I was thinking of my own profit, though, when I did it. Well, I sold some of them horses and mules and helped others to get them elsewhere.

The spring opened, and I had the busiest farm and finest prospect I have ever seen. I was running a big force, and every nigger on the plantation had a full crop about half pitched, when all at once I got a notice from the Regulators, just about like the one you publish, only they didn't require me to leave, only to stop selling horses to niggers and letting them crop on shares. They said they had made up their minds that no nigger should straddle his own horse or ride in his own cart in this county.

I saw in a minute that it meant ruin to Exum Davis either way. If I gave in to them, I discouraged my hands, spoilt my crop, and would be swamped by my fertilizer account in the fall. If I didn't, the cussed fools would be deviling and worrying my hands, ham-stringing their stock, and my crop would be short. It didn't take me long to decide. I made up my mind to fight.

It wasn't an hour after I read that notice, before I had every horse and mule on the place hauling pine logs for a stockade, though I didn't let anybody know what I had on hand.

Then I went off to Gainsborough to see the post commander there, Colonel Ricker. He is a good fellow and a gentleman, if he is a Yankee. I told him square out what the matter was, and he let me have as many old guns as I wanted (part of them surrendered arms and part extra guns of his command), and a couple boxes of ammunition.

When I got back, I told the boys what was up, and distributed the arms. We put our horses in the woods that night, stood to our arms all night, put up the stockade next day, and sent word to the Regulators that they might go to hell.

We've kept at work, being mighty careful not to be surprised, and have not been disturbed yet. I don't reckon we shall be, but there is no telling. I say, Stand your ground. They say you're a 'Yank,' but that don't make any difference. Law's law, and right's right, and I hope you will give anybody that comes to disturb you as warm a welcome as they would get here from

Yours respectfully,

Exum Davis

Start of Ch. 18, "Congratulation and Condolence," in *A Fool's Errand* by Albion Tourgée.

9. A Baptist Deacon Writes

Many Generations Will Pass

Michael W. Perry

The author of this letter was mentioned earlier in *A Fool's Errand*. George Garnet was an exceptionally decent guy. He came from a long-established Southern family that had owned slaves. Becoming convinced that slavery was wrong but having little money to free them, he bought slaves who wanted to be free and allowed them to work for their freedom. With that money, he then bought, employed, and freed other slaves. He illustrates that, even in an evil system, it is possible to do more than simply refuse to participate. Someone can fight against evil and do good. Keep in mind that, while this letter centers on the trouble he experienced from his church, he probably faced even greater hostility from the broader community. Those who freed slaves were often hated.

As a deacon in a Baptist church, Garnet tried to get it to support a Sabbath school for black children like those above. Although left unstated, the 'offense' he had committed in their eyes probably did not lie in teaching religion but in teaching those children to read and write. In that day, Sabbath schools did both. Notice also his mention of Lily, the "fair-haired child who fills the sad old house with sunshine." She must have been a most cheerful and happy child.

When you read the letter from his church, notice that George is condemned not for what he did but because some found him a "means of offense." Right and wrong should not be dictated by what others like or dislike. Sometimes those offended are wrong and should be told to change or shut up.

The next was from the old doctor, George D. Garnet—

My Dear Colonel,

I was sorry to see that the feeling against you, because you are of Northern birth, which has been smoldering ever since you came among us, has at last burst into a flame. I have been expecting it all the time, and so can not say I am surprised, but it has been so long in showing itself, that I was truly in hopes that you would escape further molestation.

I know that I had no reason to anticipate such a result, because you represent a development utterly antagonistic to that in the midst of which you are placed, and are so imbued with its spirit that you can not lay aside nor conceal its characteristics. That civilization by which you are surrounded has never been tolerant of opinions which do not harmonize with its ideas. Based and builded on slavery, the ideas which were a part of that institution, or which were necessary to its protection and development, have become ingrained, and essential to the existence of the community. It was this development which was even more dangerous and inimical to the nation than the institution itself.

You must remember, dear Colonel, that neither the nature, habits of thought, nor prejudices of men, are changed by war or its results. The institution of slavery is abolished, but the prejudice, intolerance, and bitterness which it fostered and nourished, are still alive, and will live until those who were raised beneath its glare have moldered back to dust. A new generation—perhaps many new generations—must arise before the North and the South can be one people, or the prejudices, resentments, and ideas of slavery, intensified by unsuccessful war, can be obliterated.

I hope you will not be discouraged. Your course is the right one, and by pursuing it steadily you will sow the seed of future good. You may not live to reap its advantages, or to see others gather its fair fruits. But, as God is the God of truth and right, he will send a husbandman who will some time gather full sheaves from your seeding, if you do not faint.

To show you that not only you who are from the North are made to feel the weight of disapproval which our Southern society visits upon those who do not accord with all its sentiments, I enclose you a certificate which I received from the church at Mayfield the other day. I have been a member and a deacon of this church for almost quarter of a century. I was lately informed that my name had been dropped from the church-roll.

Upon inquiry, I found that I had been expelled by vote of the church, without a trial. I demanded a certificate of the fact as a vindication of my character, and the enclosed is what was given me. It is neither more nor less than I had expected for some time. But it comes hard to a man who has reached his threescore years, and now sees his children pointed at in scorn, contemned and ostracized by the church of God, because their father does what he conceives to be his Christian duty.

With warmest regards for yourself and wife, and the fair-haired child who fills the sad old house with sunshine, I remain,

Yours very truly,

George D. Garnet

The enclosure to which he referred read as follows—

To Whom It May Concern,

This is to certify, that on the first day of April, 1867, the deacons and members of the Baptist Church, at Mayfield, in regular church meeting assembled, Brother R. Lawrence acting as moderator, did unanimously pass the following resolution—

"*Resolved*, That brother Deacon George D. Garnet be dropped from the roll of this church, because he walketh not with us.' And subsequently, on the same day, at the request of brother George D. Garnet, and to show that it was not from his bad moral character that the said church refuses longer to fellowship with him, the following was added to said resolution as explanatory of it; to wit, 'but persists, after repeated warnings and advice, upon organizing, encouraging, and teaching in a negro sabbath school, by which he has made himself a stumbling-block and means of offense to many of the members of said church."

(Signed)

John Senter, Clerk

Robert Lawrence, Deacon and Moderator

Middle of Ch. 18, "Congratulation and Condolence," in *A Fool's Errand* by Albion Tourgée.

10. A Southern Lawyer Writes

The Strength of Prejudice

Michael W. Perry

The picture above shows how scraggly cotton plants look at harvest time. In a typical Southern thunderstorm, the plants offer the soil little protection from heavy rain and erosion. That's one reason why cotton so rapidly depletes the soil. Each year the soil gets a little poorer and the harvest a little smaller.

Now imagine you're one of the boys or girls in that picture. Think of the hot sun, the stooping over and over again to pick the cotton, and the care you must take so none of the dried leaf stays with the white fibers. There's also the heavy bag you must drag behind you, a bag that may weigh more than you do. If you had to spend day after day doing that, how much energy would you have for school work? Probably little or none. In *To Kill a Mockingbird*, Harper Lee has Scout say this about her first day of school.

> Miss Caroline began the day by reading us a story about cats. The cats had long conversations with one another, they wore cunning little clothes and lived in a warm house beneath a kitchen stove. By the time Mrs. Cat called the drugstore for an order of chocolate malted mice the class was wriggling like a bucketful of catawba worms. Miss Caroline seemed unaware that the ragged, denim-shirted and flour-sack-skirted first grade, most of whom had chopped cotton and fed hogs from the time they were able to walk, were immune to imaginative literature.

> Sadly, the grind of agricultural child labor left those children without the energy or imagination to benefit from school. Learning little from what schooling they had, they grew up like their parents, repeating the vicious cycle of poverty.

The picture at the start of this chapter is from 1913 Texas, so that vile post-Civil-War cycle was already almost half a century old. It was still there almost fifty years later for Edward R. Murrow's moving 1960 documentary about migrant workers, *Harvest of Shame*, which opens with these lines.

> This is not taking place in the Congo. It has nothing to do with Johannes-burg or Cape Town. It is not Nyasaland or Nigeria. This is Florida. These are citizens of the United States, 1960. This is a shape-up for migrant workers. The hawkers are chanting the going piece rate at the various fields. This is the way the humans who harvest the food for the best-fed people in the world get hired. One farmer looked at this and said, "We used to own our slaves. Now we just rent them."

Keep in mind that, when Comfort Servosse refers to the writer that follows as a "Union man," he doesn't mean a former Union soldier like himself. He means a Southerner who supported the Union cause during the war, often at great cost.

This letter explains some of the problems Comfort faces. The war has not changed the widespread belief that blacks are an inferior people deserving of slavery and with no right to own land, ride horses, or have guns. They are for all practical purposes less than fully human. For a modern day parallel, think of those today who deny any rights to the "fetus." Both attempt to dehumanize by using words derived from Latin, as if describing someone with a foreign word somehow makes them less than human. Evil does not change.

Of course, there are differences. Slavery and the dehumanization of black people were ancient evils. In the U.S., slavery was centuries old when the debate began to heat up in the early nineteenth century. That's why, when the U.S. Supreme Court voted seven-to-two in favor of slavery in the *Dred Scott* decision—hoping to end the debate once and for all—it changed almost nothing. In contrast, when that same court and by that same vote legalized abortion in 1973, it overturned the laws of all fifty states. *Roe v. Wade* was far more radical than *Dred*.

There is also a startling historical parallel. *Both* decisions were decided by an identical vote released on precisely the *same day* in the nation's four-year political calendar. That is shocking. Here is how that's so.

Under our original Constitution, presidents were inaugurated on March 4. *Dred* was made public two days later on March 6, 1857. To reduce the delay before a new president took office, the twentieth amendment (1933) moved the inaugural date to January 20. That means that when *Roe* was released on January 22, 1973, it was also precisely two days after a presidential inaugural. In both cases the reason for choosing that date was the same—to bury a decision the Court knew was controversial in the flurry of news following a presidential inauguration. In both, the court was being more political than legal. And in both cases the Court was hideously and unspeakably wrong.

The Civil War and Attitudes toward Black People

THERE'S ANOTHER CHANGE THAT Tourgée mentions so often in his book that it must be important. Over and over again, he has people tell Comfort that the war worsened and hardened the attitude of many whites toward black people. Before the war, he is told, only the more wealthy Southerners benefited from slavery. Support for slavery in defiance of Northern opposition was little more than regional pride—something akin to preferring grits to Boston beans. "Don't mess with our way of life," many Southerners were saying. That's why slavery was often defended as state's rights rather than white supremacy.

Northern attitudes closely mirrored those in the South. Most Northerners weren't abolitionists and often disliked them. Their objections focused on issues closer to home, particularly the Fugitive Slave Act of 1850. They resented Southern attempts to draw them into the slave system more than they did slavery itself. They also turned to state's rights to defend their regional views. In 1854 the Wisconsin Supreme Court went so far as to declare the Fugitive Slave Act unconstitutional.

The Civil War changed attitudes in the North and South. It was long, costly and bloody, depriving many families of a father or a son. The North may have entered the war to preserve the union, but by the war's end few in the North wanted it to end on any terms other than the abolition of slavery. Many weren't that concerned about slavery itself. They simply wanted to prevent another war by removing the cause. Southern resistance to civil rights for blacks exploited that indifference. A bad bargain was struck. Southern acceptance of the union would be traded for Northern acceptance of white supremacy.

In the South, the cost of the war had been even greater than in the North because most of the fighting took place there. After the war, the natural human tendency to look for meaning in suffering was twisted by those responsible for the war. A costly and bloody war to defend slavery mutated after defeat into a violent and covert war for white supremacy to justify all the pointless blood shed. It was foolish to let those who had caused the war define its meaning. They should have been punished rather than rewarded with respect and political power.

The letter Comfort received follows. Written by a lawyer to a lawyer, it uses legal terms. A writ of *venire facis* requires those summoned to appear before a court for jury duty. Keep in mind that at this time there are still restrictions on voting by those who fought for the Confederacy, and Union troops were stationed in the South to ensure that black people could vote. The result was a brief period during which good and decent men such as this Thomas Denton could hold high office, typically as Republicans, and vigorously prosecute a white man for killing a black man. When Lily rides to save her father, she will also ride to save the man who wrote this letter. Remember that as you read.

The next letter was from Thomas Denton, a Union man of considerable eminence who occupied the important position of public pros-
ecutor in the courts of the State. He wrote a letter which is significant in
many ways of the public sentiment of the day—

Colonel Comfort Servosse

Dear Sir,

I notice by your letter in *The Gazette* that you are not only angry, but also
surprised, at the outrageous demands of the Regulators. Your anger is but
natural, but your surprise, you will allow me to say, shows 'an understanding
simple and unschooled.'

**That you should be unable to measure the strength of prejudice in the
Southern mind is not strange. You should remember that the war has
rather intensified than diminished the pride, the arrogance, and the sec-
tional rancor and malevolence of the Southern people.**

If you will consider it for a moment, you will see that this is the natural
and unavoidable result of such a struggle. All that made the Southern slaveholder and rebel what he was, still characterizes him since the surrender.
The dogma of State-sovereignty has been prevented from receiving practical
development, but as a theory it is as vital and as sacred as ever. The *fact* of
slavery is destroyed: the *right to enslave* is yet as devoutly held as ever. The
right of a white man to certain political privileges is admitted: the right of a
colored man to such, it will require generations to establish.

It is not at you as an individual that the blow is struck. But these people
feel that you, by the very fact of Northern birth and service in the Federal
army, represent a power which has deprived them of property, liberty, and a
right to control their own, and that now, in sheer wantonness of insult, you
are encouraging the colored people to do those two things which are more
sacred than any other to the Southern mind; to wit, *to buy and hold land and
to ride their own horses.* You can not understand why they should feel so, because you were never submitted to the same influences. You have a right to
be angry, but your surprise is incredible to them, and pitiable to me.

To show you to what extent prejudice will extend, permit me to relate an
incident yet fresh in my mind. During a recent trial in the court at Martins-
ville I had occasion to challenge the jurors upon the trial of an indictment
of a white man for killing a negro.

The Court, after some hesitation, permitted me to ask each juror this
question, 'Have you any feeling which would prevent you from convicting
a white man for the murder of a negro, should the evidence show him to be
guilty?' Strange and discreditable as it may appear to you, it became necessary, in addition to the regular panel, to order *three writs of venire, of fifty
each, before twelve men could be found who could answer this simple question in
the negative.*

When prejudice goes so far that a hundred and fifty men acknowledge upon their oaths that they will not convict a white man for killing a negro, you must not be surprised that the *ante bellum* [before the Civil War] dislike and distrust of Northern men should show itself in the same manner. The South has been changed only in so far as the overwhelming power of the conqueror has rendered change imperative. In its old domain, prejudice is still as bitter and unreasoning as ever.

Perhaps I ought not to reproach you for expressing surprise, since it was not clear even to me, a native, until I had carefully studied the cause and effect. While I sincerely regret the unfortunate folly of these men, and hope it may extend no farther, I must still beg you to consider that it is only what must always be expected under such circumstances as the recent past has witnessed.

If you have any clew [clue] to the persons guilty of this act, or if I can be of any service in freeing you from annoyances, please to consider me, both personally and officially,

Yours to command,

Thomas Denton

Middle of Ch. 18, "Congratulation and Condolence," in *A Fool's Errand* by Albion Tourgée.

11. Two Women Write

Lonely Roads
Michael W. Perry

The final two letters were written by women to Comfort' Servosse's brave young wife. You might want to imagine either as the woman pictured above with her baby.

The first letter hints at the danger Comfort also faces, especially when he travels. At that time sheriffs were still being appointed by occupation military commanders rather than elected by a local population intimidated by the Klan. That's why her brave and good husband had to be killed.

The other two were directed to Metta. The first was from the wife of a Northern man who had settled in a neighboring State, and whom Metta had met at the house of a common friend some months before. It was edged with black and told a sad story:

My Dear Mrs. Servosse,

I have desired to write you for several days, but have been too over-whelmed with grief to do so. You have probably seen in the papers the ac-count of my husband's death. You know he was appointed sheriff of this county a few months ago by the general commanding the district. There was a great deal of feeling about the matter, and I begged him not to accept. Somehow I had a presentiment of evil to come from it, but he laughed at my fears, said he should only do his duty, and there could be no cause of increased hostility against him.

Indeed, I think he had an idea, that, when the people found out that his only purpose was to administer the office fairly, they would respect his motives, and be more friendly than they had been for the past few months. He never would believe that the hostility towards Northern men was anything more than a temporary fever.

After he entered upon the office, there were many threats made against him, and I begged him not to expose himself. But he did not know what fear was, and rode all over the county at all times, in the performance of his duties, coming home every night when it was possible, however, because he knew of my anxiety. One week ago today he was detained at the courthouse later than usual. You know we live about five miles from the county seat. As night came on I grew very anxious about him. I seemed to know that danger threatened him. Finally I became so uneasy that I had my mare saddled and rode to meet him, as I frequently did. The road is almost directly westward, winding through an overhanging forest, with only here and there a plantation road leading off to a neighbor's house.

It was almost sundown when I started. Would to God it had been earlier! Perhaps I might have saved him then. I had gone about a mile, when, rising a little eminence, I saw him coming down the slope beyond, and at little branch at the foot of the hill, I stopped to wait for him. He waved his hat as he saw me, and struck into a brisk canter.

I wanted to give the mare the whip and gallop to him, but I feared he would see my alarm and count it childish, so I sat and waited. He had come half the distance, when suddenly there was a puff of smoke from the roadside. I did not wait even to hear the report, but with a cry of despair struck my horse and rushed forward like the wind. I saw him fall from his horse, which rushed madly by me. Then I saw three miscreants steal away from a leafy blind, behind which they had been hidden. And then I had my poor murdered husband in my arms, heard his last struggling gasp, and felt his warm heart-blood gushing over my hands as I clasped him to my breast. I knew nothing more until I was at home with my dead.

Oh, my dear friend, I can not picture to you my desolation! It is so horrible! If he had died in battle, I could have endured it. Even accident or swift disease, it seems to me, I could have borne. But this horrible, causeless murder fills me with rage and hate as well as grief. Why did we ever come to this accursed land! And oh, my friend, do not neglect my warning! Do not cease your entreaty until your husband hears your prayers. Do not risk the fate which has befallen me.

Yours in hopeless sorrow,

Alice E. Coleman

Your True Friend

THE OTHER LETTER WAS in a neat, feminine hand, written on the coarse, dingy paper known as "Confederate paper," which was the only kind accessible during the blockade. It was evidently written by a woman of culture. It was not signed with any name, but only "Your true friend," and bore the postmark of Verdenton:

> My Dear Mrs. Servosse,
>
> Though you do not know who I am, I have seen you, and am sure you are not only a lady, but a sensible, true-hearted woman. Though a stranger, I would not have you suffer grief, or incur trouble, if in my power to prevent it.
>
> Please, then, dear madam, listen to the advice of a sincere well-wisher, and do all in your power to persuade your husband to leave this part of the country. I am sure he can not be a bad man, or you would not love him so well. But you must know that his ideas are very obnoxious to us Southern people, and if he stays here, and continues to express them as he has hitherto, I feel that there will be trouble.
>
> You know our Southern gentlemen can not endure any reflections upon their conduct or motives; and the hopes and aspirations which gathered around the Confederacy are all the dearer from the fate of our 'Lost Cause.' I know whereof I write. [The next sentence had been commenced with the words "My husband," which had been so nearly erased that they could only be read with difficulty.] Several gentlemen were speaking of the matter in my hearing only last night, and I tremble to think what may occur if you do not heed my warning.
>
> **O dear lady! Let me beg you, as a Christian woman, to implore your husband to go away. You do not know what sorrow you will save, not only yourself, but others who would mourn almost as deeply as you, and perhaps more bitterly.** The war is over and oh! If you have mourned as much as I over its havoc, you will be willing to do and suffer any thing in order to avoid further bloodshed, violence, evil, and sorrow. May God guide you!
>
> I can only sign myself
> Your True Friend

The Fool Responds

METTA TOOK THESE LETTERS to the Fool, and laid them silently before him. Her face looked gray and wan, and there was the shadow of a great fear in her eyes, as she did so. He read them over carefully, laid them down, and looked up into her face as he said, "Well?"

"I thought I ought to show them to you, dear husband," she said with quivering lip. And then the pent-up tears overflowed the swollen lids, as she buried her head on his breast, and, clasped in his arms, wept long and convulsively. When her grief was somewhat soothed, he said, "What do you wish me to do, Metta?"

"Whatever you think to be your duty, my dear husband," she replied, the sunshine of wifely devotion showing through the last drops of the shower.

He kissed her forehead and lips—kissed away the briny tears from her eyes. "We will stay," said the Fool.

The subject of removal from their adopted home was never again mooted between them.

Last part of Ch. 18, Congratulation and Condolence," in *A Fool's Errand* by Albion Tourgée.

12. Choosing State Delegates

Speaking Up

Michael W. Perry

We've just read letters from several people describing how difficult life was after the Civil War for those who opposed white supremacy. In this chapter we see how that harsh treatment affected a larger group of mostly kind-hearted Southerners who lacked education, self-confidence, and experience in politics. Think of them as the parents of the two little girls pictured above. Notice that their home is so small, the back door is only a few yards from the front. It may have had only one or two rooms and was cold in winter, hot in summer. Notice too how the big sister holds the hand of her little sister. Probably both her parents must work in the fields so, as young as she is, she has to care for her trusting sister. The poor must often grow up fast—too fast. That leaves too little time to be a child.

To be good against such a ruthless and all pervasive evil, you must be strong and either be a leader yourself or have experienced people leading you. That's what Comfort Servosse means when he writes in this chapter about being "accustomed to command" and to "participation in matters of public interest."

Culture also mattered. The decades-old national debate over slavery had poisoned Southern culture, changing it from that of the famous Virginians who'd helped shape our Constitution and the less known frontier Baptists who gave us our Bill of Rights. Notice how the author wonders how "the spirit of ready and hearty co-operation and participation in matters of public interest which is almost the birthright of the Northern citizen" left him "vexed and troubled at the retiring hesitancy of the [Southern] Union men by whom he was surrounded. Why a hundred or a thousand men should come together for a particular purpose, and then 'hem and haw,' and wait for someone to move first, he could not understand."

As a child who grew up in the segregated South, I know what he meant. I experienced that same frustration. In high school, I called it the 'they say' problem. Adults seemed able to bring up a controversial subject only by referring vaguely to what 'they say'—with no names given. That's because taking a personal stand on a race-related topic in the Old South was dangerous. Crushing debate about slavery and white supremacy created a culture where debating anything was difficult. Remember those three ancestors of mine who were murdered for what they believed. That's what life was like in the Old South.

Crushing Dissent

Two groups were to blame for that passivity and silence. One had economic motives and the other political ones. We've already discussed this, but it's worth repeating since few today seem willing to discuss it.

In the latter half of the nineteenth century, plantation owners and their close kin (businesses such as timber companies and later cotton mills) dominated Southern economic life. They could make life unpleasant for a small farmer who needed their help in tough times. When the owners hired extra hands during planting and harvest, paying in scarce cash, they could take into account a man's politics. When a poor farmer's mule died and he needed to ask a nearby plantation owner for the loan of one for his spring plowing, he had best not be a troublemaker. It he was, his children would go hungry the next winter. That created fear—lots of fear. Never forget that.

The Democratic party was an even greater source of fear. Once it returned to power in the early to mid-1870s, the party of slavery became the party of segregation with a vengeance. It could and did use government to crush dissent. Those who made trouble or didn't vote for it, found themselves deprived of the benefits and protections that they had a right to receive.

Harper Lee described just that in *To Kill a Mockingbird* when she has Atticus tell his children that, among the reasons for Mr. Cunningham's poverty, was his stubborn refusal to do as the Democratic party dictated: "If he held his mouth right, Mr. Cunningham could get a WPA job, but his land would go to ruin if he left it, and he was willing to go hungry to keep his land and vote as he pleased."

The WPA, stood first for Works Progress Administration and later for the Work Project Administration. As a New Deal program, it gave jobs to the unemployed, typically building parks and schools for public use. That provided some income for those out of work, but did little to help them escape poverty. That was deliberate. The poor must be kept dependent.

How was that done? The WPA paid the 'prevailing wage' in a region, which in the South was woefully low, and working hours were limited to thirty a week. Paying more and working more would have outraged planters, who wanted wages kept low. What the WPA offered was what they wanted—just enough money to keep their laborers from starving during the months when their labor wasn't needed. Mr. Cunningham was right to stay away from the WPA. It was a dead end.

Documentary writers have described the same protest votes for Republicans as fiction writers such as Harper Lee. James Agee's *Cotton Tenants* describes what it was like to be a sharecropper in 1930s Alabama. One of the rare joys for one white sharecropper was voting Republican, he said, to anger those in politics who treated him badly.

> Fields still pays his poll tax. Barring tobacco and occasional drinks, it is his one luxury. He votes only when there is a Republican to vote for. He does that out of independence and spite. At first they made him trouble, of a mild sort, but they just let him go now. It gives him a lot of pleasure.

The fictional Mr. Cunningham and the real Mr. Fields were fortunate. The 1930s were not like the horrors of the 1870s. By the later date, the Democratic party so dominated Southern life that it didn't feel a need to make more than mild trouble for its critics. With only rare exceptions, they didn't need to lynch or shoot.

Black People—Lead by the Worst

FINALLY, AS BADLY AS life was for the independent farmers and tradesmen who made up the bulk of Unionist whites, the black people of the South had it far worse. Unionists were unfamiliar with leadership, but had been permitted some political freedom. Just before the Civil War, many openly voted against succession. After the war, they found a home in the Republican party.

In contrast, blacks were "unused to political assemblies" altogether. They had *never* been allowed to vote or express their opinions freely. In fact, fears of a slave revolt made any meeting outside a small church service illegal. With the exception of black preachers, who were expected to limit what they said to feelings in the present or life in the hereafter, the only leaders that blacks were allowed to have were the brutal slave overseers and slave drivers with their whips, who did as their white owners directed. Black culture is still haunted by the fact that the worst blacks were trained to lead, while the rest were expected to obey. That's a dreadful legacy to live with.

We need to be grimly realistic. It took a century for politics in the *white* South to escape domination by the political descendants of those plantation owners and the Democratic party. In the black community, change has come even more slowly. Even today, *black* politics is often dominated by the corrupt and self-serving political descendants of those slave overseers. Even today, dissent and independence within the black community is ruthlessly crushed. Most revealing of all, everyone must toe the Democratic party line just like whites did under segregation.

State Constitutional Conventions

Now FOR A LITTLE background. The Constitutional Convention described below was to create a new state constitution that complied with terms set by the victorious North. At this time many supporters of the Confederacy were barred from voting, so the new constitution will be decided by the votes of blacks and Unionist whites. Later, many of these state constitutions were replaced by ones that limited the political power of poor blacks by preventing them from voting. They also unfairly distributed votes in the state legislature, giving more political power to Black Belt counties dominated by wealthy planters and less to whites in the hilly, Unionist counties.

The Colonel Nathan Rehnn mentioned in this chapter is the same well-respected gentleman who persuaded Comfort to speak at the earlier meeting. He takes social conventions seriously, so before the Civil War he never challenged slavery. But Rehn is also a good-hearted man. He refused to separate the families of his slaves, even though that was common. That's why—although he is a former slave owner—the black people at this meeting are delighted to see him. He has their respect. He may change his mind slowly, but when he does, his new commitment is real. That's also why his appearance at this meeting creates a stir among whites. There was something about his integrity that everyone respects, something so inspiring that even his present poverty could not erase. Think of him as the opposite of the ever-shifting Colonel Vaghn, who was not even respected by those whose cause he so zealously serves.

You might examine the principles to be included in the new state constitution. These are Southerners, mostly the impoverished and poorly educated whites who are often blamed today for segregation and racism. Yet they call, first and foremost for: "Equal civil and political rights to all men." Segregation in the South didn't come from these poor whites. It was imposed from the top down by the Democratic party and was intended to serve the interests of large landowners who exploited both poor blacks and whites.

When Comfort spoke at the earlier meeting, he warned that if the champions of white supremacy didn't allow at least the better educated and more successful blacks to vote, political pressure would grow to accept all blacks and whites, however poor, as voters and jurors. That's now happening, as a tentative alliance is forming between poor whites and blacks. To win, the Democratic party must destroy that alliance. To do that it will feed racial hatred.

The third item refers to the fact that many offices in the South were appointed rather than elected, and the fourth to the brutal laws that had as their primary purpose the punishment of crimes by slaves. There were 17 crimes for which someone could be put to death. This would reduce them to one (murder) or two (probably murder and rape). The fifth refers to the fact that, across much of the South, wealthy plantation owners were allowed to determine the value of their land for tax purposes and pay less for the value of their land than poor farmers. That often left local governments starved for money. The last item, "An effective system of public schools," shows the value these poorly educated people, both black and white, attached to giving their children a good education. That brings up someone who was attending this meeting, the brave John Walters.

John Walters During the Civil War

TOURGÉE FIRST REFERRED TO John Walters, mentioned at the close of this chapter, in Chapter 19 of *A Fool's Errand*. Most Unionists of draft age who did not want to fight for the Confederacy either hid in the woods, like my great-great-grandfather, or went north to enlist in the Union army, like his brothers. Walters did neither. He shows that if you're firm enough and don't cause trouble, you *may* be left alone, although perhaps not without an occasional struggle to assert your rights. As one person put it, to keep your integrity intact, you must be "no man to trifle with." In that chapter, a friend explained what happened during the Civil War to Walters, whose health any medical board would know was excellent. He was a skilled fighter, as this description makes clear:

> "He was living in Rockford when the war began, in business, making money, and a member of the Methodist Church. He wanted to go away at the first, but his wife said she didn't want to leave her people. So John Walters staid right where he was, and went on trading, and minding his own business, the same as before.... He wasn't no man to trifle with, and so he went on unmolested.
>
> "Finally a young conscript officer came to the town, and talked pretty loud about what he would do. Some things he said came to Walters's ears, and he went over to see him, carryin' a walking-stick in his hand. They met on the porch. I never knew what passed, but a man who saw it told me that the officer drew his pistol, an' another man caught Walters's right arm. I don't reckon anybody knows just how it was done—not even Walters himself. They were all there in a crowd, but when it broke up Walters had the pistol, the officer had a bullet somewhere through his jaw, another man had a broken arm, and another had somehow tumbled off the porch and sprained his foot, so that he could not walk for a month. Walters was the only one unhurt. He reported here next day, was examined by a medical board, and somehow pronounced unfit for duty."

As you can see, Walters was a man's man. Fortunately, during the war with the fate of slavery still uncertain, the white supremacists had more important things on their minds than a lone nonconformist who minded his own business and knew how to defend himself. But after the war, when the fate of the South lay in politics rather than military action, they could not tolerate someone who was taking his convictions into politics. Later, we will see what they do to him, the father of two daughters much like those two little girls pictured at the start of this chapter.

When the time for the election of delegates to a Constitutional Convention was near at hand, the Union men of the county held a meeting to nominate candidates. The colored people, as yet unused to political assemblages, but with an indistinct impression that their rights and interests were involved, attended in large numbers. The Union men were few and not of that class who were accustomed to the lead and control of such meetings. The place of assembly selected was an old country schoolhouse some two miles from the county seat, and situated in a beautiful grove.

Accustomed to Command

THE FOOL, PARTLY FROM curiosity, and partly to give such aid and countenance as he might to a movement which was based upon a recognition and support of the Federal Union as contra-distinguished from the idea of voluntary secession and disintegration, attended the meeting, though hardly half-convinced of the practicability and wisdom of the proposed plan of reconstruction. By this time he was well known in the county, and, quite unconsciously to himself, regarded as a leader in the movement.

Accustomed to command for four years and previous to that time imbued with the spirit of ready and hearty co-operation and participation in matters of public interest which is almost the birthright of the Northern citizen, he was vexed and troubled at the retiring hesitancy of the Union men by whom he was surrounded. Why a hundred or a thousand men should come together for a particular purpose, and then "hem and haw," and wait for some one to move first, he could not understand.

When he came on the ground, the hour for which the meeting had been appointed had already arrived. The colored people had gathered in a dense mass on one side of the platform, waiting in earnest expectancy to take whatever part might be allotted to them in the performance of the new and untried duties of citizenship.

The white men were squatted about in little groups, conversing in low, uneasy tones, and glancing suspiciously at every new-comer. A little at one side was Colonel Ezekiel Vaughn, with a few cronies, laughing and talking boisterously about the different men who were taking part in the movement. This seemed to have a wonderfully depressing effect upon the white Unionists, who evidently dreaded his clamorous ridicule and feared that some disturbance might ensue, should they attempt to proceed.

"Well," said the Fool, as he approached a group of a dozen or more, seated in a circle under a giant oak, "why don't you begin?"

"Hist!," said one of those whom he addressed. "Don't you see those fellows?," at the same time nodding and winking towards Vaughn and his crowd.

"See them?" he replied, as he glanced towards them. "Yes. Why?"

"They've come here for a row," answered the other.

"Pshaw!" said the Fool. "They don't want any row. But, if they do, let them have it."

"But we can't do any thing if they have made up their minds to break up the meeting," said the Unionist.

"Break up the meeting! Fudge! Are we not enough to take care of that squad of non-combatant fire-eaters?"

"Oh, yes! But then—they would make a heap of trouble," was the reply. "Don't you think we had better put it off, and have a private understanding with our people that they shall come here on a certain day and be sure and not let Colonel Vaughn or any of his crowd know about it?"

"No, I don't!," answered the Fool promptly. "If we are going to be cowed and browbeaten out of doing our duty by a crowd of men who never did anything but talk, we may as well give up and go home. If not, let us stay and do our duty as good citizens."

"Why don't you open your show, Servosse?" asked Vaughn, in a loud and taunting voice, as he approached the group. "I tell you we are getting mighty tired of waitin,' and them niggers is just bustin' for a chance to begin votin'."

"Hello, Vaughn!," said the Fool, in a voice equally loud, but more jovial. "Are you here? Then we will begin at once. We were just waiting for the monkey before the show began. But, if you are on hand, we are all ready."

There was a laugh, and Vaughn retired disconcerted. But one of those with whom the Fool had been conversing drew him aside, and said with great seriousness—"Now, Colonel, you will excuse me, but I am afraid you will get yourself into trouble if you talk to these folks in that way. You see they are not used to it."

"Then let them get used to it," said the Fool carelessly. "If Vaughn did not want a sharp retort, he should not have made an insolent remark."

"That's so, Colonel, but you see they are used to doin' and sayin' any thing they choose in regard to people who happen to differ with them. Why, I remember when a man was prosecuted here in this very county for havin' a seditious book—one about slavery, you know— in his possession, and lendin' it to a friend. And people were almost afraid to speak to him, or go bail for him. You Northern people don't know any thing about what we call public opinion here."

"I'm sure I don't want to know, if it means that a man shall not speak his opinion freely and throw stones when another throws them at him," said the Fool determinedly.

"Yet," said the Union man, "it is folly to defy and provoke such a spirit unnecessarily."

"I agree with you there, my friend," was the Fool's answer. "But, if one has principles which are worth supporting or fighting for, they ought also to be worth standing up for against ridicule and arrogance."

"It would seem so, but it won't do—not in this country, anyhow," said the Unionist with a sigh.

Colonel Nathan Rhenn Arrives

At this point there were symptoms of excitement among the crowd; and a faint, straggling cheer broke out, as Colonel Rhenn rode up, and dismounted from his horse, which he tied to an overhanging bough, and came forward, holding his well-worn beaver [hat] in his left hand, bowing, and shaking hands with his neighbors, and returning with slight but grave courtesy the boisterous greeting of the colored people. This arrival at once seemed to give confidence to those who had before evidently regarded the movement as a disagreeable if not a dangerous duty.

Nathan Rhenn was a gentleman of a type peculiarly Southern and exceedingly rare. He was of an old but not now wealthy family. His connections were good, but not high. Before the war he had been in comfortable circumstances only—now he was actually poor. Yet at no time had he abated one jot of that innate gentility which had always marked his deportment. He was clad now in "butter-nut-gray" homespun, wore black woolen gloves on his hands, a high black stock on his neck, with a high, narrow-brimmed, and rather dingy beaver hat, and would have been a figure highly provocative of mirth, had it not been for his considerate, graceful, and self-respecting courtesy.

Since the meeting at which he presided, when the Fool made his maiden speech upon a political question, Colonel Rhenn had rarely attended public meetings, and was known as one whose status (despite his former Unionism, which was unquestioned) was very doubtful. He was known to be one who would not have attended the meeting unless he intended to give in his adhesion to the cause which it had assembled to promote. He was considered, therefore, an accession of very great importance, by those who were present, to the cause of Reconstruction. Hardly had he greeted his many friends, when some one arose and said—

"I nominate Nathan Rhenn as chairman of this meeting."

Nathan Rhenn's Speech

IT WAS UNANIMOUSLY CONCURRED in, and the new arrival, with many grave bows and protestations, permitted himself to be led to the platform. Upon taking his seat as chairman, he made a brief speech, in substance as follows:

"Fellow Citizens, I have come here today for the purpose of giving my support and countenance to a movement in support of what are known as the Reconstruction Acts, which I presume to be the reason that you have honored me by making me your chairman.

"As you are well aware, I have always been a Union man. I believe that under all circumstances, and by all persons and parties, I have been accorded that distinction. At the same time, I have never been, or been considered, an abolitionist. I was a slaveholder, and belonged to a race of slaveholders, and never felt any conscientious scruples at remaining such. I did not pass upon slavery, it is true, as a new or an abstract question, but considered it as I found it, solely in relation to myself.

"I did not buy nor sell, except when I bought a woman that she might not be sold away from her husband, and sold one man, at his own request, that he might go with his wife. The act of buying and selling human beings, I admit, was repulsive to me, but I accepted the institution as I found it, and did not feel called upon to attempt its overthrow.

"In the attempt which was made to disrupt the government, this institution has been destroyed; and it is the question in regard to the future political relations of those who were, as it were, but yesterday slaves, which produces the present differences of opinion among our people, and promises future contact.

"If it were the simple question whether we should now be restored to the American Union, and take our place as one of the co-ordinate States, which we had to decide, there would be no difference of opinion. Only an insignificant minority of our people would oppose such restoration upon any terms which did not embrace the conferring of political power upon the freed people.

"Many think this an unwise and impracticable measure. Others believe it to be imposed upon us by the conquerors, simply as an act of wanton and gross insult, for the purpose of adding to the degradation of an already humiliated foe. The fact, also, that every one who had been an officer of the old government, and then served the Confederacy in any voluntary capacity, is barred from the right of suffrage, while his recent slave is given the power to vote, occasions much ill feeling.

"While I deem the exclusion wise and necessary, though it must strike some who are undeserving, I confess that I have had my fears in regard to the latter measure. After mature and earnest reflection, however, I have become satisfied, that, at the least, the best thing we can do is to accept what is offered, show our willingness to submit to whatever may be deemed wise and proper, and trust that the future may establish the right. Therefore I have come here today to co-operate with you. And now, gentlemen, what is your pleasure?"

For once there was a scarcity of candidates. No one seemed to desire a position which promised to be onerous, without honor, and of little profit, which it was felt would cast odium upon the individual, and social and religious ostracism upon his family. The names of the chairman and another were submitted, but the chairman stated that, having been a member of the Legislature before the war, and a justice of the peace during the Confederacy, he believed himself disqualified. Then the Fool's name was substituted for that of the chairman, and the nomination was made.

According to custom, the candidates were called upon to make speeches in acceptance; and the Fool in so doing acknowledged himself quite unprepared to state the line of conduct he should propose in the convention, beyond the acquaintance of the conditions prescribed in the Acts under which the election would be held, but promised to set it forth in a printed circular, that all might read and understand his position.

The Convention Document

THE NEXT WEEK THIS document came out. It does not seem half so revolutionary as it really was. It read:

I shall, if elected, favor:

1. Equal civil and political rights to all men.

2. The abolition of property qualifications for voters, officers, and jurors.

3. Election by the people of all officers—legislative, executive, and judicial—in the state, the counties, the municipalities.

4. Penal reform: the abolition of the whipping-post, the stocks, and the branding-iron; and the reduction of capital felonies from seventeen to one, or at most two.

5. Uniform and *ad valorem* [according to value] taxation upon property, and a limitation of capitation tax to not more than three days labor upon the public roads in each year, or an equivalent thereof.

6. An effective system of public schools.

The Fool had no idea that he was committing an enormity, but from that day he became an outlaw in the land where he hoped to have made a home and which he desired faithfully to serve.

There was a short, sharp canvass, a quiet election, and one day there came to the Fool's address an official document bearing the imprint of the "Headquarters of the Military District" in which he lived, certifying that "Comfort Servosse had been duly elected a delegate to the Constitutional Convention to be held pursuant to the acts of Congress." With him went as members of that body some old friends whom we have met in these pages. Among them John Walters, who was the delegate-elect from his county.

Ch. 23, "The Die is Cast," in *A Fool's Errand* by Albion Tourgée.

13. SHAMED BY THE KLAN

Pride and Prejudice

Michael W. Perry

As all this was happening, Lily was growing into her teens and discovering what we've seen thus far. In this chapter, Comfort mentions her exposure to the unpleasantness of their life. I am including those troubles, so you'll understand what will pass through her mind when that most important of all nights comes.

Yes, I'm aware that knowing about these events isn't pleasant for you as a reader and still more aware that events are about to turn far worse. But does mean that, when the need for her ride comes, Lily is prepared, and that, if you read along with me, you'll be prepared too. You'll know why she didn't hesitate to undertake her ride through that terrifying, Klan-infested night.

Comfort introduced Squire Nathaniel Hyman in Chapter 10 of *A Fool's Errand*, explaining that he was one of their nearest neighbors and "a queer old gossip, who is so anxious to be on good terms with everybody that he has hard times to keep anybody on his side." That eagerness to please must have made it difficult for Hyman to be a judge and having an independent son wasn't making life any easier for him. Imagine him, before his health turned bad, minding his own business and seeding his fields much like the man in the picture above.

Notice that the Regulators have become the Ku Klux Klan. That matters little. Foulness by any name remains foul. Notice too the high sense of honor Hyman feels—the shame that his son has been badly beaten by some unknown with no chance of getting a 'gentleman's revenge.' Pride played an important role in Southern culture.

Notice that simply voting Republican is enough to earn even someone who minds their own business the noxious label 'Radical.' Sadly, political prejudice has changed little between now and then. Bigots, it seems, never even change. They still attack the character of good people.

Finally, there's Theophilis Jones, the preacher that Servosse contacts to help Hyman's son when he moves to Indiana. Comfort is probably right to point out that this "fanatic" was a bit too inclined to see everything that happens as God doing something especially for his sake. It may also be true that denouncing slavery was, for this preacher not so much a matter of working to end slavery for the sake of the black people themselves than of providing a situation where these two preachers could preach and be persecuted, thus acquiring what they think is merit in God's eyes.

That said, it's also true that, having taken up the task of helping the son of someone who once harmed him, "duty and religion" would keep him faithful. In that limited sphere, he was a good man in an era when goodness was scarce.

One morning in the early winter, Squire Hyman came to Warrington at a most unusual hour. Comfort and his family were just sitting down to their early breakfast when he was announced. The servant stated that he had declined to join in the meal, but had taken a seat by the sitting-room fire. Lily, who was a prime favorite with the old man, went at once to persuade him to come and breakfast with them. She returned with the unexpected visitor, but no persuasions could induce him to partake with them. He seemed very much disturbed, and said, as he sat down in the chimney corner:

"No, I thank you kindly. I just came over to have a little chat, and perhaps get a little neighborly advice, if so be the colonel would be good enough to give it."

"I hope there is nothing wrong with you at home," said Servosse, with real anxiety, for the old man seemed greatly disturbed.

"I'm afraid, Colonel," he replied, with a deep sigh, "that there's a good deal of wrong, a good deal—a heap more and a heap worse than I had ever counted on."

"Why, no one sick, I hope?" said the colonel.

"No, not sick exactly," was the reply, "worse'n that. The truth is, Colonel, the Ku-Klux took out my boy Jesse last night, and beat him nigh about to death."

"Shocking! You don't say!," burst from his listeners. The meal was abandoned, and, gathering near the old man, they listened to his story.

"You see," he said, "Jesse had been into town yesterday, and came home late last night. So far as I can learn, it must have been nine o'clock or so when he started out—at least, 'twan't far from twelve o'clock when he came through the little piece of timber on the far side of my house (you know the place well, Colonel, and you too, Madam, for you have ridden by it often—just in the hollow, this side the blacksmith's shop). When all at once a crowd of men burst out of the woods and bushes, all hidden with masks and gowns, and after some parley took him into the woods, tied him to a tree, and beat him horribly with hickories.

Jesse said he hadn't no chance to fight at all. They were all on him almost afore he knew it. He did kick about a little, and managed to pull the mask off from one fellow's face. This seemed to make them madder than ever, though they needn't have been, for he says he didn't know the man from Adam, even when he saw his face. However, that didn't make no difference. They took him out and whipped him, because they said he was a 'nigger-loving Radical.'"

"Poor fellow! Is he seriously injured?," asked Comfort in alarm.

"I don't know as to that, Colonel," answered Hyman, "and it don't much matter. He's been whipped, and it could not be worse if he were dead. Indeed," continued the old man as he gazed sadly into the fire, "I would rather know that he was dead. He'd better be dead than be so disgraced! Did you ever know, Colonel, that the Supreme Court of this State once decided that whipping was worse than hanging?"

"No," said Comfort. "I never heard of such a thing."

"They did, though," said the old squire. "I don't recollect the precise case, but you will find it in our [published court] reports, if you care to look for it. You see the Legislature had changed the punishment for some crime from hanging to whipping and had repealed the old law. The result was, that some fellow, who was afterwards convicted of an offense committed before the passage of the act, appealed on the ground that whipping was an aggravation of the death penalty, and the Court held with him.

They were right too—just right. I'd a heap rather my poor Jesse was dead than to think of him lying there, and mourning and groaning in his shame. If it had been openly done, it would not have been so bad. Then he could have killed the man who did it or been killed in the attempt to get a gentleman's revenge. But to be whipped like a dog and not even know who did it, to think that the very one who comes to sympathize as a friend may be one of the crowd that did it—oh! It is too much, too much!"

"Indeed," said the Fool, with an awkward attempt at consolation, "it is too bad, but you must console yourself, Squire, with the reflection that your son has never done any thing to deserve such treatment at his neighbor's hands."

"That's the worst part on't, Colonel," said the old man hotly. "He's a good boy, Jesse is, an' he always has been a good boy. I don't say it 'cause he's mine, nor 'cause he's the only one that's left, but because it's true; and everybody knows it's true. He's never been wild nor dissipated—not given to drinkin' nor frolickin'. He was nothin' but a boy when the war came on, but when my older boy, Phil—the same as was killed at Gettysburg—went away, Jesse took hold as steady and regular as an old man to help me on the plantation. You know I'm gittin' old, and hain't been able to git about much this many a year, so as to look after the hands, an' keep things a-goin' as they ought to be.

Well, boy as he was, Jesse raised two as good crops as we've had on the plantation in a long time. Then when they called for the Junior Reserves, toward the last of the war, he went and 'listed in the regular army 'bout Richmond, and took his share of the fightin' from that on.

An' when it was over, an' the niggers free, an' all that, he didn't stop to dawdle round, and cuss about it, but went right to work, hired our old niggers—every one of whom would lay down his life for Jesse—an' just said to me, 'Now, Dad, don't you have any trouble. You just sit quiet, and smoke yer pipe, an' poke 'round occasionally to see that things is goin' right round the house an' barn-lot, an' keep Ma from grievin' about Phil, and I'll run the plantation.' An' when I told him how bad off I was, owin' for some of the niggers that was now free, and a right smart of security-debts beside, and the State-script and bank stock worth almost nothin', he didn't wince nor falter, but just said, 'You just be easy, Pa. I'll take care of them things. You must keep Ma's spirits up, and I'll look out for the rest.'

"You know how that boy's worked, Colonel, early and late, year after year, as if he had nothing to look forward to in life only payin' his old father's debts, and makin' of us comfortable. He never meddled with nobody else's business, but just stuck to his own all the time—*all the time!* An' then to think he should be whipped, by our own folks too, last like a nigger!—and all because he was a Radical!

"S'pose he was a Radical, Colonel, hadn't he a right to be? You're a Radical, ain't ye? And a carpetbagger too? Have they any right to take *you* out an' whip you? I reckon you don't think so, but it's a heap worse to mistreat one of our own folks—one that fought for the South, and not agin her. Don't ye think so, Colonel?

"Well, it's natural you shouldn't see the difference, but I do. S'pose he *was* a Radical? He didn't have nothing to say about it—just went an' voted on 'lection-day, and come home again. Are they goin' to whip men, an' ruin them, for that? I declare, Colonel, I'm an old man, and a man of peace too, and a magistrate. But I swear to God, if I knew who it was that had done this business, I'd let him know I could send a load of buckshot home yet—damned if I wouldn't!

"Beg pardon, Madam," he continued, as he remembered Metta's presence, "but you must allow for the feelings of a father. I'm not often betrayed into such rudeness, Madam—not often.

"But Colonel," he went on meditatively, "do you know I don't think that was more than half the reason the Ku-Klux beat Jesse?"

"No?" said the Fool. "What else had he done to awaken their animosity?"

"He's been your friend, Colonel—always your friend, and he thinks, and I think too, that what he's been made to suffer has been more on your account than his own. You know they've been a-threatenin' and warnin' you for some time, and you haven't paid no heed to it. When they rode off last night, they told Jesse he might tell his 'damned Radical Yankee friend Servosse that they were comin' for him next time.'

"Jesse's mighty troubled about it, for he thinks a heap of you all, and he wanted me to come right over here, and let you know, so that, bein' forewarned, you might be forearmed."

"Poor fellow!" said the Fool. "It was very kind and thoughtful of him. It is altogether too bad that any one should suffer merely for being my friend."

"Well, you know how our people are, Colonel," said the old man, with the impulses of a life still strong upon him to make excuse for that people whose thought he had always endorsed hitherto, and whose acts he had always excused, if he could not altogether approve. "You know how they are. They can't stand nobody else meddlin' with their institutions, and your ideas are *so* radical! I shouldn't have wondered if it had been you—candidly, Colonel, I shouldn't—but that they should do so to my boy, one that's native here, of good family (if I do say it), and that never troubled nobody—it's too bad, too bad!"

"Yes, indeed!" said the Fool. "And I must go and see him at once. I don't suppose I can do him any good, but I must let him know how I sympathize with him."

Helping Hyman's Son

"THAT BRINGS ME AROUND to the rest of my errand," said the old man. "I am so upset by this thing, that I like to have clean forgotten it. He 'llowed you'd be comin' to see him as soon as you heard of it, and he wanted me to tell you that he couldn't see anybody now (not while he's in this condition, you know). But he—he wanted I should say to you— say to you," he repeated, with the tears running over his face, "that he was goin' to Injianny [Indiana] tonight, and he would be glad if you could give him some letters to any friends you may have in the West. You know he can't stay here any more (not after this), and he thought it might be well enough to have some introduction, so as not to be exactly goin' among strangers, you know."

"He will take the train at Verdenton, I suppose," said the Fool.

"Yes, I spose so," answered the old man. "He hain't made no arrangements yet, an' it'll be a hard thing for him to ride there in his condition."

"Has he any particular point to which he wishes to go?"

"None at all—just to get away, you know. That's all he goes for."

"Yes," said the Fool thoughtfully. Then, after a moment, he continued decisively, "See here, Squire! You tell the boy not to trouble himself about the matter, but keep quiet, and I will arrange it for him. He must not think of going tonight, but you may give out that he has gone. I will come for him tonight, and bring him here. And after a time he can go West and find himself among friends."

This arrangement was carried out, almost against the will of the one most concerned. And it was under the roof of the "carpetbagger" that the outraged "native" found refuge before he fled from the savage displeasure of the people who could not suffer him to differ with them in opinion.

In his behalf the fool wrote a letter to the Reverend Theophilus Jones, detailing to him the event which this chapter narrates, and the condition of the young man at that time. To this letter he received the following reply:

Wedgeworth, Kan

My Dear Sir,

Your very interesting letter has awakened strange memories. It is only twelve years ago that Brother James Stiles and myself were interrupted in the midst of a gospel service at a place called Flat Rock by a mob, which was said to have been put upon our track by your neighbor Nathaniel Hyman, because we preached the word of God as it had been delivered unto us, and denounced the sin of slavery according to the light that was given us.

We were sorely beaten with many stripes. But we continued instant in prayer for them who did despitefully use us, calling out to each other to be of good cheer, and, even in the midst of their scourging, praying, in the words of the blessed Saviour on the cross, "Father, forgive them, for they know not what they do."

When they loosed our bonds, we gave thanks that we were permitted to bear testimony to the truth, even with our blood, and went on our way rejoicing, tarrying not in those coasts, however, since we perceived that this people were joined to their idols, and given up to sin. We said unto our persecutors, in the words of the apostle, "The Lord reward thee according to thy works."

Verily, the Lord hath heard the cry of his servants, and hath not forgotten their stripes. My heart was hushed with holy awe when I read in your letter that the son of this man, who caused *us* to be scourged, had suffered a like chastisement at the hands of wicked men—perhaps the very hands by which we were smitten aforetime. Through all these years the God of Sabaoth hath not forgotten our cry, nor to reward the evil-doers according to their works."

Well may we exclaim, as we look back at these intervening years of wonder-working events, "What hath God wrought!" As the war went on, and I saw the bulwarks of slavery crumbling away, until finally the light of freedom shone upon the slave, I rejoiced at the wonderful power of God, who wrought out the ends of his glory through the instrumentality of human passion and human greed.

How it reproached our weak murmurings and want of faith! Who could have believed that all the evils which slavery was for so many years piling up as a sin-offering in mockery of the Most High and his mandates—the blood, the tears, the groans, and woes of God's stricken and crying people—were so soon to become the forces which should destroy the oppressor, root and branch! Ah! If that grand old St. John of this new dispensation of liberty—John Brown—could have foreseen this in the hour of his ignominious death! But perhaps he did see it, and the sting of death was removed by the beatific vision.

Nothing of it all, however, has so humbled and terrified me as this immediate and fearful retribution visited on one of my persecutors. God knows I had never entertained feelings of malice or revenge towards them. I have never forgotten to pray for these, my enemies, as we are commanded to do in the canon of Holy Scripture. But I had never thought to see the hand of God thus visibly stretched forth to avenge my wrongs. The very thought has humbled me more than I can express, and I have been moved to ask myself whether this occasion does open to me a way of duty which is in strictest harmony with the dictates of our holy religion.

The young man who has suffered for his father's sin, and of whom you speak so highly, you say desires to escape from what he considers his shame, though it ought to be deemed his glory. Why not let him come hither, my friend—for as such I can not but esteem you henceforth—and let me thank the good Father by succoring the son of him who persecuted me? Gladly, humbly, will I perform this duty as an act of praise and thanksgiving to Him who ruleth and over-ruleth all things to his glory. Faithfully, as He was faithful to me, would I perform such trust, tenderly and humbly, so that the young man should never know whose hand was extended to do him kindness. Please to consider this suggestion, and, if it accord with your views, send him to me, assured that I will intermit no effort in his behalf.

I am in truth,

Thy servant and brother in the Lord,

Theophilus Jones

The Fool knew that the fanatic was in serious earnest, and that, despite his ready assumption of the divine act as having been performed in his individual behalf, there was a sort of chivalric devotion to what he deemed duty and religion, which would make him untiring in the performance of his self-imposed trust. So the castigated son of the old squire went to the free West to begin life anew under the protection and patronage of the man whose back was striped at his father's instigation, in the good old days "befo' the wah."

Ch. 29, "Footing Up the Ledger," in *A Fool's Errand* by Albion Tourgée.

14. John Walters Disappears

Press Hatred

Michael W. Perry

The chapter that follows, now split into three parts, wasn't in my first draft of *Lily's Ride* for the same reason that Albert Tourgée hesitated to include it. He explained why in a note: "This account of an incredible barbarity is based on the sworn statement of a colored person who overheard just such an account, given of just such a performance, by one of the actors in it. It is too horrid to print, but too true to omit." Notice what he was saying. This story may be in a novel, but what it describes actually happened. It's real as you and I. *It is history.*

Why include it? First, I want you to give a strong sense for what life was like back then. Lily grew up in a world filled with hatred and violence. When she awoke each morning she knew that her father's life hung by the thinnest of threads. There were those who, given the opportunity, would kill him just as brutally and coldly as they will John Walters. That's why she never doubts the warning she gets, and why she begins her brave ride.

Second, I hope you develop a healthy suspicion for the news you read and hear. The newspapers lied about John Walters then. They may lie about someone as good as he is today There seems to be something about journalism that attracts the prejudiced. Perhaps they're drawn by the power to attack those they dislike. Short of murder, few evils are worse than destroying a person's reputation. That's as true now as then. The proper response is the same contempt you'd feel for a physician who kills his patients through incompetence or malice. He clearly should not be in medicine, like they should not be in journalism.

Notice too that this dishonest reporting wasn't just in the Southern press. Even a little child could see that only *one* group had a reason to kill John—the Democratic party that would soon be facing him in an election. In fact the first article, written when John was merely missing, hopes that the "worst thing" that could happen to him has happened—meaning his death. Yet the Northern press blindly echoed the lies of their Southern counterparts. Journalism apparently attracts both bigots *and* people lacking enough common sense to connect A to B by a dotted line. Taking into account its prejudices, the press is remarkably easy to manipulate.

Also, take special note when the news media or someone they quote accuses someone of being 'radical." Historically, it's a great compliment. The word entered our political vocabulary when it was used by Democrats to slander those who wanted to put an end to slavery—mostly abolitionists and Republicans. When slavery ended, its meaning shifted slightly to those who opposed white supremacy—again mostly Republicans—who were then branded scalawags and carpetbaggers. That's the meaning in this book. Today that term is used in the abortion debate and again typically used of pro-life Republicans and social conservatives in general. Perhaps because they live in an echo chamber of their own creation, journalist rarely learn from their mistakes. They repeat them over and over again, feeding generation after generation of misery.

Third, never forget who John Walters was. He was a poor Southern white who looked much like the man whose picture is at the start of this chapter. He was a member of a group that's branded today as a racist. But he was kind and good-hearted man who'd never had a chance for a good education. He had spent untold hours, after long and exhausting days in the fields, educating himself. He desperately wanted the two daughters he loved to have the schooling he'd been denied. That's why he was speaking out and risking his life. That's also why, although he's white, he had many ardent black supporters. Like him, they wanted a good education for their children. In that day, studying hard wasn't just for whites. I can't say that enough. It was the Klan who taught black people—through violence, burning and lynchings—that blacks should not read and study hard. Black people who live today as if studying and learning is something 'white' or bad are the foolish puppets of long-dead Klansmen.

Fourth, we need to understand the circumstances of the black people who play such an important role in this story. This was not Comfort's county in the hill country of North Carolina. This was a Black Belt county where blacks, as former slaves, were a majority of the population. That gave them power. If they were allowed to vote—and especially if they were allied with the county's poorer whites—they decide who holds political office. That was why so much hatred was directed at them.

Never forget, though, that these newly freed slaves faced a terrible problem. Most were illiterate. That was not their fault. Across the slave-owning South, teaching them to read had been a crime. In addition, outside their churches, few had any experience with leadership. For generations, they'd been the ones taking orders. That's why the blacks in this story often seem passive. They were used to being bossed about and mistreated. They were not used to leading.

Yes, there was one exception—a most depressing one that I mentioned earlier. Within the black community there were slave overseers and drivers who served planters well. Slavery would have been far less successful if a slave owner had to be out in the cotton fields all day under a blazing sun rather than sipping mint juleps [iced bourbon with sweetened mint] in the shade of a veranda. It was those blacks who whipped slaves and drove them relentlessly who made slavery work. For that, they were well-rewarded. Although rarely mentioned, after the Civil War, they would continue to serve their white masters. They don't enter our story because Tourgée doesn't mention them. But be aware that they exist. Every group has traitors.

Alliance of Poor Blacks and Whites

ALL THAT EXPLAINS WHY in this Black Belt county the political alliance between poor blacks and whites mattered so much. Slaves received no education. Poor whites received only a little education, but that was enough to make some literate. Slaves were beaten if they didn't obey. These poor whites usually had small farms or some trade that earned them a living. Most had little experience giving orders. But some had a fiercely independent spirit that made it easier for natural leaders to develop. One of those leaders was John Walters.

The problem these poor whites and blacks faced was that there were so few among them qualified to hold political office. That's why John Walters was willing make a deal with what he hoped were a better sort of Democrats—a vain hope that proved to be. His supporters, a clear majority in that county, did not have a bad agenda. They're good people who would support any candidate who enforced the laws fairly and provided good schools for all children, black and white.

Last and foulest of all were the evil doers in this dreadful tale This meeting, with several hundred people attending, was for Democrats only. It's goal was to crush the growing alliance between poor blacks and whites. That's why they were furious that John Walters, that alliance's leader, sat among them taking notes.

That's why they lure him away and kill him within sight of his daughters playing on a hillside. Can you think of anything fouler than that? Most of the killing in this era were done by surrogates of the Democratic party, especially the Klan. This murder was done by the party itself. I think you can see why I describe it not only as a hate group but as an extraordinarily violent one.

Also, notice the history that you hear today says little or nothing about these murderers, preferring instead to blame poor whites. The Democratic party's evil has been as concealed from our eyes as the good done by those wonderful church-going Yankee women who came South to teach black children to read. Silence itself can be a great wrong. Silence can be a terrible lie. In fact, it can be as evil as slander.

Tourgée will tell what happened from several points of view. We turn to the first telling—the newspaper accounts of what happened. Yes, I know that names such as General DeBang (Confederate army), the Honorable John Snortout (probably a judge), and Colonel Whiteheat (perhaps a wealthy planter) are obviously made up. They were given fake names for legal reasons. The people behind this story are real and might have harassed Tourée by suing him.

Also, the term *scalawag*—used here for the first time in this story—was originally a word for sickly, worthless cattle. Much like carpetbaggers, used of Northerners who came South after the Civil War, it was a smear word for Southerners who opposed white supremacy and typically voted Republican. Some of my ancestors were undoubtedly scalawags, a fact in which I take great pride. You might want to adopt a similar attitude. If you're going to be hated, make sure you are hated for the right reasons and take pride in it.

Last and most important of all, remember that Lily heard her parents talk about this. She understood what happened to John Walters, the father of two wonderful little girls, could also happen to her father. Put yourself in her shoes.

Now I'll explain something that will help you understand these. The murder you'll read about was certainly evil, but you may not realize just how evil it was. Viewed one way, there are three kinds of evil. What we might call *basic evil* slanders, attacks and even kills until forced to stop by force or the law. Basic evil certainly existed here. A good man, a wonderful husband, and a loving father was murdered.

But this evil goes deeper still. Beyond basic evil lies *denialist evil*. These are those who deny any responsibility for the evil they did. "We're innocent," they say. "We had nothing to do with what happened." When today's Neo-Nazis claim that the deaths of millions of Jews during World War II had nothing to do with Nazism—that all those people died of hunger and disease in the confusion of war—they're practicing denialist evil. That happened here too. Those who killed John did their best to cover it up by hiding his body and claiming he had left the building.

But that still falls short of what actually happened here. Beyond basic evil and denialist evil lies something far worse—*accusatory evil*. These depraved people understand that crimes require a criminal, so they manufacture one from innocent people. Neo-Nazis claim that the Jews either killed their own people or made it look like they were killed when they weren't. In this story, those who killed John Walters claim that either the blacks who loved John killed him or that his white Republican friends did. That is far worse than 'mere' murder—far viler.

This matters because, if you know how to tell the difference between basic, denialist, and accusatory evil, you'll not be fooled by such people. If you react passively, however, you may think that denialists and accusers are innocent. After all, the denialists are telling you they're innocent and the accusers are pointing to others as the real criminals. Don't fall for that.

If you understand these evils, you'll know that dubious denials suggest guilt and that unjust accusations are telling evidence of great guilt. Good people don't attack innocent people. Guilty people do. The greater the crime and the louder the accusations, the greater should be your suspicions. That's as true then as now. Also keep in mind that those who practice denialist and accusatory evil are far less like to repent and change their ways. They seem incapable of reform. All we can do stop their evil deeds. Now we turn to the newspapers.

The newspapers told it first.

1. The Dunboro' Herald of May 17, 18—, said:
"THE GOOD PEOPLE OF Rockford County met in convention at the courthouse today, to nominate candidates for county offices, and to discuss the political situation. Since the military usurpation took away from the people the right of self-government, and made them subservient to the will of the degraded Radical niggers, and the infamous scalawags and carpetbaggers who unite with and lead them, the honest people of Rockford have had no voice in her government. They have now concluded that the time has come when they will make one more effort to control their own affairs.

They met today as one man, and listened to the burning words of such soul-stirring orators as General De Bang, Honorable John Snortout, and Colonel Whiteheat, until it was evident, from their wild enthusiasm, that the white people of Rockford intend to rule her affairs again. **There was a rumor, just as our informant left, of some trouble or difficulty in connection with John Walters, the notorious**

Rockford Radical. We did not learn what it was, and do not care. The worst thing that could occur to him would be the best thing for the rest of the county."

2. The Moccason Gaptler (published the next day) said:

"WE LEARN, THAT, AFTER the meeting at Rockford Courthouse yesterday, there was considerable excitement among the colored population over the disappearance of their great leader, the infamous Walters. It seems that he had the cheek to attend the meeting and sat taking notes of the speeches during the whole time. His presence caused considerable remark. For, although it was a public meeting, it was not supposed that he would have the impudence to show himself among decent white people, after joining the niggers to insult, oppress, and degrade them. It is said that the speakers, especially the Honorable John Snortout, alluded to him in terms which he richly deserves.

It became noised through the meeting that he was taking notes of the speeches for the purpose of having troops sent to Rockford. It is even said that inquiry was made of him as to his object in taking notes—to which he impudently responded that his purpose was known to himself, which was quite sufficient.

After the meeting adjourned, it seems he could not be found, and a great outcry was raised among the niggers on account of his disappearance. Search was immediately instituted, and all the niggers of the town, as well as hundreds from the adjoining country, came pouring in, surrounding the courthouse, and clamoring for the keys. They were very much excited, and did not hesitate to declare that their leader had been murdered by the gentlemen at the meeting. This infamous charge against some four or five hundred of the best men of Rockford was borne with exemplary patience by that law-abiding people.

The meeting quietly dispersed, and the niggers continued their search. It is believed that Walters has taken himself off at this time for the purpose of producing an impression that he has been murdered, and thereby having troops sent to that county to influence the coming election. No trace of him had been found at last accounts."

3. The Ringfield Swashbuckler (two days afterwards) said:

"THE NIGGERS OF ROCKFORD are in tribulation, but the white people of the good old county will sleep easier. It appears, that, after the adjournment of the mass meeting held by the good people of that county at the courthouse on the 17th inst[ant], Walters, the infamous scalawag leader of the nigger Radicals, who have ruled the county since the military usurpation, could not be found. He was supposed to have been in attendance on the meeting as a spy upon its action. But several of the most respectable citizens say that he left a considerable time before its close.

At once, upon its becoming known that he was missing, there was great excitement among the niggers. And when, towards morning, his body was found in one of the offices upon the lower floor of the courthouse, there was great apprehension for a time that the town would be burned by the infuriated blacks.

The manner of his death is a mystery. It is generally believed that some of the leading negroes, who have for some time been growing restive under his dictatorship, waylaid him as he came down from the meeting, killed him, put his body in this room, and then raised an alarm over his disappearance, hoping thereby at once to get rid of a troublesome leader, and produce the impression that he was murdered by his opponents, and for political effect. Of course such a claim [that he was murdered by his opponents] is too ridiculous to be entertained for a moment. We learn that an inquest was held, but nothing was elicited to cast any light upon the mystery."

4. The Verdenton Gazette, in its next issue, remarked:
"THE DEATH OF THAT infamous Radical, Walters of Rockford County, is making a great excitement. The Radicals pretend to believe that he was killed by the Democrats, who had been holding a nominating convention in the courthouse that afternoon. It is far more probable, indeed some circumstances which have since come to light, render it almost certain, that his death was procured by certain of his Radical associates. The carpetbaggers and scalawags who run that party are fully aware of the fate which awaits them on election day, unless something can be done to fire the negro heart and bring troops into the State. It is therefore generally believed that this killing of Walters was a cold-blooded assassination planned by the Radicals at the Capital and executed by their minions. It is even asserted that Morton was heard to declare, not many days ago, that we would 'hear h_ll from the South in less than a week.'

In addition to this, it is said that a very reputable man, residing in the western part of that county, declares that he saw Colonel Tom Kelly, the chairman of the Radical committee for this district, driving

rapidly away from Rockford very soon after four o'clock on that evening—about the time the murder must have been committed. Perhaps Mr. Tom Kelly will now rise and explain what he was doing in
Rockford at that time."

5. *The Central Keynote (published a week afterwards) said:*
"WHETHER THE RADICAL BUMMER Walters was killed by some of his
nigger understrappers, by some of his carpetbag scalawag associates who
were jealous of his power, by his own relatives, or by some paramour of
his wife who was anxious that she should obtain the large amount of
insurance which he had upon his life, we do not know. But one thing we
do know, that the State is well rid of a miserable, unprincipled Radical
and infamous scoundrel, who ought to have been a carpetbagger, but,
we are sorry to admit, was a native. We sincerely trust that the state at
large may share the good fortune of the county of Rockford very soon,
and be equally well rid of his Radical associates."

The National Trumpet

THE NATIONAL TRUMPET, WHICH was the Radical organ for the State,
very naturally gave a different version of the affair, denounced it as a
most outrageous political murder, and inveighed most bitterly against
what it termed the inhuman barbarity of the opposition journals, which,
not content with the death of Walters, sought to slay his good name by
slanderous imputation, and to blast the reputation of the stricken widow
with baseless hints of complicity in his death.

**It pronounced him "a faithful husband, a tender father, and a
stanch friend—one who from obscure parentage had raised himself
through poverty and ignorance to competence, had aided orphan
brothers and sisters, supported a widowed mother, and maintained a
good Christian character until expelled from his church on account
of his political opinions.** His courage and organizing ability were unquestioned, and under his lead it was well known that nothing could
prevent the County of Rockford from continuing to give overwhelming
Radical majorities. John Walters was guilty of this offence, no more!
And for this he was killed! He gave up his life for the rights of the people—the right of equal manhood suffrage—as clearly as any soldier who
fell upon the battlefield died for liberty! The time will come when his
name will be remembered by a grateful people as that of a martyr of
their freedom."

The Northern Press

So THE ACT PASSED into current history, and the great journal of the North recorded with much minuteness, and with appropriate headlines and display, the fact that John Walters, a man of infamous character, and a prominent politician, and leader of the negroes in Rockford County, was killed by stabbing and strangling. By whom the crime was committed was by no means clear, they said, nor yet the motive. But one thing seemed to be well established—that it was not done from any political incentive whatever. It was true he was a leading Radical politician in a county having a decided colored majority, which was made effective almost solely by his organizing power. But it was certain that only personal feeling of some sort or another was at the bottom of this murder.

Thus it first came to the Fool's ears. He had known the man, not intimately, but well, having seen him often since their meeting at the League, and had grown into a sincere regard for him. He knew of his energy and daring, knew of his own premonitions as to his fate, and the coolness with which he had prepared himself to meet it.

But the Fool had only half believed that it would come—at least not so soon or suddenly, nor in a form so horrible, nor with such ghastly accompaniment of *post mortem* [after death] barbarity. It was strange how unreasoning he was in his sorrowful anger. He would not hear a word as to any other hypothesis of his friend's death, except that it was a political murder, coolly planned, and executed with the assent of the entire meeting of respectable men who were passing patriotic resolutions above the scene of its perpetration. It was very unreasonable, but perhaps not unnatural, that he should do so.

Ch. 30, "A Thrice-Told Tale," Part I, in *A Fool's Errand* by Albion Tourgée.

15. John's Close Friend

Informing Yourself

Michael W. Perry

If you've ever been part of a news event or seen an article on a topic you know well, you realize that news stories are often wrong. Their worst failures often come when they portray bad people as good and good people as bad. The very situations where they should do their best are the ones where they do their worst.

In this chapter, Comfort discovers what actually happened in that courthouse from a reliable source. Keep in mind that there was no reason the local papers couldn't have interviewed this friend of John Walters or his wife, who may have looked much like the worried woman pictured above with her two daughters. They didn't, because they had a dishonest 'story' to tell and no interest in seeing any evidence to the contrary.

Learn from these events. Be suspicious about what you read. Always look for better informed and more truthful sources. If you find a source that lies or distorts, consider that a grave insult and leave that source forever discredited in your mind. In short, never be a passive reader. Always think.

As you read this chapter, recall what I said earlier about the wealthy planters who wanted to keep blacks and whites poorly educated. Downtrodden whites did *not* benefit from keeping black people down. They merely suffered a little less. The real beneficiary of racism were those who wanted to exploit both blacks and whites as cheap labor.

Notice too that these poor, illiterate blacks quickly reach the correct conclusions about John's death, while the press—both Northern and Southern—never did. Truth only comes to those who seek it.

Upon the second day after this unfortunate occurrence, there came to the Fool's house one who had been an eye-and-ear witness of all that had occurred in Rockford on that occasion, except the tragic act which has been once already narrated. This man said:

"I was with John Walters when he went to the meeting, and went up and sat with him for a short time. I had tried to dissuade him from going there at all. There had been a good deal of excitement in the county for some time. The Ku-Klux had been riding about, and his life had been threatened a good many times. Only a few days before, a crowd of them had come, and, after riding about the town, had left at his house a coffin, with a notice stuck on to it with a knife. He knew he was in great danger and told me repeatedly that he thought they would get him before it was over.

On this day he was heavily armed and very foolishly carried with him a considerable sum of money, which he had received the day before, and intended to bring here and put in bank the next day. He had been very careful about showing himself upon the street for some time, especially after dark. I don't suppose he had been out after sundown in six months. He said that it was necessary for him to go to this meeting for two reasons: First, to let them know that he was not afraid to do so. And, second, that he might know what course the opposition intended to pursue in the coming campaign.

"There was a very full attendance at the meeting, and, when Walters came in, there were a heap of sour looks cast at him. He sat down, took out his book, and began taking notes. The speakers turned on him the worst abuse you ever heard, Colonel. But he just smiled that quiet, scornful smile of his and went on taking his notes as if no one was near him.

"By and by it got so hot that I thought we had better get out of there. I told him so in a whisper. But he just looked up and said I could go. He should stay till it was over. He wanted to see some parties there who had made some proposition to him about a compromise-ticket for county officers. He was greatly in favor of this. For, although we had a large majority in the county, we had really only one or two candidates competent to fill the county offices. It was by his advice that, at the election before, our folks had supported the Democratic candidate for sheriff and other county-officers. He said it would never do to put ignorant and incompetent men in such places.

"He was greatly troubled about his own lack of education and studied hard to make it up. I've often heard him mourn his lack of early advantages. I think it was the only thing that used to make him right-down mad. He used to say that was what every poor man owed to slavery. And he appeared to think that institution had done him as much harm, and he had as good a right to hate it, as if he had been a nigger. He could read pretty peart [lively and quickly], but writing always come hard to him

"I heard him one time talking about his little gal, who was just beginning to learn to read. He said he was determined she should have what he missed because he happened to be a poor man's son in a slave country, and that was an education.

John's Family

OH! HE WAS VERY bitter in his denunciation of the slave-holding aristocracy and would persist in declaring that they had starved the souls of the poor people and kept them from the tree of knowledge just to promote their own selfish aims and enhance their own wealth. It's the only thing I've ever heard John Walters grow eloquent upon (you know he was a man of few words). But I've heard him sometimes on the stump when he seemed to get out of himself and be another man, in the wild eloquence with which he urged the need of education and deplored the manner in which he had been robbed of its privileges and advantages.

"I remember he said once that he never asked grace before meat at his own table nor conducted family worship in his own house, as he did every day, without feeling ashamed of the ignorance which hung like a millstone about his neck. He thought that even his little eight-year-old must be ashamed of her papa's blunders.

"I thought of all these things while the speakers were abusing him, and the people were turning towards him with black looks and threatening gestures and wondered what would come of it all.

"When it got too hot for me, I left, and went back to his house. His wife was taking on terribly. She is not a very strong woman, but she thought a heap of John. She asked me all about what he was doing at the meeting and then took on worse than ever. She pointed to their two children who were playing on the lawn back of the house, and said, 'Poor things, poor things! They'll be fatherless and alone pretty soon. Why won't John quit this foolish fight for what will do him no good, get away from here, and go West, where he and his children can have a white man's chance? Why won't he listen to me?' She kept on crying and mourning, and begged me to speak to John about it—*if* he ever came home.

"I tried to comfort her, and we sat by the door, the little children playing on the green slope before us, until the meeting was over, and the people began to pass by on their way homeward. I noticed that Mrs. Walters seemed very restless, and every now and then looked anxiously over toward the courthouse. Finally she called to some colored men who were passing and asked if the meeting was over. They told her it was. And she then asked if they had seen her husband since it closed. And, when they said they had not, she threw up her hands, and moaned, and cried, 'They've killed him! They've killed him! I knew it! Oh, my God!' and just kept taking on terribly.

"I went over into the town at once, and began to make inquiries. None of our friends had seen him. But, as soon as they found I was inquiring for him, several of the white people kindly volunteered information in regard to him. This one had seen him in this place, and another in that, and another remembered hearing a third man speak of having seen him in still a different direction, and all about the same time.

Growing Suspicion

"THIS DISAGREEMENT OF THE reports which were made, as well as the fact that none of the colored people had seen him (though there were many more of them, and each felt a peculiar interest in him, so that they would be more likely to notice and remark his presence than the others), strengthened a dim suspicion that had been growing in the minds of all. So that, instead of waiting to go to the points indicated to ascertain their truth, the report went out at once that he was missing—had been killed.

"**I never knew before what a hold he had on the colored people. Every one seemed as distressed as if he had lost a brother. Men, women,** and children crowded into the streets. Moans and imprecations were about equally mingled in the surging crowds who hurried toward the courthouse.

"From the first moment there was no question as to his death. It was assumed as a fact. And the conclusion was at once arrived at, that his body was concealed somewhere about the courthouse. Strangely enough the fragments of the crowd who had been in attendance on the meeting gathered quietly about one or two of the stores, talked with each other in low tones, offered neither remonstrance, aid, nor ridicule of the search that was going on, and finally broke away by twos and threes, silently and solemnly to their homes.

"Every moment the excitement grew more intense among the colored people. In an incredibly brief time the crowd had swelled from a couple of dozen to as many hundred. And, in an hour or two, more than a thousand were gathered. The white people of the town looked on gloomily and silently, but took no part in the search.

The courthouse was at once surrounded, and every room examined into which access could be obtained, for the keys of some of them were said to have been lost, and one especially, it was claimed, had not been opened for many months. All trace of the key of this room seemed to have been lost by the officials in whose custody the law presumed it to have been.

"Then some of the white people came with very positive reports that Walters had been seen going out of town towards Dunboro', where it was known that he intended to go on the morrow. Several of the leading citizens came out at this time, and endeavored to convince the colored people of the folly of their course. The Honorable John Snortout was especially active in this endeavor.

They might as well have talked to the wind. The colored people clung to their hypothesis with a sort of blind instinctive conviction of its truth, which nothing could move. As it came on dark, fires were lighted, and a regular line of sentries put around the building. Meantime attempts were made to get a glimpse of the interior of the rooms of which they could obtain no keys, by peering through the closed windows. Clambering from one window ledge to another, they flashed the light of blazing torches into them, but in vain. Nothing could be seen.

"And so the night dragged on, and the crowd grew hourly greater with accessions from the country, and the conviction grew stronger that in one of these rooms they would find the nameless horror which they sought, and which they yet would not behold.

"Yet this half-barbarous crowd were strangely regardful of law. They did not violate anybody's right. Neither locks nor windows were broken. They sought the keys far and near, but they did no violence. They were sure their lost leader was within—dying or dead, they knew not which. They called him by name, but knew he could not answer. None slept of the colored people—they waited, watched, and mourned.

A Terrible Discovery

"Just in the gray of the morning light, one of those who had been most active and assiduous in the search mounted on the shoulders of a friend, and peered into the window of the most suspected room on the first floor. Shading his eyes with his hand, he scanned the dim-lighted interior, and was about to give up the quest, when his eye fell upon something mysterious and appalling. On the inside of the window-ledge he saw —*a single drop of blood!* Another look and he saw, or thought he saw, the well-known hat which their leader had been wont to wear.

"'Here he is—in there!,' he shouted, as he leaped down, and started for the corridor. They had no longer any need of key. The door flew apart as if made of pasteboard, before the brawny shoulders that pressed against it. In that room they found their worst fears confirmed. There, pressed down into a box, with a pile of firewood heaped upon him, a stab in his throat, and a hard cord drawn taut about his neck, stark and cold, was the body of John Walters—the Radical!

There was very little blood in the room, only a few drops on the floor, and one drop on the window-sill! The stab in his throat had cut the artery. Where was the blood? The physician who examined the body said he must have bled internally."

From the foregoing narrative it was evident to the Fool that between three and five o'clock of the day before, while the meeting of respectable white citizens was in progress in the room above, John Walters had either been killed in that room, or murdered elsewhere, and brought thither. The manner of his death was evident. The motive was not doubtful, since strangely enough, this "bad man" seems to have had no personal enemies. In some mysterious manner the universal sentiment of execration that prevailed against him in the community had found an instrument, and John Walters, the Radical leader of Rockford, had met the doom which he might reasonably have expected when he presumed to organize the colored voters of that county in opposition to the wish and desire of its white inhabitants.

The coroner's jury, after a tedious examination of every person that could be found who would be likely, on ordinary principles, to know nothing whatever of the matter, returned that the death was "caused by some person or persons unknown." Which verdict was, no doubt, in strict conformity with the evidence taken.

Ch. 30, "A Thrice-Told Tale," Part II, in *A Fool's Errand* by Albion Tourgée.

16. John's Murder Overheard

Writing Dialect

Michael W. Perry

Like me, you might pass over the girl's white dress in the picture above without a second glance. Don't do that. For you and I, having clean, bright clothing is easy. We simply toss them into a washer with a powerful detergent. But that wasn't true for her. Dirt roads and messy farm wagons made it hard to keep clothes clean. She had to work hard, scrubbing by hand with mere soap to get that dress spotless. Sometimes we forget how easy we have it.

Some words spoken in this chapter may be hard to follow because of the heavy dialect. Today, that's considered demeaning. At the time this book was written, however, writing dialect was considered the mark of a good writer. Charles Dickens and Mark Twain often used it. If you have trouble, try saying the words to yourself. The spelling may be different, but the sound is similar.

Remember what I said about those who wanted to make it impossible for a black to testify against a white? This chapter illustrates why and also shows why these people slandered their white opponents and gave them nasty labels such as radical, carpetbagger and scalawag. They wanted to discredit in advance anything these people might say. Libels and slanders like that suggest guilt.

Keep in mind too how incredibly brave these three black servants were. Caught listening, these murderers would have killed them too, perhaps burying their bodies deep in a swamp, and claimed they'd run off with the family silver. This people really are evil, although as the chapter notes, they "were all of good families, and of undoubted respectability." Never confuse moral character with nice homes and polite manners.

Also, the "Jerry" who appears at the start of this chapter was same godly Uncle Jerry Hunt whose emotional preaching was described in Metta's earlier letter (chapter 7), and who warned Comfort he was about to be attacked. We'll meet him again in Chapter 27.

"Kunnel, dar's a man h'yer dat wants ter tell you sumfin'. He says he won't tell nobody else but you, widout your positive orders."

The speaker was old Jerry. He stood at the door of the Fool's library or office and had with him a colored man, whom he introduced as Nat Haskell. This man had one of those expressionless faces, which, however, bear a look of furtive observation, so characteristic of the colored man who has been reared under the influences of slavery.

"Well," said Comfort, "what is it?"

"Didn't you know Mars' John Walters?," asked the colored man cautiously.

"Yes, certainly!," answered Comfort.

An' ain't you de gemman as come an' tried ter find out who 'twas dat killed him?"

"Yes."

"Wal, den, you's de one I want ter see, an dat's what I want ter see ye about."

"Why, what do you know about that?"

"I don't know nothin,' but I done heard somefin' that may lead you to fine out who 'tis. Dat's what I come fer."

"Where do you live?"

The Story Begins

"I LIVES WID OLE man Billy Barksdill, 'bout five miles below Rockford Courthouse. That is, I did live dar. I hain't no notion o' goin' back dar any mo'."

"Were you in Rockford that day?"

"No, sah!"

"Then how do you come to know anything about the matter?"

"Wal, yer see, Kunnel, I was wukkin' fer Mr. Barksdill, ez I tole ye. An' dat night, jest arter I come in from de fiel', he called me ter come an' take care of a hoss. I know'd dat hoss right well. 'Twas a gray filly dat Mars' Marcus Thompson he'd rid by our place dat mornin'. Arter I'd put the critter away, an' fed it, I went inter de kitchen ter git my supper. I sot down ter de table, an' de cook — dat's Mariar, my ole 'ooman—she brings me my supper, an' den goes back inter de dinin'-room ter wash up de dishes de white folks hed been usin'.'

Presen'ly she come back mighty still like, an' says, 'Nat, come h'yer, quick!' An' wid dat she starts back agin.

"'Sh—! take off yer shoes,' she says, half whispering ez we git ter de dinin'-room do'.

"I slips outer my shoes, an' we goes in. Der wa'n't no light in de room. But she led me a-till we come nigh de do' a-twixt de dinin'-room an' de settin'-room. Dar we stopped an' listened, an' I could hear Mr. Barksdill an' Mr. Marcus Thompson talkin' togeder mighty plain. Cynthy Rouse—dat's anudder servant-gal—she was dar too, a-crouchin' down by de do', dat wasn't shet close, But dar wa'n't no light in de settin'room, but de fire. When I come, Cynthy puts her hand on her lips, shakes her head, an' says, 'H'sh!' an' put her head down to listen agin. The fust words I heard was ole Mr. Barksdill—he's sorter half-def, yer knows—a-sayin', right peart:

"'It must a' been a good day's work, in fact, if we've got rid o' John Walters finally. How was it done? I did hear der was some notion o' sendin' a committee from de meetin' ter tell him he must leave. But I hadn't no notion he'd du it. He's pluck to de back-bone, John Walters is. Whatever else he may be, we must allow, Thompson, dat he ain't nobody's fool nor coward. An' I 'llowed, dat, ef de meetin' should do dat, jest ez likely's not some o' dat committee mout git hurt. Ye didn't try dat, I reckon?'

"'No,' answered Mars' Thompson, 'we didn't hav no need ter du dat. De brazen-faced cuss hed the impudense ter come ter the meetin' hisself!'

"'Dar now, you don't tell me!,' sed old man Barksdill. 'Wal, now, what was I sayin'?—he's pluck.'

"'Yes, and he sot dar as cool as a cucumber, a-takin' notes ob all dat went on,' says Mr. Thompson.

"'You don't! Wal, I declar'!,' sez the ole man.

"'Yes, de damned fool hadn't a bit more sense dan to show his head dar, when we'd met most a-purpose to fine a way to get rid of him. He mout 'a' knowed what would come on't.'

"'Wal, what did? I s'pose de people was pretty hot, an' perhaps dar was smart of a row.'

"'Not a bit, Mr. Barksdill! Jest de quietest affair you ever heard on. De fac' is, some one on us hed made an appintment wid Walters, ter see him 'bout what we called a fusion ticket we purtended ez we wanted ter git up. So some on' em signified to him dat we wanted ter see him, an' we got him down inter the old County Clerk's office, an' shet de do'. Dar was ten on us, an' he seed de game we was up to in a second—but he didn't even wince.

"Well, gentlemen," sez he, ez cool ez if he'd been settin' over on his own porch, which we could see ez plain ez day from de winder, "what d'ye want o' me? Der seems tu be enough on ye ter du ez you've a mine ter. Go I mout ez well ask yer will an' pleasure."'

"'Law sakes!,' sez de ole man, 'but dat wuz monstroua cool.'

"'Cool? I should tink it was, ez cool es hell,' sez t'oder one. 'Den some on 'em took out a paper dat hed been drawed up aforehand fer him ter sign, an' handed it over tu him. He read it over kinder slow like, an', when he got frough, handed it back, an' sed, "I can't sign dat paper, gentlemen."'

"'What was de paper?'

"'Noffin, only jest a statement dat he, as leader ob de Radical party in dis county, hed been de gitter-up ob all de devilment done here in de last two or free years, includin' de burnin' o' Hunt's barn; an' dat he done dese tings under de direction ob de Radical leaders at de capital. We tole him, ef he'd sign dis, an' agree tu leab de State in ten days, we'd let him off safe an' sound.'

'An' he wouldn't do it?,' bust in de ole man.

"'Do it? Hell! He sed we mout kill him, but we couldn't make him sign no sech paper ez dat. Dat made de boys mad. You know, we didn't want ter kill him, dough we hed no notion ob backin' out after goin' dat far. In fac', we couldn't.'

"'No mo' you couldn't, I should say,' put in Mars' Barksdill. "'Ob course not! An' I fought fer a minit de boys would jest hack an' tear him to pieces, dey was so mad. I tried ter pacify 'em, an' persuade him to sign de paper, an' not force us to sech extremes. But he wouldn't hear tu me, an' fust I know'd, he hed jumped back an' pulled out a pistol. De lowdown, ornary cuss! Ef it hadn't been fer Buck Hoyt, who caught his arm, an' Jim Bradshaw, dat whipped a slip-noose over his neck, an' pulled him back, der's no knowin' what he might 'a' done wid dat ten-shooter o' his.'

"'He's a nasty hand wid shootin'-irons,' sed the ole man.

"'Wal,' says Thompson, 'dey got him down, an' frottled him, an' tuk de pistol away from him, an' every ting he had in the weepon line. Den dey let him up, an' all agreed dat sech a pestiferous, lyin', deceitful cuss ought ter be killed. We told him so, an' dat he could hev jest five minutes ter git ready in. He didn't never flinch, but jest sed, "I s'pose I ken be allowed ter pray." An', widout waitin' fer an answer, he jes' kneeled down, an' prayed fer all his frien's an' neighbors, an' fer each one ob us too. Dis prayin' fer us wuz gittin' a little tu damn pussonal, so Jim Bradshaw, dat held de cord, gin it a jerk, ha' tole him we didn't want no more o' dat. Den he got up, an' I axed him ef der wuz any ting else he wanted ter do or say afore he died. You see, I fought he might like ter make some 'rangement 'bout his property or his family, an' I wanted to gib him a white man's chance.' it's done. It's damned encouragin' to dem dat takes de risk!

"'Ob co'se, ob co'se,' said Mars' Barksdill, 'an' very proper an' considerate of ye, tu.'

Seeing his Daughters
"'I FOUGHT SO, CERTAIN,' said Thompson. 'Wal, he axed us to let him look out o' de winder, at his childern playin' on de slope o' de hill over by his house. Dar was some o' de boys didn't want to do dat, but I persuaded 'em to let him. His hands was tied, an' de cord was 'roun' his neck, so't he couldn't git away nohow. De lower sash hed been raised; but we had some two or three fellows standin' outside anyhow. So we led him to de winder, an' he looked at his two gals a smart while. I declar' it come hard to see de tears a-standin' in his eyes, an' know what was waitin' fer him; but it couldn't be helped den. An', jest while I was tinkin' ub dis, he made a spring, and, wid all dat agin him, managed to git his left leg ober de winder-sill, an' I'm not at all sure't he wouldn't 'a' wriggled hisself out entirely, ef Jack Cannon hadn't 'a' gathered a stick of wood, an' dropped it over his leg till it straightened out ez limp ez a rag. We pulled him back in, an' frew him on de long table dat's in de room. He jest give one groan when he seed all was over. It was de fust

an' last. Der wasn't no use tryin' ter hold de boys back no longer. Jim Brad he drew de cord till it fairly cut inter de flesh. Den dey turned him half over, all on us holdin' his arms an' legs, an' Jack Cannon stuck a knife inter his throat.

He bled like a hog. Be we caught de blood in a bucket, an' arterward let it down out de winder in a bag to de fellers outside; so't der wa'n't a drop o' blood, no any mark ub the squabble in de room. We stowed him away in de wood-box, an', arter it comes on a good an' dark, de boys are goin' to take him ober, an' stow him away under dat damned nigger school house o' his; an' den you se we'll claim de niggers done it, an' perhaps hev some on 'em up, an' try 'em for it.'

"'Good Lord!,' sed ole man Barksdill arter a minit. 'So he's dead!'

"'Dead!," said Thompson wid a queer laugh. 'You may count on dat—ez dead ez Julius Caesar! De county's well rid o' de wust man dat was ebber in it.'

"'Yes, yes!," said de ole man, 'a bad fellow, no doubt, might bad; dough I dunno ez he ever done any ting so *very* except hold political meetin's wid de niggers, an' put all sorts o' crazy notions in de heads, makin 'em lazy, an' no 'count, an' impudent to white folks.'

"'An' ain't dat 'nough?," said Thompson.

"'Oh, ob co'se!' Mars' Barksdill sai: 'dat's mighty bad—but arter all'—

"'Well, what? said Mars' Thompson, kinder hot like.

"'Oh, well, noffin'!—dat is, noffin' to speak of. I was no friend o' John Walters; but I would 'a' felt better ef he'd been killed in a fa'r fight, an' not shut up like a wolf in a trap, an' killed in… in…'

"'In cold blood, I s'pose you mean,' put in Thompson quick and husky. Fer he was a-gittin' mad.

"'Wal, yes, it does look so,' said ole Mars', kinder 'pologizin' like.

"'Ob co'ese,' said Thompson, 'it'll do fer you ter set dar an' fine fault wid what's done. Here de whole county's been wishin' somebody would rid 'em ub John Walters fer two years an' mo.' Everybody's been a-cussin' an' bilin',' an' tellin' what ought ter be done; an' now dat some of us hez hed the pluck ter go in an' *du* the very ting ye've been talkin' on, ye stan' back, an' draw on an affidavy face, an' say yer sorry it's done. It's damned encourgin' to dem dat takes der risk! Perhaps de next fing you do'll be tu go an' tell on us.'

"De ole man wouldn't stan' dat. We heard him rise up, an' gay, mighty grand like—

"'Mr. Thompson!'

"Jest then, Cynthy, who's a mighty excitable gal, an', besides dat, used ter live with Mrs. Walters, an' so knew de one dey'd been talkin' on right well, bust out a-sobbin' an' a-moanin', an' we hed to hold a hand over her mouf, an' half tote her out ob de room ez fast ez we could. I heard Mars' Thompson say, 'Who's in dar?' An' den Mars' Barksdill he lights de can'le, an' comes an' opens de dinin'-room do'. But, Lor' bress ye! Der wan't nobody in dar — nobody at all."

"What did you do then?"

"Nuffin' at all. Jest waited, an' kep' still. Cynthy an' 'Riar an' me we talks it over a little, an' concluded ez we'd better not let on dat we knowed any fing about it. So when Bob Watson come over some time 'fore mornin', an' whistled me out, an' tole me dat Mars' Walters was a-missin', an' dat eberybody ob de colored folks was a-huntin' for him, an' de whole town jest alive an' a-light all night, I didn't say noffin', only, arter a while I turns to Bob an' I says, says I,—

"'Bob, dey won't never fine him.' An' he sez, sez he, 'Dat's my notion too.' So we passed de time o' day, an' he went home, an' I turned in ter sleep agin."

"Have you ever told any one else of this?" asked the Fool. "Nary one," was the reply. "A few days arterwards, ole man Barksdill he questioned me some, an' arter dat de gals telled me dat he axed dem some questions 'bout what we know'd or hed heard 'bout Mr. Walters. But he didn't git no satisfaction outer me, dat's shore, an' I don't reckon he did out ob de gals. Howsomever, 'twan't long afore he an' his boys begun ter talk right smart 'bout what would happen ter any nigger ez should testify agin any white man ez havin' any fing to do along o' Mr. Walters. An' finally Mr. Barksdill he tole me—an' I found dat he tole de wimmen too—dat any nigger dat knowed any fing 'bout dat matter would be a heap more likely to die ob ole age ef he lived in anudder State. Dig scart de gals nigh about to deaff, an' I 'llowed dar was a heap o' sense in it myself. So we lit out; an' I never hinted a word about it afore, only to Uncle Jerry h'yer, an' he brought me to you, sah."

Upon further investigation, Servosse learned several facts strongly confirmatory of this strange story, the details of which harmonized with wonderful accuracy with all the known facts of the bloody deed.

The men named as the associates of Thompson, it appeared, were all present at the meeting. Some of them had before been suspected of complicity in the act, while others had not been thought of in connection with it. They were all of good families, and of undoubted respectability. The two women, being separately examined, confirmed, with only such variation as rendered their accounts still more convincing, the story which has been given.

Ch. 30, "A Thrice-Told Tale," Part III, in *A Fool's Errand* by Albion Tourgée.

17. KLAN ATTACKS UNCLE JERRY

Taking a Stand

Michael W. Perry

I was walking around Seattle's popular Green Lake one afternoon, when I came on a man who was throwing knives at a tree just a few yards from the paved walkway around the lake—a walkway that at that time of day was filled with mothers and small children. Not good, I thought. A knife could easily bounce off that tree and put out the eye of a little boy or girl.

I kept walking, but I could tell from the faces of those mothers that this guy bothered them too. A hundred yards further on was the lake's waterfront activity center, so I stopped to ask its staff to do something. They responded by telling me that they'd been ordered *not* to do anything about odd-acting people.

Lawyers are behind that, I thought, and that got my blood to boiling. Only a few months earlier I'd won a copyright lawsuit brought by bullying Manhattan lawyers. I wasn't going to let lawyers tell *me* what to do, particularly with little children at risk. Unable to get help from city-paid staff, I walked back toward the knife thrower, once again noticing just how terrified these mothers were. Somebody had to act, and it looked like that would be me.

I came upon a man in his thirties and asked him to linger on the sidelines, phoning for help if matters got out of control. Without a word, he scurried away like a frightened mouse. "Worthless," I thought.

"Well," I reminded myself, "You spent almost two years as the director of a group home. You know how to deal with drug addicts and crazy people. And you spent several months as the assistant director of a homeless shelter in Alaska dealing with street people. You even calmed down someone threatening you with a razor-sharp case cutter. You can handle this knife thrower."

I knew to remain relaxed but firm, stating what must be done clearly without being threatening, which only sets off the craziness. That's what I did. I walked up to him, pointed out the danger, and politely suggested he pick a tree away from people for his knife-throwing.

I've had enough experience to know that this guy was likely to be either stupid or crazy. He was crazy and became belligerent—suggesting that what he was doing was OK because thousand of people die on highways every year. I told him that didn't matter and that, if he didn't stop, I'd call the police. He said, "Go ahead," so I pulled out my cell phone.

I'm about average in height and weight, so at that point, I became aware that he was a big guy with a few inches and forty pounds on me. He was moving toward me, so I backed away while talking to the 911 operator. He has at least five knives, I thought, so if he kept coming, I'll toss my pack at him to throw off his aim and run like mad. He was fat and couldn't run fast. I'd already seen how poor his throwing was, so I knew that once I was at least twenty feet away, I'd be safe.

Fortunately, I didn't have to run. Coming up at just the right time was a big guy, someone who was at least six-foot-five and muscular—much bigger than the knife guy. He intercepted the knife guy, talked with him, and forced him to back away. "Whew," I thought, "that was close."

A couple of minutes later, the big guy and I had a man-to-man talk. He'd seen what I'd seen and thought he should do something, but had hesitated until he saw me walk up to the knife thrower. Then he acted. Together, we made a good team—I provided the words, and he provided the muscle to end a dangerous situation. In some situations, all you can do is act, believing that the help you need will come. In our story, when her father's life is in danger Lily will do just that.

Far Greater Risk

Now MULTIPLY THE RISK I took a thousand fold, and you have a taste of what this chapter is about. To prepare you for it, I'll use my experience at that lake to explain what Tourgée, a battle-hardened Union officer, meant when he said of Uncle Jerry's stand: "When experience, wealth, and intelligence combine against ignorance, poverty, and inexperience, resistance is useless. Then the appeal to arms may be heroic, but it is the heroism of folly, the faith—or hope rather—of the fool."

Why was it foolish? **First, there was a huge difference in *experience*.** Most of the Klansmen riding that night were well-trained soldiers. They knew how to patrol and stand guard much like I know how to handle drug-addled and mentally deranged people. That's what Tourgée meant when he sets the Klan's *experience* against the *inexperience* of Uncle Jerry's little black neighborhood.

Yes, those black people knew the danger they faced and had planned a response. But when danger actually threatened, their plans fell flat. Why? Because it's much harder to *do* something difficult when you've not done it before than it is to simply *talk* about doing it.

That's particularly true for recently freed slaves. Remember, for generations any display of resistance on their part had been met with swift retribution. The result was an instinctive, deeply ingrained cultural response to hide from danger and do nothing—precisely what that black community does this night. Centuries of habit embedded into a group's culture can't be overcome that easily.

The importance of experience applies equally well to situations that don't involve physical danger. For an illustration, you might read a book I wrote, *My Nights with Leukemia*. It's about when I worked night shift caring for children with cancer at one of the nation's top children's hospitals.

In it, I describe how, after several months working with those children, I realized that I'd developed an intuition that warned me when a child was in trouble. Twice, I intervened to get their treatment changed. No, that wasn't what I was *supposed* to do. I was a member of the nursing staff and was supposed to follow a physician's orders, simply recording numbers in flow sheets and not following hunches. But stopping their chemotherapy was what I knew I *should* do. Along with learning *when* a child was in trouble came enough experience to know *how* to get those medical orders changed. Experience had taught me *what* to do. In the account we are reading now, these unfortunate former slaves had no experience with fighting back. They were confused and lost.

Second is the contrast Tourgée makes between the *wealth* of the Klan riders and the *poverty* of that black community. Ignore the shrill 'power to the people' rhetoric of academics. The difference was practical and down-to-earth. The poor bring less to a fight and that matters.

That difference starts with the timing. The Klan struck on a Saturday evening. Most of those poor blacks had been working from sunrise to sunset under a blazingly hot sun for the past six days. My grandparents' generation called that being "bone-tired." They meant being so tired from working in the fields that your bones as well as your muscles ache. These poor blacks were bone tired. It's why, when the Klan broke into Uncle Jerry's house, he was sound asleep. He was exhausted.

Yes, this black neighborhood should have had patrols out to warn them that the Klan was coming and yes, they should have been alert and ready to move into position to fight at a moment's notice. But these people were tired, perhaps tireder than you or I have been in our entire lives. After two months of diligence, they'd let their guard down. The Klan could afford to wait and did.

There were other rich versus poor factors. Someone on horseback, particularly someone on one of the powerful horses that were out that night, is intimidating to someone on foot. Someone who is carrying the latest repeating rifle is terrifying to someone who only has an ancient, single-shot flintlock that's perhaps good only for shooting squirrels and may not even fire reliably. Money made this a most unequal clash.

Third, there's the contrast Tourgée draws between *intelligence* of the Klan and the *ignorance* of this poor black community. And no, he did not mean IQs. The concept of IQ had yet to be invented. He was not saying that one group was smart and the other stupid. He was talking about something that's as necessary in a life crisis as experience. A better choice of words might have been to contrast *knowledge* with *ignorance*. This is intelligence in the sense of military intelligence. It's something one side knows that the other does not know.

Experiences are skills we get from what we have done. Knowledge are skills we learn from what others say or write. Most of those Klansmen could read and that meant they had read books about soldiering and newspaper articles about what the Klan had done in other parts of the state. That gave them an advantage.

You see that in their planning. They not only delegated men to cover the black community, they had ten members in the white community whose homes they especially watched—people known to oppose the Klan. That 'trick' was something they may have known because they read about it.

When I cared for those children with cancer, I depended on both my experience and my knowledge. One night, I became convinced that a boy I was caring for was in serious trouble. That was the voice of *experience* speaking. But I faced a problem. How could I get the resident on duty that night to do something? There, my *knowledge* came into play. I'd read enough to know that two tests—a complete blood count and a blood chemistry—told a lot about a leukemia patient's status. The resident had already ordered a complete blood count, so I persuaded him to include a blood chemistry. A short time later, that second test came back with all alarms ringing. That boy's blood chemistry was way out of kilter and he was rushed to the ICU. Both my personal experience and my book-read knowledge mattered.

There's fourth factor we must keep in mind—*confidence*. Someone who believes they can handle risks will take risks. They will assume that everything can be made to work even if something unexpected happens. That was me with that crazy knife thrower. I'd handled enough similar situations to believe I could handle this one. A group who has been crushed by generations of slavery, never being allowed to succeed on their own, will lack that confidence. The result is paralysis. That's what happened on this terrible night. The people in this black community remained in their homes, failing to do even what they could do.

The *confidence* to act is where *experience* and *knowledge* come together. One afternoon, while I was working at that children's hospital, I walked passed the room of a teen girl with leukemia. She was coughing a peculiar, tickle-in-the-throat cough that I knew from experience might mean she was getting air in her central line (like an IV but more sophisticated). I darted in, checked her line, and saw air rather than fluid. In an instant, with my right hand I turned off her IV pump while with my left I pulled the pillow out from under her head. At the same time I asked her to roll on her left side. Less than four seconds after I'd heard her coughing, I had her in a protective position that would keep those dangerous air bubbles away from her head or heart.

That's what confidence does. We act because, almost without thinking, we know what to do. It's what soldiers, firefighters and police mean when they talk about their 'training kicking in.' Unfortunately, that night all too many Klansmen had done evil so many times that doing it had become instinctive. The same wasn't true of their black victims. They needed to do something new. They needed to fight back and that they could not do.

The same lack of confidence was also true of the nearby white community. Comfort gives details he heard from "some trusty friends" who are clearly whites and who remain in their homes too. It seems likely that the Klan horsemen posted as sentinels knew which white homes also needed to be watched. Not every white supported what the Klan was doing.

Later, when we get to Lily's brave ride, keep all this in mind. That night she had to face new things. She'd never ridden her father's powerful thoroughbred before, and she'd probably never imagined riding through the Klan-infested night to warn her father. But she *had* faced dangers so many times growing up that responding decisively had become instinctive with her. Danger meant action. What she needed to do came quickly to her mind. In the next chapter, we get a hint of how she learned to be brave and decisive.

Now for a look at what happens in this chapter. It opens by describing Uncle Jerry's response when he discovered the Democratic party's brutal and carefully planned murder of John Walters. That's "the narrative" that so outrages him. The Jim Bradshaw who was spying on the black church service had slipped the noose around John Walter's neck, playing a major role in the murder. Uncle Jerry's revelation must be all the more terrifying for Bradshaw because it seems to come directly from God.

Note also that at least some of the Klan riders that night were wearing black robes rather than white. I did a little research. That color may designate those who have specific roles, such as sentry, but the reason could be practical. At night, someone in black is much harder to see. Someone who simply wants to scare people wears white to appear spooky. Someone who plans to kill wears black to be almost invisible. These Klansmen planned to kill.

Notice also that what follows was not at an isolated farmhouse. It happened in the "colored suburb" of a largely white town within sight and hearing of the town's population. Confident it won't be hindered, the Klan was aggressive and bold. Evil can be like that. Also, this chapter doesn't tell all that happened. Later, we'll find out more about this murder from one of those involved in the killing.

Finally, remember the terror that evil creates depends on a unique set of circumstances. In a different era, that ability to intimidate can fade. As I looked for pictures to use in this book, I came across quite a few of Klansmen in their white robes. At the time those pictures were taken, the sight of them would have terrified most people, both black and white. One person in this chapter says that he'd have rather joined General Picket's almost suicidal charge at Gettysburg than to face the wrath of the Klan. But for me, living long after the power of the Klan has been broken, these thugs in white sheets look silly. We may laugh about them now, but we should never forget that we have our own terror groups to face down.

Uncle Jerry was much excited by the narrative which he had heard. For a long time the outrages which had been perpetrated upon his race and their friends, the daily tale of suffering and horror which came to his ears, had been working on his excitable temperament, until it needed only the horrible recital which Nat had given, to destroy entirely his self-control. During its repetition he had uttered numerous ejaculations expressive of his excitement. And, when he went away with his friend, he was in a sort of semi-unconscious state, his wide-open eyes full of a strange light, and muttering brokenly as he went along the road to his own house, short ejaculatory remarks:

"Lor' God ob Isr'el! Lor', Lor', whar is yer gone? Don't ye h'yer de cry ob de pore no mo'? Whar is de 'venger ob blood?"

These and many similar expressions fell from his lips as he wandered about his garden and lot that evening. To Nat, who had returned with him, and was his guest, he said but little. He seemed absorbed in dreamy thought.

Uncle Jerry's Defiance
EVEN BEFORE THIS TIME, **Uncle Jerry had been noted for his openly expressed defiance of the Ku-Klux, his boldness in denouncing**

them, and the persistence with which he urged the colored men of his vicinity to organize and resist the aggressions of that body.

In this he had been partially successful. A considerable number of the inhabitants of the colored suburb had armed themselves, had appointed a leader and lieutenants, and agreed upon signals, on hearing which all were to rally for defense at certain designated points.

He had infused into his duller-minded associates the firm conviction which possessed himself—that it was better to die in resisting such oppression than to live under it. He had an idea that his race must, in a sense, achieve its own liberty, establish its own manhood, by a stubborn resistance to aggression—an idea which it is altogether probable would have been the correct and proper one, had not the odds of ignorance and prejudice been so decidedly against them.

As matters stood, however, it was the sheerest folly. When experience, wealth, and intelligence combine against ignorance, poverty, and inexperience, resistance is useless. Then the appeal to arms may be heroic, but it is the heroism of folly, the faith—or hope rather—of the fool.

Nevertheless, chiefly through Uncle Jerry's persuasions, and because of his prominence and acknowledged leadership, this spirit had gone out among the colored men of the county. A determination to resist and retaliate such outrages had become general among them.

The first effect of this determined stand upon their part seemed to have been to prevent the repetition of these offenses. For several weeks no one had been beaten or scourged in that county, and the impression seemed to gain ground that there would be no more. This was especially strong after two full moons had passed without disturbance, since it was at those seasons that the disguised horsemen were particularly active. This fact had tended strongly to confirm old Jerry in his theory of resistance, and at the same time had relaxed the vigilance of himself and his neighbors.

A Fateful Prayer Meeting

THE NIGHT OF THE day on which he had listened to the recital given by Nat was the time for the regular weekly prayer meeting at the schoolhouse. Of course he attended, and, as it chanced, there were several white men also in attendance—strangers, it seemed—who sat in the back part of the audience, and seemed to be making light of the exercises. This was an indignity which always aroused the strongest feeling on the part of Uncle Jerry. To such he was accustomed to say, with a sweet-voiced boldness:

"We's allers glad ter hab de white folks come to our meetin's, an' allers tinks it may do us good, an' dem tu. It sartin can't hurt nobody tu be prayed fer. An' we prays for 'em, an' hopes dey prays for us, an' hopes de good Lord'll bress us all. But when white folks comes an' laughs at our weak praars—dat hurts. We knows we ain't larned, nor great, nor perfic, but we tries to do our best. An' when you all laughs at us, we can't help tinkin' dat we mout 'a' done better ef we hadn't been kep' slaves all our lives by you uns."

Few could continue to mock after this reproof. On this occasion, when the meeting had progressed for some time, the conduct of the white visitors became very annoying. Two or three times, it was noticed that Uncle Jerry raised his head and stretched forward his hands upon his staves, as if he would speak. But each time, upon second thought, it seemed, he abandoned the idea.

Finally it could be endured no longer, and he arose, and walked toward them, speaking in an unusually harsh and aggrieved tone as he did so. When he came within two or three steps of them, he took both staves in his left hand, raised the right, with the finger pointing toward them as steady as a rifle barrel, and became at once rigid and silent. At first the mockers attempted ridicule. But the pale, still face, and fixed, staring eyes, as well as the awe stricken hush of the colored portion of the congregation, soon reduced them to silence.

When at length his tongue was loosed, and he poured forth one of his wonderful rhapsodies, a mortal terror seemed to take hold upon his hearers, and they sat listening to his burning words, while he told the story of the Ku-Klux, and ended his horrible portraiture with a detailed statement of the manner in which John Walters had been killed, giving the names of those engaged, and the part taken by each in the bloody deed. He painted as by magic the scene of the murder, and gave the very tone and manner of each of those engaged in it, though he had never seen them. Before the recital was ended, there was a shriek from one of the white men, as he rose, and staggered toward the door. Then the others followed after him and silently left the house.

When the 'spell' was over, and Uncle Jerry was lying back, panting and moaning, in his seat, Nat came to him, and broke out—"Fo' God, Uncle Jerry, what ye mean?"

"What's de matter, Brudder Nat? What I done? Hurt your feelin', Brudder? Bress God, I hope not!"

"Hurt my feelin's? No!," said Nat. "You'se not likely to do dat, Bre'r Jerry. But, Lor' bress us! D'you kno' one o' dem ar men waz nobody else but Jim Bradshaw!"

"De Lord's will be done! He's done use his pore sahvent for his glory, wedder he will or no. Bress de Lor'!," said Uncle Jerry, with a look of resignation.

"Dat's all right, Bre'r Jerry, but I feel jes' ez ef I could trust de Lor' a heap better ef I wuz 'cross de line, an' out o' de State. So I bids you good by, Uncle Jerry! I'se gwine ter cut outen h'yer, shore."

The news of this terrible revelation soon spread far and wide among the colored people, and there was great apprehension on account of it. Uncle Jerry alone did not seem to be disturbed or alarmed. Since this last display of his strange peculiarity, he seemed to have lost all apprehension, and all feeling of annoyance or trouble, as to the future of himself or his race.

"De Lord's will be done," he said, with entire composure, whenever the matter was mentioned to him. "He knows what's best, an' he's made dis pore sahvent see dat he knows. Bress his holy name! He brings de good out ob evil, an' ober-rules de bad. He's been wid de pore culled man in de six troubles, an' he not gwine ter desart him in de sebenth! Uncle Jerry'll jes' try an' wait on de Lor', so dat when he call fer me, I jes' answers, 'H'yer, Lor'!' widdout waitin' ter ax eny questions 'bout his business."

Saturday Night Comes

So THE DAYS WENT on until a week from the Saturday night which followed his denunciation of the slayers of Walters at the meeting, and there had been no disturbance. On that night the little suburban village sank to its usual repose, after the labors and cares which Saturday night imposes upon people of low degree. The bacon and meal for the next week had been purchased, the clothes for the morrow put in order, and preparations made for that Sunday dinner which the poorest colored family manages to make a little better than the week day meal. It was nearly twelve o'clock when all became silent; and the weary workers slept all the more soundly for the six days' labor of the week which was past.

It was a chill, dreary night. A dry, harsh wind blew from the north. The moon was at the full, and shone clear and cold in the blue vault.

There was one shrill whistle, some noise of quietly moving horses, and those who looked from their windows saw a black-gowned and grimly-masked horseman sitting upon a draped horse at every corner of the streets, and before each house—grim, silent, threatening. Those who saw dared not move or give any alarm. Instinctively they knew that the enemy they had feared had come, had them in his clutches, and would work his will of them, whether they resisted or not. So, with the instinct of self-preservation, all were silent—all simulated sleep.

Five, ten, fifteen minutes the silent watch continued. A half-hour passed, and there had been no sound. Each masked sentry sat his horse as if horse and rider were only some magic statuary with which the bleak night cheated the affrighted [frightened] eye. Then a whistle sounded on the road toward Verdenton. The masked horsemen turned their horses' heads in that direction, and slowly and silently moved away. Gathering in twos, they fell into ranks with the regularity and ease of a practiced soldiery. And, as they filed on towards Verdenton, showed a cavalcade of several hundred strong, and upon one of the foremost horses rode one with a strange figure lashed securely to him.

When the few who were awake in the little village found courage to inquire as to what the silent enemy had done, they rushed from house to house with chattering teeth and trembling limbs, only to find that all were safe within, until they came to the house where old Uncle Jerry Hunt had been dwelling alone since the death of his wife six months before.

The door was open. The house was empty. The straw mattress had been thrown from the bed, and the hempen cord on which it rested had been removed.

Sunday Morning Arrives

THE SABBATH MORROW WAS well advanced when the Fool was first apprised of the raid. He at once rode into the town, arriving there just as the morning services closed, and met the people coming along the streets to their homes.

Upon the limb of a low-branching oak not more than forty steps from the Temple of Justice, hung the lifeless body of old Jerry. The wind turned it slowly to and fro. The snowy hair and beard contrasted strangely with the dusky pallor of the peaceful face, which seemed even in death to proffer a benison [blessing or benediction] to the people of God who passed to and fro from the house of prayer, unmindful both of the peace which lighted the dead face and of the rifled temple of the Holy Ghost which appealed to them for sepulture [burial].

Over all pulsed the sacred echo of the sabbath bells. The sun shone brightly. The wind rustled the autumn leaves. A few idlers sat upon the steps of the courthouse and gazed carelessly at the ghastly burden on the oak. The brightly dressed churchgoers enlivened the streets. Not a colored man was to be seen. All except the brown cadaver on the tree spoke of peace and prayer—a holy day among a godly people, with whom rested the benison of peace.

Friends Explain What Happened

THE FOOL ASKED OF some trusty friends the story of the night before. With trembling lips one told it to him,

"I heard the noise of horses—quiet and orderly, but many. Looking from the window in the clear moonlight, I saw horsemen passing down the street, taking their stations here and there, like guards who have been told off for duty, at specific points. Two stopped before my house, two opposite Mr. Haskin's, and two or three upon the corner below. They seemed to have been sent on before as a sort of picket-guard for the main body, which soon came in. I should say there were from a hundred to a hundred and fifty still in line. They were all masked and wore black robes.

The horses were disguised, too, by drapings. There were only a few mules in the whole company. They were good horses, though. One could tell that by their movements. Oh, it was a respectable crowd! No doubt about that, sir. Beggars don't ride in this country. I don't know when I have seen so many good horses together since the Yankee cavalry left here after the surrender.

They were well drilled too. Plenty of old soldiers in that crowd. Why, every thing went just like clockwork. Not a word was said—just a few whistles given. They came like a dream and went away like a mist. I thought we should have to fight for our lives, but they did not disturb any one here. They gathered down by the courthouse. I could not see precisely what they were at, but, from my back upper window, saw them down about the tree.

After a while a signal was given, and just at that time a match was struck, and I saw a dark body swing down under the limb. I knew then they had hung somebody, but had no idea who it was. To tell the truth, I had a notion it was you, Colonel. I saw several citizens go out and speak to these men on the horses. There were lights in some of the offices about the courthouse and in several of the houses about town. Every thing was as still as the grave—no shouting or loud talking, and no excitement or stir about town.

It was evident that a great many of the citizens expected the movement and were prepared to co-operate with it by manifesting no curiosity or otherwise endangering its success. I am inclined to think a good many from this town were in it. I never felt so powerless in my life. Here the town was in the hands of two or three hundred armed and disciplined men, hidden from the eye of the law, and having friends and co-workers in almost every house. I knew that resistance was useless."

"But why," asked the Fool, "has not the body been removed?"

"We have been thinking about it," was the reply; "but the truth is, it don't seem like a very safe business. And, after what we saw last night, no one feels like being the first to do what may be held an affront by those men. **I tell you, Colonel, I went through the war and saw as much danger as most men in it. But I would rather charge up the Heights of Gettysburg again than be the object of a raid by that crowd.**"

After some parley, however, some colored men were found, and a little party made up, who went out and saw the body of Uncle Jerry cut down and laid upon a box to await the coming of the coroner, who had already been notified. The inquest developed only these facts, and the sworn jurors solemnly and honestly found the cause of death unknown. One of the colored men who had watched the proceedings gave utterance to the prevailing opinion, when he said—"It don't do fer niggers to know too much! Dat's what ail Uncle Jerry!"

And indeed it did seem as if his case was one in which ignorance might have been bliss.

Ch. 31, "The Folly of Wisdom," in *A Fool's Errand* by Albion Tourgée.

18. The Dread Cavalcade

Learning to be Brave

Michael W. Perry

Remember at the start of this book when I described young Lily crouched behind her bed with a pistol ready to shoot anyone who might invade her home? The passage that gave me the inspiration for that comes in this chapter.

> The constant apprehension of attack from the masked marauders had familiarized her with danger, and given her a coolness and decision of character which nothing else could have developed. She had seen the dread cavalcade pass in the dim moonlight and had stood at her chamber-window, revolver in hand, prepared to take part in the expected defense of their home.

You might wonder why Lily's parents exposed her to such grave danger. The answer lies in a book called *The Altruistic Personality* by Samuel Oliner. It describes why some in Nazi-occupied Europe risked their lives to rescue persecuted Jews. The author asked those who'd been parents why they risked the lives of their children. They answered that teaching goodness was so important that it must be done whatever the risks. That's how Lily learned her "coolness and decision of character," and why she was ready when her big test came.

We're now to the part you've been eagerly awaiting. Lily moves into the spotlight. She has a happy and sunny disposition, so imagine the girl at the center of the picture above is her. Growing up hasn't been easy. Her family has been ostracized and her father lives in constant danger. Yet because of those troubles, she has become strong and independent. Skilled on horseback and with a gun, she knows how to take care of herself. Her character and personality are so appealing, people her age are drawn to her in spite of the hostility of their parents.

Lily, the one child of Comfort and Metta Servosse, had developed under the Southern sun, until, almost before her parents had noted the fact, she had the rounded form and softened outlines indicative of womanhood. The atmosphere in which she had lived had also developed her mind not less rapidly. From her infancy almost, owing to the peculiar circumstances which surrounded their life, she had been the constant companion and trusted confidant of her mother.

Shut out from all that may be termed 'society' by the unfortunate relations which her husband and she herself sustained to those around them, regarded either as enemies, intruders, or inferiors, by those whose culture rendered their society desirable, Metta had not sought to remove this impression, but, acting upon her husband's advice, had calmly and proudly accepted the isolation thus imposed upon her, only compensating herself by a more intimate and constant association with her husband, sharing his thoughts, entering into his plans and purposes, and interesting herself in all that interested him.

It resulted that she took the liveliest interest in all that concerned the present and future of that community in which they dwelt. Side by side with her husband she had digged [dug] into the history of the past, studied the development of the present, and earnestly endeavored to find some clew [clue] to the clouded and obscure future. In this absorbing question her heart had become weaned from many of those things which constitute so much of the ordinary life of woman. And, in the society of her husband and the care and education of her daughter, she had almost ceased to miss those social enjoyments to which she had been accustomed before their migration.

The exciting events which had occurred around them had drawn this little family into even closer relations with each other than this involuntary isolation would, of itself, have compelled. The difficulties and dangers attending the Fool's life and duties had woven themselves into the daily life of the wife and daughter until they became the one engrossing theme of their thought and the burden of their conversations. During his absence, anxiety for his safety, and, during his presence, thankfulness for his preservation, filled their hearts.

Every act of violence perpetrated by the mysterious enemy which lay hidden all about them was one more evidence of the peril which surrounded him on whom all their hopes were centered. Every call of duty which took him from their sight was another trial of their faith in the

Great Deliverer. Every absence and every return increased the intensity of their anxiety, and fixed their minds more exclusively upon those events which were passing day by day about them. Each farewell came to have the solemnity of a death bed, and each return, the solemn joy of an unexpected resurrection.

In this furnace blast of excitement and apprehension the young girl's heart and mind had matured even more rapidly than her person. A prudence unknown to one of her years who had lived in quiet times and under other conditions of society, had come to be habitual with her.

The constant apprehension of attack from the masked marauders had familiarized her with danger and given her a coolness and decision of character which nothing else could have developed. She had seen the dread cavalcade pass in the dim moonlight and had stood at her chamber window, revolver in hand, prepared to take part in the expected defense of their home.

She had learned to watch for danger, to see that all precautions were adopted against it, to be cautious what she said and to whom she said it, to weigh with suspicious doubt the words and acts of all whom she met. Many a time, while yet a mere child, she had been called upon to be her mother's consoler [counselor] in seasons of doubt and apprehended danger. A thousand times she had seen the dull gray look of agonized foreboding steal into the loved face and had bravely undertaken the duty of lightening the mother's woe. All this had ripened her mind with wonderful rapidity.

As she had shared the anxieties and perils of her parents, she had participated also in their joys. She had early been trained to the saddle. And from the very outset of their life in the new home, her pony had been the frequent companion of both Lollard and Jaca in many a long ride. As she grew older, the pony gave way to her own petted mare, and a more easy, graceful, and daring rider it was hard to find, even in that region of unrivaled horsemen and horsewomen. She had also been trained to the use of arms and handled both rifle and revolver, not only without fear, but with readiness and precision.

In person she was by no means unattractive. She had the lithe, trim figure of her mother, and, united with it, that softness of outline, delicacy of color, and ease and grace of carriage which the free, untrammeled life and soft, kindly climate of that region give in such rich measure to those reared under their influences. Her eyes were of that deep blue which evinces fortitude and sincerity, while her luxuriant hair took the character of its hue from the light in which it was viewed—"golden in the sunshine, in the shadow brown," and, touched by the moonbeam, a spray of tinted silver. It had been the joy and pride of the fond mother. Shears had never marred its glossy sheen, and it had rarely felt the restraint of twist or braid, but had hung naturally about the child's shoulders, until it fell, in a rippling cascade, to her waist.

Friends Her Age

To THESE PERSONAL ATTRIBUTES Lily joined a sunniness of temper, a sparkle and vivacity of mind, inherited from faraway French ancestors, which seemed to have been brought out by the sunny brightness of the kindred clime in which she had been reared. These charms combined to render her an exceedingly piquant and charming maiden, so that, as she rode here and there with her parents, or scrambled about the shady bridle-paths of the adjacent country alone, her beauty came to be remarked. **The young people of the vicinity began shyly to court her presence and finally opened their social circles and their hearts to her, only regretting that her parents were not "our people" and kindly exercising more or less forgetfulness of her origin.**

Among those who had seen and admired the bright presence which reigned supreme at Warrington was Melville Gurney, the son of General Marion Gurney of Pultowa County, adjoining that in which the Fool resided. Young Gurney was a splendid specimen of the stock of Southern gentlemen from which he sprung, being tall and commanding in person, of that easy grace which is rarely matched in other portions of the country and admirably adapted to excel in field-sports, in all of which he was an acknowledged proficient. His early youth had covered the period of the war, in which his father had won no little renown, and before his sixteenth birthday he had run away from home, riding his own horse, to take part in the last campaign of Early in the Valley of the Shenandoah, where his father's command was engaged.

After the last defeat he found his father lying wounded in a Federal hospital, and by unremitting exertion saved him from fatal prostration and brought him home to slow but certain recovery. The daring youngster could not, after that, confine himself to the dull routine of the college. But in his father's library and afterwards in his office, he had received a culture not less complete, although very different from what he would have gathered in the course of a collegiate career. This young man, bold, active, and endowed with a superabundant vitality, had met the little lady of Warrington at a festive gathering near his father's home a few months before the time to which our story has advanced, and with the frank impetuosity characteristic of his nativity had forthwith testified his admiration and asked an invitation to Warrington.

That the young girl should be flattered by the attentions of so charming a cavalier was but natural. It was the first time, however, that she had been asked to extend the hospitalities of her father's house to any of her associates and at once the anomalous position in which they stood to those by whom they were surrounded forced itself upon her thought. Her face flushed for an instant, and then, looking up quietly into his, she said, "Are you in earnest, Mr. Gurney? Would you really like to visit Warrington?"

The inquiry brought the young man to a serious consideration of his own request. When he had first preferred it, he had thought only of the fair creature by his side. Now, he thought of a thousand incidents which might flow from it. Bold almost to recklessness, he was sincere almost to bluntness also, even with himself. Therefore, ready as he would have been with the words of a mere outward politeness, he honestly hesitated before answering the question.

Instantly the quick perceptions and natural pride of the "carpet-bagger's" daughter were aroused, and she said somewhat haughtily but with a studied courtesy of tone, "I see, Mr. Gurney, that your request was merely intended as an empty compliment, which it is not worth the trouble either to accept or decline. Excuse me," and, having already removed her hand from his arm, she bowed lightly and turned with a smile to begin a lively conversation with a friend who stood near.

Melville's Admiration Grows

THE INCIDENT SHOWED SUCH coolness and self-control, as well as frank sincerity, that the admiration of Melville Gurney was increased rather than diminished thereby. He did not regard it as a rebuff, but as a self-respecting assertion that one who doubted as to the propriety of visiting her father's house had no right to prefer such a request to her. So he did not approach her again during the evening but watched her attentively.

And the next day, when he saw her pass his father's office, mounted upon Lollard (now full of years, but still a horse of magnificent action and unabated fire), her fair hair falling free over her dark habit until it almost touched the glossy coat of her steed, each fiber transformed by the sunlight into a gleaming thread of gold, he began to feel something of regret that he had not answered her question and pressed for an answer to his request.

General Gurney was as active and prominent a political leader upon the other side as the Fool was upon his and was looked upon as a partisan of similar intensity of conviction. Both were pronounced and positive men. They were well-matched opponents too, had more than once met upon the stump, and had served together in public bodies. There was that acquaintance between them which such association gives, without further personal relations, and perhaps something of that esteem which is sure to prevail between men often pitted against each other without decisive victory.

The general was the representative of an old and honored family, and felt, with the utmost keenness, the degradation resulting from defeat, and the subsequent elevation of the colored man to a position of political coordination with the white race. He had married early. Melville was the oldest child, and on him the hopes, aspirations, and love of the father were centered in an unusual degree.

"What do you think of Colonel Servosse, Pa?," asked the son a few moments after Lily had passed.

"Think about him? That he is the worst Radical in the State. He has the most ineradicable hate of everything Southern that I have ever known," answered the father.

"But aside from his politics—as a man, Pa, what do you think of him?"

"Oh! As a man he is well enough. In fact, better than I could wish. Personally there seems to be no weak spot in his armor. They did try to make some attack upon his character. But no one really believed it, and I am of the notion that it did us more harm than good. I never did believe it, though I have sometimes hinted at it, just because I saw that I could get under his hide in no other way. He is the coolest and most collected man I have ever met in public life."

"Is he a gentleman?"

"Well—yes, in a Northern sense," answered the father. "I have no doubt that if he had staid [stayed] at the North, and I had known him as a Northern man, I should have enjoyed him thoroughly. Everybody who is acquainted with him admits that he has fine social qualities. He is somewhat reserved to strangers. He is a man of decided ability and culture, and I count him one of the most dangerous Radicals in the State. But why do you ask?"

"Well, I thought I would like to know all sides of him," replied the son. "I had read so much of him, and had heard you speak of him so often in a semi-public manner, that I thought I would like to know your actual opinion in regard to him."

"That's right. You ought to learn everything you can of a man of his mark. You will meet his influence in the State as long as you live. He has left an impress upon it that would remain, even if he should die to-morrow."

A Note to Lily

SOON AFTERWARDS MELVILLE GURNEY wrote a note to Lily Servosse, which contained only these words:

> Miss Lily,
> Will you allow me, after mature deliberation, to renew the request which I made to you?
> Respectfully,
> Melville Gurney

Lily took this to her mother and told her all that had occurred. For the first time the mother realized that her daughter was growing into womanhood. The blushes which accompanied her narrative told that her heart was awakened. It seemed but a little while since she was only a prattling child. But now, as the mother looked on her budding beauty, she could but admit, with a pang of sorrow, that the days of girlhood were over, that the summer of love had come, and that her pretty bird was but pluming her wings for the inevitable flight. Like a prudent mother, she determined to do nothing to hasten this result, and yet to so act as to keep her daughter's confidence as implicit and spontaneous as it had hitherto been. So she only kissed the girl's blushing cheek, asking lightly, "And would you like to have him come?"

"I don't know, mama" answered Lily artlessly. "I *would* like to be more like—like our neighbors and have more young companions."

"And so you shall, my daughter," answered the mother. So it resulted, that, a few weeks after, a party was given at Warrington, and Mr. Melville Gurney, with several others of Lily's friends in Pultowa, received an invitation to be present. Metta did not see fit to confide anything of this to the Fool, who only knew that young Gurney came with others to a party given for his daughter's pleasure. It was the first time that wife or daughter had ever had a secret which the husband and father had not shared.

The first part of Ch. 35, "An Awakening," in *A Fool's Errand* by Albion Tourgée.

19. WARNED ABOUT THE KLAN

Silencing Opponents

Michael W. Perry

W e met Thomas Denton in Chapter 10 when, speaking as a Southern attorney, he wrote Comfort a letter warning, "The South has been changed only in so far as the overwhelming power of the conqueror has rendered change imperative. In its old domain, prejudice is still as bitter and unreasoning as ever."

In its zeal to restore white supremacy, the Democratic party had murdered John Walters, a leader for both poor blacks and whites and used the Klan to lynch the gentle and godly Uncle Jerry, the most outspoken voice for freedom among the blacks. But that wasn't enough.

To win back the political power the party had under slavery, it knew it must also silence its most powerful foes, educated white professionals, particularly those who had grown up in the South and could not be slandered as trouble-making "carpetbaggers." With the Democratic party not yet dominant, Denton has become a judge who is actively pursuing the Klan. To silence him, the Klan will pull together all their forces. Over a hundred riders will converge from three counties to kill one man.

Mr. Denton, the district-attorney, whose letter to Comfort Servosse has already been given to the reader, had been elected a judge of the State courts, and had recently, before the period at which we have now arrived, been very active in his efforts to suppress the operation of the Klan and punish those engaged in its raids. By so doing, he had incurred the hostility of the Klan at large and especially of that portion with which the suspected parties had been actually connected.

There had long been threats and denunciations afloat in regard to him. But he was a brave man, who did not turn aside from the path of his duty for any obstacles, and who, while he did not despise the power of the organization which he had taken by the throat, was yet utterly oblivious to threats of personal violence. He would do his duty, though the heavens fell. This was a fact well known and recognized by all who knew him. And for this very reason, most probably, it was generally believed that he would be put out of the way by the Klan before the time for the trial of its members arrived.

Denton and Servosse to Meet

IT WAS UNDER THESE circumstances that the Fool received a telegram from Judge Denton, requesting him to come to Verdenton on a certain day, and go with him to his home in an adjoining county. It was seven miles from Glenville, the nearest railroad-station, to the plantation of Judge Denton. To reach it, the chief river of that region had to be crossed on a long wooden bridge, four miles from the station. The Fool accepted this invitation and with Metta drove into Verdenton on the day named.

The railroad which ran nearest to the home of Judge Denton connected at an acute angle with that on which he was to arrive at Verdenton. Between the two was the residence of Colonel Servosse, six miles from Verdenton, and sixteen from Glenville.

The train left Verdenton at eight-and-a-half o'clock in the evening, and ran to the junction, where it awaited the coming of the northward-bound train on the other road, so that they would not arrive at Glenville until ten o'clock, and would reach the river bridge about eleven and the judge's mansion perhaps a half-hour later. By previous arrangement, his carriage would meet them at the station. Metta intended to remain until the train reached Verdenton and bring home a friend who was expected to arrive upon it.

Lily in Charge

LILY REMAINED AT HOME. She was the "only white person on the lot," to use the familiar phrase of that region, which means that upon her rested all the responsibility of the house.

The existence of a servile, or recently servile race, devolves upon the children at a very early age a sort of vice-regal power in the absence of the parents. They are expected to see that "every thing goes on right on the plantation" and about the house in such absence. And their commands are as readily obeyed by the servants and employees as those of their elders. It is this early familiarity with the affairs of the parents and ready assumption of responsibility which give to the youth of the South that air of self-control and readiness to assume command of whatever matter he may be engaged in. It is thus that they are trained to rule.

To this training, in large measure, is due the fact, that, during all the *ante bellum* [before the Civil War] period, the Southern minority [wealthy landowners] dominated and controlled the government, monopolized its honors and emoluments [advantages], and dictated its policy in spite of an overwhelming and hostile majority at the North. The Southrons are the natural rulers, leaders, and dictators of the country, as later events have conclusively proved.

It was just at sundown, and Lily was sitting on the porch at Warrington, watching the sunset glow, when a horseman came in sight and rode up to the gate. After a moment's scrutiny of the premises, he seemed satisfied and uttered the usual halloo which it is customary for one to give who desires to communicate with the household in that country. Lily rose and advanced to the steps.

"Here's a letter," said the horseman, as he held an envelope up to view, and then, as she started down the steps, threw it over the gate into the avenue and, wheeling his horse, cantered easily away. Lily picked up the letter. It was directed in a coarse, sprawling hand: "Colonel Comfort Servosse, Warrington." In the lower left hand-corner, in a more compact and business-like hand, were written the words, "Read at once." Lily read the superscription carelessly as she went up the broad avenue. It awakened no curiosity in her mind. But, after she had resumed her seat on the porch, it occurred to her that both the messenger and his horse were unknown to her.

The former was a white lad of fourteen or fifteen years of age, whom she might very well fail to recognize. What struck her as peculiar was the fact that he was evidently unacquainted with Warrington, which was a notable place in the country. And a lad of that age could hardly be found in a circuit of many miles who could not have directed the traveler to it. It was evident from the demeanor of this one that, when he first rode up, he was uncertain whether he had reached his destination and had only made sure of it by recognizing some specific object which had been described to him. In other words, he had been traveling on what is known in that country as a 'way-bill' or a description of a route received from another.

Then she remembered that she had not recognized the horse, which was a circumstance somewhat remarkable, for it was an iron-gray of notable form and action. Her love of horses led her instinctively to notice those which she saw, and her daily rides had made her familiar with every good horse in a circle of many miles. Besides this, she had been accustomed to go almost everywhere with her father, when he had occasion to make journeys not requiring more than a day's absence. So that it was quite safe to say that she knew by sight at least twice as many horses as people.

These reflections caused her to glance again a little curiously at the envelope. It occurred to her, as she did so, that the superscription was in a disguised hand. Her father had received so many letters of that character, all of threat or warning, that the bare suspicion of that fact aroused at once the apprehension of evil or danger.

Reading the Letter

WHILE SHE HAD BEEN thinking, the short Southern twilight had given place to the light of the full moon rising in the East. She went into the house and, calling for a light, glanced once more at the envelope, and then broke the seal. It read:

Colonel Servosse,

A raid of K.K. has been ordered to intercept Judge Denton on his way home tonight (the 23d inst.). It is understood that he has telegraphed to you to accompany him home. Do not do it. If you can by any means, give him warning. It is a big raid and means business.

The decree is that he shall be tied, placed in the middle of the bridge across the river, the planks taken up on each side, so as to prevent a rescue, and the bridge set on fire. I send this warning for your sake. Do not trust the telegraph. I shall try to send this by a safe hand, but tremble lest it should be too late. I dare not sign my name, but subscribe myself your

Unknown Friend

The young girl stood for a moment paralyzed with horror at the danger which threatened her father. It did not once occur to her to doubt the warning she had received. She glanced at the timepiece upon the mantel. The hands pointed to eight o'clock.

"Too late, too late!," she cried as she clasped her hands, and raised her eyes to heaven in prayerful agony. She saw that she could not reach Verdenton in time to prevent their taking the train, and she knew it would be useless to telegraph afterwards. It was evident that the wires were under the control of the Klan, and there was no probability that a message would be delivered, if sent, in time to prevent the catastrophe.

"O my dear, dear papa!," she cried, as she realized more fully the danger. "O God! Can nothing be done to save him!"

Rescuing Her Father

Then a new thought flashed upon her mind. She ran to the back porch and called sharply, but quietly, "William! *Oh*, William!"

A voice in the direction of the stables answered, "Ma'am?"

"Come here at once."

Oh, Maggie!," she called.

"Ma'am?," from the kitchen.

"Bring me a cup of coffee, some biscuits, and an egg—quick!"

"Law sakes, chile, what makes ye in sech a hurry? Supper 'll be ready direckly Miss Mettie gits home. Can't yer wait?," answered the colored woman querulously.

"Never mind. I'll do without it, if it troubles you," said Lily quietly.

"Bress my soul! No trouble at all, Miss Lily," said the woman, entirely mollified by the soft answer. "Only I couldn't see what made yer be in sech a powerful hurry. Ye'se hev 'em in a minit, honey."

"William," said Lily, as the stable-boy appeared, "put my saddle on Young Lollard and bring him round as quick as possible."

"But Miss Lily, you know dat hoss"—the servant began to expostulate.

"I know all about him, William. Don't wait to talk. Bring him out."

"All right, Miss Lily," he replied, with a bow and a scrape. But, as he went toward the stable, he soliloquized angrily, "Now, what for Miss Lily want to ride dat pertickerler hoss, you s'pose? Never did afore. Nobody but de kunnel ebber on his back, an' *he* hab his hands full wid him sometimes. Dese furrer-bred hosses jes' de debbil anyhow! Dar's dat Young Lollard now, it's jest 'bout all a man's life's wuth ter rub him down an' saddle him. Why can't she take de ole un! Here you, Lollard, come outen dar!"

He threw open the door of the log-stable where the horse had his quarters, as he spoke, and almost instantly, with a short, vicious whinney, a powerful dark-brown horse leaped into the moonlight, and with ears laid back upon his sinuous neck, white teeth bare, and thin, blood-red nostrils distended, rushed towards the servant, who, with a loud, "Dar now! Look at him! Whoa! See de dam rascal!," retreated quickly behind the door.

The horse rushed once or twice around the little stable-yard, and then stopped suddenly beside his keeper and stretched out his head for the bit, quivering in every limb with that excess of vitality which only the thoroughbred horse ever exhibits. He was anxious for the bit and saddle, because they meant exercise, a race, an opportunity to show his speed, which the thoroughbred recognizes as the one great end of his existence.

Riding Young Lollard

BEFORE THE HORSE WAS saddled, Lily had donned her riding-habit, put a revolver in her belt, as she very frequently did when riding alone, swallowed a hasty supper, scrawled a short note to her mother on the envelope of the letter she had received—which she charged William at once to carry to her—and was ready to start on a night ride to Glenville. She had only been there across the country once. But she thought she knew the way or was at least so familiar with the 'lay' of the country that she could find it.

The brawny groom with difficulty held the restless horse by the bit. But the slight girl, who stood upon the block with pale face and set teeth, gathered the reins in her hand, leaped fearlessly into the saddle, found the stirrup, and said "Let him go!" without a quaver in her voice. The man loosed his hold. The horse stood upright, and pawed the air for a moment with his feet, gave a few mighty leaps to make sure of his liberty, and then, stretching out his neck, bounded

forward in a race which would require all the mettle of his endless line of noble sires.

Almost without words, her errand had become known to the household of servants. And as she flew down the road, her bright hair gleaming in the moonlight, old Maggie, sobbing and tearful, was yet so impressed with admiration, that she could only say—

"De Lor' bress her! 'Pears like dat chile ain't 'fear'd o' noffin'!"

As she was borne like an arrow down the avenue and turned into the Glenville road, Lily heard the whistle of the train as it left the depot at Verdenton and knew that upon her coolness and resolution alone depended the life of her father.

The last part of Ch. 35, "An Awakening," in *A Fool's Errand* by Albion Tourgée.

20. Racing Against the Klan

Young Lollard

Michael W. Perry

Like people, horses have family trees. Young Lollard had Lollard, the horse that Comfort rode during the Civil War, as his sire (father) and was a descendant of both Glencoe and Emancipator through his mare (mother). Glencoe (1831–1857) was a famous British race horse. Transported to the U.S. in 1836, he became one of the first thoroughbreds to be brought into this country. Emancipator apparently came over about the same time.

As your read, keep in mind that there are no signs on these country roads, and Lily has only been this way once before. That's why she keeps praying for guidance. One wrong turn, and she will reach Glenville too late. As she rides this high-strung and powerful horse, she must keep her mind clear and calm.

Now for more background. Many of my readers know far more about horses than I'll ever learn, and I envy you. But for those who don't, I will draw on my limited expertise. Years ago, I was invited to a party at a Texas ranch and had a chance to go riding. I could tell that the horse offered to me didn't like people from how it glared at me. I'm not easily deterred though, so I got on him. For this story, I'll call him Meanie.

After a couple of minutes, Meanie had enough of me and headed for a nearby live oak tree despite my pulling back on the reins. Fortunately, its branches were high enough, I could duck down and make it through. Then Meanie headed for a tree whose branches were so low, I didn't see how he could make it through, much less me. When we reach the tree, I grabbed its branches and lowered myself to the ground. Meanie stopped a few yards off and glanced back at me with disdain. "I showed you," he seemed be thinking. Still not deterred, I got back on.

At that point a teen daughter in the family who owned the ranch came up. Handling Meanie was easy, she said. Pulling back on the reins, she went on, wouldn't make him stop. I knew that. However, she explained, if I yanked the reins far to one side, he'd *have* to turn that way. He had no choice. And if I then yanked the reins far to the other side, he'd have to turn yet again. Those two sharp turns would force him almost to a stop.

She was right. Meanie soon learned he could no longer scrape me off his back. He made one attempt to bite me on the foot, which I blocked by yanking the reins. After that, he settled down and rode quite well. He now knew who was the boss.

Young Lollard isn't a mean horse, but he is high-spirited and difficult to control. As Lily starts out, she can do little more than use the reins to get him headed in the right direction. But as you will see, she's not able to pull back on the reins and make him slow down. Instead, she keeps them tightly drawn, so she can sense instantly if he turns sharply to either side. If she's thrown to the ground and injured, she'll never reach her father in time. Only later, as she's crossing the river, is she able to take control. She has won Young Lollard's trust and respect.

It was perhaps well for the accomplishment of her purpose, that, for some time after setting out on her perilous journey, Lily Servosse had enough to do to maintain her seat, and guide and control her horse. Young Lollard, whom the servant had so earnestly remonstrated against her taking, added to the noted pedigree of his sire the special excellences of the Glencoe strain of his dam, from whom he inherited also a darker coat and that touch of native savageness which characterizes the stock of Emancipator.

Upon both sides his blood was as pure as that of the great kings of the turf, and what we have termed his savagery was more excess of spirit than any inclination to do mischief. It was that uncontrollable desire of the thoroughbred horse to be always doing his best, which made him restless of the bit and curb, while the native sagacity of his race had led him to practice somewhat on the fears of his groom.

With that care which only the true lover of the horse can appreciate, Colonel Servosse had watched over the growth and training of Young Lollard, hoping to see him rival, if he did not surpass, the excellences of his sire. In everything but temper, he had been gratified at the result. In build, power, speed, and endurance, the horse offered all that the most fastidious could desire. In order to prevent the one defect of a quick temper from developing into a vice, the colonel had established an inflexible rule that no one should ride him but himself.

His great interest in the colt had led Lily, who inherited all her father's love for the noble animal, to look very carefully during his enforced absences after the welfare of his favorite. Once or twice she had summarily discharged grooms who were guilty of disobeying her father's injunctions and had always made it a rule to visit his stall every day so that, although she had never ridden him, the horse was familiar with her person and voice.

Dashing Away

IT WAS WELL FOR her that this was the case. For as he dashed away with the speed of the wind, she felt how powerless she was to restrain him by means of the bit. Nor did she attempt it. Merely feeling his mouth and keeping her eye upon the road before him, in order that no sudden start to right or left should take her by surprise, she coolly kept her seat and tried to soothe him by her voice.

With head outstretched, and sinewy neck strained to its uttermost, he flew over the ground in a wild, mad race with the evening wind, as it seemed. Without jerk or strain, but easily and steadily as the falcon flies, the high-bred horse skimmed along the ground. A mile, two, three miles were made, in time that would have done honor to the staying quality of his sires, and still his pace had not slackened.

He was now nearing the river into which fell the creek that ran by Warrington. As he went down the long slope that led to the ford, his rider tried in vain to check his speed. Pressure upon the bit but resulted in an impatient shaking of the head, and laying back of the ears. He kept up his magnificent stride until he had reached the very verge of the river.

There he stopped, threw up his head in inquiry, as he gazed upon the fretted waters lighted up by the full moon, glanced back at his rider, and, with a word of encouragement from her, marched proudly into the waters, casting up a silvery spray at every step. Lily did not miss this opportunity to establish more intimate relations with her steed. She patted his neck, praised him lavishly, and took occasion to assume control of him while he was in the deepest part of the channel, turning him this way and that much more than was needful, simply to accustom him to obey her will.

When he came out on the other bank, he would have resumed his gallop almost at once, but she required him to walk to the top of the hill. The night was growing chilly by this time. As the wind struck her at the hilltop, she remembered that she had thrown a hooded water-proof about her before starting. She stopped her horse and, taking off her hat, gathered her long hair into a mass, and thrust it into the hood, which she drew over her head and pressed her hat down on it. Then she gathered the reins, and they went on in that long, steady stride which marks the high-bred horse when he gets thoroughly down to his work.

Finding Her Way

ONCE OR TWICE SHE drew rein to examine the landmarks and deter-mine which road to take. Sometimes her way lay through the forest, and she was startled by the cry of the owl. Anon it was through the reedy bottom land, and the half-wild hogs, starting from their lairs, gave her an instant's fright. The moon cast strange shadows around her. But still she pushed on, with this one only thought in her mind, that her father's life was at stake, and she alone could save him.

She had written to her mother to go back to Verdenton and tele-graph to her father, but she put no hope in that. How she trembled, as she passed each fork in the rough and ill-marked country road, lest she should take the right-hand when she ought to turn to the left, and so lose precious, priceless moments! How her heart beat with joy when she came upon any remembered landmark! And all the time her mind was full of tumultuous prayer. Sometimes it bubbled over her lips in tender, disjointed accents.

"Father! Papa, dear, dear Papa!," she cried to the bright still night that lay around, and then the tears burst over the quivering lids, and ran down the fair cheeks in torrents. She pressed her hand to her heart as she fancied that a gleam of redder light shot athwart the northern sky, and she thought of a terrible bonfire that would rage and glow above that horizon if she failed to bring timely warning of the danger.

How her heart throbbed with thankfulness as she galloped through an avenue of giant oaks at a crossroads where she remembered stopping with her father one day! He had told her that it was half way from Glen-ville to Warrington. He had watered their horses there, and she remem-bered every word of pleasant badinage [joking] he had addressed to her as they rode home. Had one ever before so dear, so tender a parent?

The tears came again, but she drove them back with a half-involun-tary laugh. "Not now, not now!," she said. "No, nor at all. They shall not come at all, for I will save him. O God, help me! I am but a weak girl. Why did the letter come so late? But I *will* save him! Help me, Heaven! Guide and help!"

She glanced at her watch as she passed from under the shade of the oaks and, as she held the dial up to the moonlight, gave a scream of joy. It was just past the stroke of nine. She had still an hour, and half the distance had been accomplished in half that time.

She had no fear of her horse. Pressing on now in the swinging fox-walk which he took whenever the character of the road or the mood of his rider demanded, there was no sign of weariness. As he threw his head upon one side and the other, as if asking to be allowed to press on, she saw his dark eye gleam with the fire of the inveterate racer. His thin nostrils were distended, but his breath came regularly and full. She had not forgotten, even in her haste and fright, the lessons her father had taught. But, as soon as she could control her horse, she had spared him, and compelled him to husband his strength. Her spirits rose at the prospect.

She even caroled a bit of exultant song as Young Lollard swept on through a forest of towering pines, with a white sand-cushion stretched beneath his feet. The fragrance of the pines came to her nostrils, and with it the thought of frankincense, and that brought up the hymns of her childhood. The Star in the East, the Babe of Bethlehem, the Great Deliverer—all swept across her wrapt vision; and then came the price-less promise, "I will not leave thee, nor forsake."

The first part of Ch. 36, "A Race Against Time," in *A Fool's Errand* by Albion Tourgée.

....

Hymns that Lily Sang that Night
Michael W. Perry

The first hymn Lily sang, "The Star in the East," is an old folk hymn written by Reginald Heber in 1811 and popular among Baptists and Methodists. Notice its call for God's aid and guidance. You might want to say the words to yourself to get a feel for what she was feeling that night.

Hail the blest morn! See the great Mediator
Down from the regions of glory descend.
Shepherds go worship the babe in the manger;
Lo! For his guard the bright angels attend.
Brightest and best of the sons of the morning,

Dawn on our darkness and lend us thine aid.
Star in the East, the horizon adorning,
Guide where our infant Redeemer is laid.

There are several nineteenth century hymns called "The Babe of Bethlehem." Here are words from the one that seems to have been the most popular and from the fourth and fifth stanzas, which seem to apply best to her night ride.

On the same night a glorious light to shepherds there appeared,
  Bright angels said, "Be not afraid, although we much alarm you,
  The angels said, "Be not afraid, although we much alarm you,
  We do appear good news to bear, as now we will inform you.

"The city's name is Bethlehem, in which God hath appointed,
  This glorious morn a Savior's born, for him God hath anointed;
  By this you'll know, if you will go, to see this little stranger,
  His lovely charms in Mary's arms, both lying in a manger."

And finally, there's the last hymn, "Come, Great Deliverer, Come" written by the blind Fanny Crosby in 1877. Here's the second and third verses. You'll see how relevant they are.

I have no place, no shelter from the night,
Come, Great Deliv'rer, come;
One look from Thee would give me light,
Come, Great Deliv'rer, come.

My path is lone, and weary are my feet,
Come, Great Deliv'rer, come;
Mine eyes look up Thy loving smile to meet,
Come, Great Deliv'rer, come.

And now the refrain:
I've wandered far away o'er mountains cold,
I've wandered far away from home;
O take me now, and bring me to Thy fold,
Come, Great Deliv'rer, come.

21. TRAPPED BY THE KLAN

Fleet Steeds

Michael W. Perry

The line from the poem that Lily will quote in this chapter comes from a wonderfully romantic poem by Sir Robert Scott that was once memorized by every schoolchild in Britain and Ireland. It's called "Lochinvar" and is part of a much longer poem called "Marmion." In the tale, the parents of a maiden had refused to give their daughter's hand in marriage to brave Lochinvar as he went off to war, pledging her instead to a less brave man. On her wedding day, Lochinvar returns alone riding a fast steed. Entering the crowded wedding hall, he says:

"I long woo'd your daughter, my suit you denied;—
Love swells like the Solway, but ebbs like its tide—
And now I am come, with this lost love of mine,
To lead but one measure, drink one cup of wine.
There are maidens in Scotland more lovely by far,
That would gladly be bride to the young Lochinvar."

One touch to her hand, and one word in her ear,
When they reach'd the hall-door, and the charger stood near;
So light to the croupe the fair lady he swung,
So light to the saddle before her he sprung!
"She is won! We are gone, over bank, bush, and scaur;
They'll have fleet steeds that follow," quoth young Lochinvar.

There was mounting 'mong Graemes of the Netherby clan;
Forsters, Fenwicks, and Musgraves, they rode and they ran:
There was racing and chasing on Cannobie Lee,
But the lost bride of Netherby ne'er did they see.
So daring in love, and so dauntless in war,
Have ye e'er heard of gallant like young Lochinvar?

The Soloway is a firth (bay) on the border between Scotland and England. Because of its shape, the tide rises quickly—sometimes so fast a man cannot outrun it—but it falls slowly. Lochinvar is saying that the love he felt for this young woman came upon him quickly, and that he will not easily forget her or be deterred from winning her hand.

Now we return to Lily's brave ride. As your read, consider the skill it took for Lilly to keep her high-strung stallion calm at night in the presence of over a hundred strange horses and men. Notice also her talent at using the stars to tell directions, as well as how she could navigate by the lay of the land, using hills and streams to tell where she was. This is a girl who knows how to handle difficult situations and, armed with a gun, is ready for trouble.

Finally, after being held back by the Klan, Lily must push Young Lollard to his limits to reach Glendale in time. Even her horse senses her urgency and runs flat out, holding nothing back.

Still on and on the brave horse bore her with untiring limb. Half the remaining distance is now consumed, and she comes to a place where the road forks, not once, but into four branches. It is in the midst of a level old field covered with a thick growth of scrubby pines. Through the masses of thick green are white lanes which stretch away in every direction, with no visible difference save in the density or frequency of the shadows which fall across them.

She tries to think which of the many intersecting paths lead to her destination. She tries this and then that for a few steps, consults the stars to determine in what direction Glenville lies, and has almost decided upon the first to the right, when she hears a sound which turns her blood to ice in her veins.

The Klan Arrives

A SHRILL WHISTLE SOUNDS to the left—once, twice, thrice—and then it is answered from the road in front. There are two others. O God! If she but knew which road to take! She knows well enough the meaning of those signals. She has heard them before. The masked cavaliers are closing in upon her. And, as if frozen to stone, she sits her horse in the clear moonlight and can not choose.

She is not thinking of herself. It is not for herself that she fears. But there has come over her a horrible numbing sensation that she is lost, that she does not know which road leads to those she seeks to save, and at the same time there comes the certain conviction that to err would be fatal.

There are but two roads now to choose from, since she has heard the fateful signals from the left and front. But how much depends upon that choice! "It must be this," she says to herself. And, as she says it, the sickening conviction comes, "No, no—it is the other!"

She hears hoof-strokes upon the road in front, on that to her left, and now, too, on that which turns sheer to the right. From one to the other the whistle sounds—sharp, short signals. **Her heart sinks within her. She has halted at the very rendezvous of the enemy. They are all about her. To attempt to ride down either road now is to invite destruction.**

She woke from her stupor when the first horseman came in sight, and thanked God for her dark horse and colorless habit. She urged Young Lollard among the dense scrub-pines which grew between the two roads from which she knew that she must choose, turned his head back toward the point of intersection, drew her revolver, leaned over upon his neck, and peered through the overhanging branches. She patted her horse's head and whispered to him softly to keep him still.

Hardly had she placed herself in hiding, before the open space around the intersecting roads was alive with disguised horsemen. She could catch glimpses of their figures as she gazed through the clustering spines. Three men came into the road which ran along to the right of where she stood. They were hardly five steps from where she lay, panting, but determined, on the faithful horse, which moved not a muscle. Once he had neighed before they came so near. But there were so many horses neighing and snuffing, that no one had heeded it.

She remembered a little flask which Maggie had put into her pocket. It was whiskey. She put up her revolver, drew out the flask, opened it, poured some in her hand, and, leaning forward, rubbed it on the horse's nose. He did not offer to neigh again.

The Klan Debates

ONE OF THE MEN who stood near her spoke, "Gentlemen, I am the East Commander of Camp No. 5 of Pultowa County."

"And I, of Camp No. 8, of Wayne."

"And I, of No. 12, Sevier."

"You are the men I expected to meet," said the first.

"We were ordered to report to you," said the others.

"This is Bentley's Cross, then, I presume."

"The same."

"Four miles from Glenville, I believe?"

"Nigh about that," said one of the others.

"We leave this road about a mile and a half from this place?"

"Yes, and cross by a country way to the river-road."

"What is the distance to the river road by this route?"

"Not far from five miles."

"It is now about half-past nine, so that there is no haste. How many men have you each?"

"Thirty-two from No. 8."

"Thirty-one from No. 12."

"I have myself *forty*. Are yours informed of the work on hand?"

"Not a word."

"Are we quite secure here?"

"I have had the roads picketed since sundown," answered one. "I myself just came from the south, not ten minutes before you signaled."

"Ah! I thought I heard a horse on that road."

"Has the party we want left Verdenton?"

"A messenger from Glenville says he is on the train with the carpetbagger Servosse."

"Going home with him?"

"Yes."

"The decree does not cover Servosse?"

"No."

"I don't half like the business, anyhow, and am not inclined to go beyond express orders. What do you say about it?," asked the leader.

"Hadn't we better say the decree covers both?," asked one.

"I can't do it," said the leader with decision.

"You remember our rules," said the third, "'when a party is made up by details from different camps, it shall constitute a camp so far as to regulate its own action and all matters pertaining to such action which the officer in command may see fit to submit to it shall be decided by a majority vote.' I think this had better be left to the camp?"

"I agree with you," said the leader. "But, before we do so, let's have a drink."

He produced a flask, and they all partook of its contents. Then they went back to the intersection of the roads, mounted their horses, and the leader commanded, "Attention!"

The men gathered closer, and then all was still. Then the leader said, in words distinctly heard by the trembling girl.

"Gentlemen, we have met here, under a solemn and duly authenticated decree of a properly organized camp of the county of Rockford, to execute for them the extreme penalty of our order upon Thomas Denton, in the way and manner therein prescribed. This unpleasant duty of course will be done as becomes earnest men. We are, however, informed that there will be with the said Denton at the time we are directed to take him another notorious Radical well known to you all, Colonel Comfort Servosse. He is not included in the decree, and I now submit for your determination the question, 'What shall be done with him?'"

There was a moment's buzz in the crowd.

One careless-toned fellow said that he thought it would be well enough to wait till they caught their hare before cooking it. It was not the first time a squad had thought they had Servosse in their power, but they had never ruffled a hair of his head yet.

The leader commanded, "Order!" And one of the associate Commanders moved that the same decree be made against him as against the said Denton. Then the vote was taken. All were in the affirmative, except the loud-voiced young man who had spoken before, who said with emphasis—"No, by Granny! I'm not in favor of killing anybody! I'll have you know, gentlemen, it's neither a pleasant nor a safe business. First we know, we'll all be running our necks into hemp. It's what we call murder, gentlemen, in civilized and Christian countries!"

"Order!" cried the commander.

"Oh, you needn't yell at me!," said the young man fearlessly. "I'm not afraid of anybody here, nor all of you. Mel Gurney and I came just to take some friends' places who couldn't obey the summons—we're not bound to stay, but I suppose I shall go along. I don't like it, though, and, if I get much sicker, I shall leave. You can count on that!"

"If you stir from your place," said the leader sternly, "I shall put a bullet through you."

"Oh, you go to hell!," retorted the other. You don't expect to frighten one of the old Louisiana Tigers [Confederate soldiers from that state were known for their bravery] in that way, do you? Now look here, Jake Carver," he continued, drawing a huge navy revolver and cocking it coolly, "don't try any such little game on me, 'cause, if ye do, there may be more'n one of us fit for a spy-glass [small drinking glass] when it's over."

Lily Slips Away

AT THIS, CONSIDERABLE CONFUSION arose, and Lily, with her revolver ready cocked in her hand, turned, and cautiously made her way to the road which had been indicated as the one which led to Glenville. Just as her horse stepped into the path, an overhanging limb caught her hat and pulled it off, together with the hood of her waterproof, so that her hair fell down again upon her shoulders. She hardly noticed the fact in her excitement, and, if she had, could not have stopped to repair the accident. She kept her horse upon the shady side, walking upon the grass as much as possible to prevent attracting attention, watching on all sides for any scattered members of the Klan.

She had proceeded thus about a hundred and fifty yards, when she came to a turn in the road, and saw, sitting before her in the moonlight, one of the disguised horsemen, evidently a sentry who had been stationed there to see that no one came upon the camp unexpectedly. He was facing the other way, but just at that instant turned, and, seeing her indistinctly in the shadow, cried out at once, "Who's there? Halt!"

They were not twenty yards apart. Young Lollard was trembling with excitement under the tightly-drawn rein. Lily thought of her father half-prayerfully, half-fiercely, bowed close over her horse's neck, and braced herself in the saddle, with every muscle as tense as those of the tiger waiting for his leap. Almost before the words were out of the sentry's mouth, she had given Young Lollard the spur and shot like an arrow into the bright moonlight, straight towards the black muffled horseman.

"My God!," he cried, amazed at the sudden apparition.

She was close upon him in an instant. There was a shot. His startled horse sprang aside, and Lily, urging Young Lollard to his utmost speed, was flying down the road toward Glenville.

She heard an uproar behind—shouts and one or two shots. On, on, she sped. She knew now every foot of the road beyond. She looked back and saw her pursuers swarming out of the wood into the moonlight. Just then she was in shadow.

A mile, two miles, were passed. She drew in her horse to listen. There was the noise of a horse's hoofs coming down a hill she had just descended, as her gallant steed bore her, almost with undiminished stride, up the opposite slope. She laughed, even in her terrible excitement, at the very thought that any one should attempt to overtake her.

"They'll have fleet steeds that follow, quoth young Lochinvar," she hummed as she patted Young Lollard's outstretched neck.

She turned when they reached the summit, her long hair streaming backward in the moonlight like a golden banner and saw the solitary horseman on the opposite slope, then turned back, and passed over the hill. He halted as she dashed out of sight and after a moment turned round and soon met the entire camp, now in perfect order, galloping forward dark and silent as fate. The Commander halted as they met the returning sentinel. "What was it," he asked quickly.

"Nothing," replied the sentinel carelessly. "I was sitting there at the turn examining my revolver, when a rabbit ran across the road, and frightened my mare. She jumped, and the pistol went off. It happened to graze my left arm, so I could not hold the reins. And she like to have taken me into Glenville before I could pull her up."

"I'm glad that's all," said the officer, with a sigh of relief. "Did it hurt you much?"

"Well, it's used that arm up for the present."

A hasty examination showed this to be true, and the reckless-talking young man was detailed to accompany him to some place for treatment and safety, while the others passed on to perform their horrible task.

The train from Verdenton had reached and left Glenville. The in-comers had been divided between the rival hotels, the porters had removed the luggage, and the agent was just entering his office, when a foam-flecked horse with bloody nostrils and fiery eyes, ridden by a young girl with a white, set face, and fair, flowing hair, dashed up to the station.

"Judge Denton!," the rider shrieked.

The agent had but time to motion with his hand, and she had swept on towards a carriage which was being swiftly driven away from the station and which was just visible at the turn of the village street.

"Papa, Papa!," shrieked the girlish voice as she swept on.

A frightened face glanced backward from the carriage, and in an instant Comfort Servosse was standing in the path of the rushing steed.

"Ho, Lollard!," he shouted, in a voice which rang over the sleepy town like a trumpet-note.

The amazed horse veered quickly to one side and stopped as if stricken to stone, while Lily fell insensible into her father's arms. When she recovered, he was bending over her with a look in his eyes which she will never forget.

The last of Ch. 36, "A Race Against Time," in *A Fool's Errand* by Albion Tourgée.

22. Lily's Southern Admirers

Falling Insensible

Michael W. Perry

Yes, the previous chapter does end with Lily falling 'insensible into her father's arms.' I don't like that any more than you do. That is, however, a common pattern in nineteenth-century novels, where women seem to swoon into a man's arms at the slightest provocation. But it makes no sense. She had endured much, so there's no reason for her—having found her father and safety—to suddenly collapse, unable to deliver the message she'd risked so much to carry. So feel free to rewrite it in your head and have her calmly deliver the warning about the Klan to her dad, after which she says, "I'm hungry. After Young Lollard is taken care of, could we get something to eat?" Yes, much better!

Of course, the plots today are often just as bad in the opposite direction. In them, Lily, who is described as 'slight' in size, would have left at least a dozen of these husky male Klansman on the ground in a crumpled heap simply by using a few martial arts kicks. In real life, that's no more likely than a sudden faint. The Lily of this tale is wise enough that, when she rides alone, she's armed.

In this chapter, two young men, Southern born and bred, discuss how impressed they are with the pluck—spirited and determined courage—and skill of this Yankee girl. Both express an eagerness to marry her but, fortunately for Lily's peace of mind, only one is free to do so.

Note the blunt honesty of John Burleson. In his remarks you'll get a succinct statement of the mistakes the South makes after the war when it returns power to the Democratic party, along with the failures of Northern Republicans to defend their allies and supporters in the South. It was a shoddy time to live.

Lily had faltered out her message of horror even in the unconscious moments when she was being carried in her father's arms to the hotel. Indeed, her unexpected appearance and clamorous haste to prevent her father's departure from the town, would have been sufficient to inform him that she knew of some danger that impended. Her unconscious mutterings had still further advised him of the character of the danger and the fact that she herself had narrowly escaped.

This was all he could glean from her. Her over-taxed system had given way with excitement and fatigue, and, fortunately for her, she slept. A physician was called, who, after examination of her condition, directed that she should in no event be aroused. A telegram from Metta, which should have been delivered on the arrival of the train, confirmed the conclusion at which Servosse had arrived.

He left the bedside of the daughter who to his eyes had grown to womanhood since the noon of the day before, but once during the night, and that was but to telegraph to Metta, to provide that Young Lollard should be well cared for, and to consult with Judge Denton, who had remained with them in the town. It was by no means certain that the danger had passed by, so these two men concluded to watch until morning.

It was broad daylight when Lily opened her eyes, to find her father holding her hand and gazing upon her with inexpressible affection. She told him all as soon as her weakness and her sobs would permit and was more than repaid for all she had dared and suffered by the fervent embrace and the tremulous "God bless you, my daughter!," which followed her recital. Then he ordered some refreshments for her and recommended further sleep, while he went to recount her story to his friend.

Somehow the story seemed to have leaked out during the night, and everyone about the town was aware of its main features. That there had been a raid intended, nay, that it had even been organized, and proceeded to the bridge across the river, for the purpose of intercepting Judge Denton on his way home, was undoubted. That the party had rendezvoused at Bentley's Cross Roads was also known, as well as the fact that the judge's carriage had been stopped and turned back, just on the outskirts of Glenville, by the arrival of the daughter of Colonel Servosse, bareheaded and mounted on a foaming steed.

That she had come from Warrington was presumed, and that she must have passed Bentley's Cross about the time of the rendezvous was more than probable. Added to this was the fact that a countryman coming to market early had brought in a lady's riding-hat which he had found at the very spot where the Klan had met. He was closely examined as to the appearance of the ground, and the precise point at which he found it. Of course, it was by no means sure that it was Miss Lily's hat, but such was evidently the impression.

John and Melville Discuss Lily

THE LOUD-VOICED YOUNG MAN [John Burleson] who had been detailed to take care of the wounded sentinel, and who had come into the same town with his charge, volunteered to ascertain that fact and took the hat into his possession. Returning to the hotel and entering the room where a young man lounged upon the bed, with his left arm in a sling, he exclaimed, "I thought it was mighty queer that a rabbit had made Melville Gurney shoot himself and let his horse run away too. I think I understand it now."

He laid the hat upon the bed beside his friend as he spoke. Melville Gurney recognized it in an instant, but he tried to betray no emotion, as he asked, "Well, what is it you understand, John Burleson?"

"The whole thing. I see it now from beginning to end. The little Yankee girl had just come to the Cross when our bands began to close in on her. She hid in the pines—probably right there at the Forks, and no doubt saw and heard every thing that went on. By Gad! She's a plucky little piece! But how the deuce do you suppose she kept that horse still, with a hundred horses all around her? Gad! It was close quarters!

"Then, as she is coming out, she stumbles on Mr. Melville Gurney standing sentry over that devil's gang of respectable murderers, shoots him before he has time to say Jack Robinson, and comes sailing in here like a bird, on that magnificent thoroughbred, overhauls Judge Denton's carriage, and saves her father's life like a heroine and a lady too, as she is. Dang my buttons if I ain't ready to kiss the hem of her garments even! Mel Gurney, I'll be hanged if I don't envy you the pleasure of being shot by such a splendid plucky little girl! D'ye know her? Ever met her?"

"Yes."

"Of course. They say she knows almost as many people as her father, who, by the way, Mel, is no slouch, either. I know him and like him too, if he is a carpetbagger. I'm glad I put in a good word for him last night. No doubt she heard me. Mel Gurney, I'm in luck for once. Give me that

hat! What am I going to do with it? Why, restore it to the owner, make my peace with her pa and Judge Denton, and in the fullness of time offer her my hand and heart."

"Pshaw!" exclaimed Gurney.

"Pshaw? My dear friend, you seem smitten with a big disgust all at once. Perhaps you would like to take my place? Remember you can't have all the good things. It's enough for you to have her sling a lump of cold lead through your carcass. Be thankful for what you enjoy and don't envy other people their little pleasures."

"I wish you would stop fooling and talk sense for a moment, Burleson," said Gurney fretfully.

"Hear him now! As if I had been doing any thing else! By Gad! The more sense I talk, the less I am appreciated. Witness Jake Carver last night and Mel Gurney this morning. I'm no spring-chicken and, allowing me to be the judge, I feel free to say that I have never listened to more sound and convincing sense than flowed from these lips on those two occasions," responded Burleson.

"Are you in earnest?" asked Gurney.

"What, about the sense? Entirely so."

"No, about Miss Lily Servosse," said Gurney.

"And the proffer of my heart and hand?" answered Burleson. "No. *Unfortunately*—don't you blow on me and tell that I ever used that word. But in earnest truth I never came nearer feeling it, unfortunately, I say, I am, as you have reason to know, under bonds to confer my precious personality upon another—a Miss Lily too, (thank Heaven for the name, at least!)—and so must deny myself the distinguished privilege I for a moment dreamed of. No, I'm not in earnest about that part of it."

"Well, I am," said Gurney emphatically.

"The devil you say!" exclaimed Burleson in surprise. "You don't mean it!"

"I will win and wed Lily Servosse, if I can," said Gurney modestly.

"Well, *I* swear!" exclaimed Burleson. But do you know, old fellow, I don't think you put that in the hypothetical without reason? It's my notion you'll have a hard time of it, even if you manage to pull through at all on that line. Remember, old fellow, your family, position, and all that, won't count a rush for you in this matter. These carpetbaggers don't care a continental cuss how many niggers your ancestors had. Then your father is an especial antagonist of Servosse. And for yourself—all that I can see that you have to put up is, that you went along with a crowd of respectable gentlemen to kill her father and would have done so, but for her nerve. In fact, you can claim very justly that you would have prevented her saving him, if she had not shot you, and effected her escape."

"That is not so. Her father was not included in the decree, and I had no reason to suppose he would be in company with Denton," interrupted Gurney.

Gurney's Problem

"WELL, WE WILL SAY on your way to roast—yes, by Heaven!—to *roast alive*—Judge Denton! Think of that, will you? General Gurney's son, in the middle of the nineteenth century, nay, almost in its last quarter—in the blaze of American freedom and civilization at all events—goes out by night to broil a neighbor, without even the cannibal's excuse of hunger! Bah! That's a fine plea for a lover, isn't it?"

"My God, Burleson!," cried Gurney, jumping up. "You don't think she'll look at it in that light, do you?"

"Why not? Oughtn't any decent woman to do so, not to say a carpet-bagger's daughter? I vow I shouldn't blame her if she took another shot at you for your impudence!"

"Nor I either, Burleson, that's a fact!" said Gurney musingly.

"Ha, ha, ha!," laughed Burleson. "I understand that rabbit story now. You recognized Miss Lily?"

"Of course," said Gurney simply.

"'Of course,' it is, indeed!," said Burleson. "I might have known it would have taken more than one broken arm to make Mel Gurney let a rider run his guard unhurt. You recognized her and galloped after her to prevent suspicion and on the way invented that story about the rabbit and your pistol going off. By Gad! It was a gallant thing, old fellow, if we were on a heathen errand. Give me your hand, my boy! It's not so bad, after all. Perhaps Miss Lily might make a decent man of you in time, though we both ought to be hanged, that's a fact!"

"I never thought of it in that way, Burleson; but it *is* horrible," said Gurney, with a shudder.

"Horrible?—It's hellish, Mel Gurney! That's what it is! If I were the Yankees and had the power of the government, I wouldn't see these things go on one hour. By Gad! I'm ashamed of them as Americans!

When the war was going on and we met them in battle, there was always one satisfaction, whoever got 'fanned out'—it was always our own folks that did it, and one couldn't well help being proud of the job. I tell you what, Mel, there's been many a time when I could hardly tell which I was proudest of—Yank or Reb.

There was Gettysburg, now! You know I was in the artillery, and had a better chance to see the *ensemble* of a battle than one in the infantry line. We had been pouring a perfect hell of shot upon the cemetery for an hour, when the charge was ordered, and we ceased firing. We were black and grim, and almost deaf with the continuous roar. I remember the sweat poured down the sooty faces of my gun-mates, and I don't suppose there was a dry rag about them.

Some leaned on the smoking piece and some threw themselves on the ground. But every one kept his eyes riveted on that line of bright steel and dirty gray which was sweeping up to the low wall that we had been salting with fire so long. We thought they would go over it as the sea breaches a sand-dike. But we were mistaken. Those men who had hung to their ground through it all, sent their plague of leaden death in our fellows' faces and met them at the point of the bayonet as coolly and stubbornly as if it were but the opening of the ball, instead of its last *gallopade* [dance]. Bad as I felt when our fellows fell back, I could have given three cheers for those Yanks with a will. I thought then, that if the worst came, as I always believed it would, we could have a genuine pride in our conquerors.

"And so I had, until this Ku-Klux business came up. I told our fellows on the start, they would burn their fingers. For I could not forget that the men they were whipping and hanging were the friends of those same Yankees—the only friends they had here too—and I had no idea that *such* men would suffer them to be abused at that rate.

Some of the boys got the notion, however, that I was afraid. And I went in just to show them I was not. **For a time I looked every day for an earthquake, and, when it didn't come, I felt an unutterable contempt for the whole Yankee nation, and damn me if I don't feel it yet. I really pity this man, Servosse! He feels ashamed of his people and knows that even the white Republicans—poor shotes [young pigs] as many of them are—despise the whining, canting sycophancy which makes their Northern allies abandon helpless friends to powerful enemies.** I tell you what, Mel Gurney, if we Southerners had come out ahead and had such friends as these niggers and Union men, with now and then one of our own kidney [kind or class of people], scattered through the North, we would have gone through *hell-fire* before we would have deserted them in this way!"

"That is no justification to us, though," said Gurney, who was now walking back and forth across the room, quite forgetful of the pain of his arm.

"On the contrary, it makes it worse," said Burleson. "We are advancing the power of a party to which we are devoted, it is true; but in so doing we are merely putting power in the hands of its worst elements, against whom we shall have to rebel sooner or later. The leaders in these cowardly raids—such men as Jake Carver and a hundred more whom I could name—will be our representatives, senators, legislators, judges, and so forth, hereafter.

It is the simple rule of human nature. Leadership in any public movement is the sure pathway to public honor. It has been so since the war. Look at the men to whom we have given civic honors. How many of them would have been heard of, but for their soldiering? In that case, I don't complain of it. They were all brave men, though some were great fools. But when it comes to preferring midnight murderers and brutal assassins for legislators and governors and judges, and the like, simply *because* they were leaders in crime, I swear, Mel Gurney, it comes hard! Some time or other we shall be sick and ashamed of it."

"I am that now," said Gurney.

"No doubt—especially since you have thought how Lily Servosse must look at it. Now, I'll tell you what, Mel, I like you, and I like Servosse's little girl too. I believe you can get her—after a while, you know—if you've got pluck enough to own up and reform, 'repent and be baptized' you know. And it *will* be a baptism to you, you can bet on that—a baptism of fire!"

"You don't suppose I'd 'peach,' do you, John Burleson?" said Gurney, turning indignantly towards his friend.

"Hell! You don't think I've turned fool, do you?," asked Burleson, with equal indignation. "See here, Gurney, you and I were boys together. Did you ever know me to do a mean thing?"

"Never!"

Leaving the Klan

"WELL NOW, LISTEN. I'M going to bolt this whole business. I'm not going to tell on anybody else (you know I'd be drawn and quartered first). But I'm going to own up *my* connection with it, tell as much as I can, without implicating any one else, and do my best to break it up. I never thought of just this way of doing it before, and should not have hit on it now but for your sake."

"For my sake?" asked Gurney in surprise.

"Yes, for your sake. Don't you see you will have to own up in this way, before either father or daughter will look at you?"

"Well?"

"Well? I'll just go ahead and break the way, that's all."

"When will you begin?"

"Today—now!"

"How?"

"I shall go down upon the street and publish as much as I well can of this raid and try to laud the pluck of that young lady about half as highly as it deserves. God bless her! I would like to kiss the place where she has set her foot, just to show my appreciation of her!"

"Do you really think you had better venture upon such a course? It might be a very dangerous business," said Gurney.

"The very reason above all others why John Burleson should undertake the job. Someone must do it, and it would not do for you to be the first. It's not often one has a chance to serve his friend and do a patriotic duty at once. It's all out now, in fact. The guesses and rumors that are afloat are within an ace of the facts. There may as well be some advantage gained by that, as not. I shall take the young lady her hat"—

"Let me do that, if you please," said Gurney anxiously.

"All right, if you think you can face the fire."

The first part of Ch. 37, "A 'Reb' View of It," in *A Fool's Errand* by Albion Tourgée.

23. Breaking with the Klan

Quiting but not Exposing

Michael W. Perry

Thanks to Tourgée, we know that Klansmen were cowardly thugs. They hid their faces behind masks and their bodies inside flowing robes. Calling themselves the Invisible Empire, they operated from concealment or at night, often attacking while their victims were traveling or sleeping. When possible, they outnumbered their victims by dozens to one. They were violent, killing good black and white people, including perhaps my great-great-grandfather, to *terrorize the rest into silence*. Their goal were legalized racism and Democratic party rule. In Southern politics, the two were one and the same.

Unfortunately, in the decades to follow, the history of the Ku Klux Klan would be rewritten by notable historians, talented film makers and prominent politicians. It wasn't enough for those later apologists to remake the Klan into something harmless—say an oddly dressed fishing and hunting club. No, as I will explain in a later book, one perhaps entitled *Not Just the Klan*, those who rewrote the history of Klan transformed it into a champion of national reunion and the heroic defenders of (white) women In fact, that's the central plot of the blockbuster 1915 film *The Birth of a Nation*, which inspired a rebirth of the Klan. In this book, we'll follow Tourgée and look at the unraveling of the original Klan, whose foul deeds were so fresh and vivid in the minds of the public that even a biased press could not conceal its evil nature.

Now for some bluntness. In the previous chapter, I was quite impressed with John Burleson's honesty and good sense. In this chapter, I'm left with a bad taste in my mouth. It's not enough to talk in generalities about the evil that the Klan was doing or even to denounce certain specific crimes. Evil on that scale isn't merely to be criticized. It's to be fought, tooth and nail, to the finish. That means naming those involved and making sure they're punished.

Imagine a scale for measuring right and wrong. On one sides rests a solemn oath to keep an organization's secrets and never betray comrades. On the other is the need to bring murderers to justice, so they kill no more. Such a scale should slam down hard on the side of naming shouldn't it? No oath can justify keeping secrets that vile or leaving murderers free to kill again.

But with Burleson, the scale tilts heavily toward letting those killers go free, suffering only the insult of being called a "devil's gang of respectable murderers." To understand why he reasons so oddly, imagine a different murder, one not involving the Klan or race but still involving an oath of silence. Would Burleson remain mum? I doubt it. The reason Klansmen get a pass is that all too many Southern whites, including Burleson, agreed with the Klan's primary goal—white supremacy. They're merely squeamish about its tactics. They want the same result but with less violence.

That's the heart of the problem. Many of the Klan's critics simply don't take its crimes as seriously as they ought. They want the killing to stop, particularly when the victims are whites. That's embarrassing and unsettling. But they don't want prior murders to be punished because the motivation behind them is seen as noble. That fatally weakens what they're doing. That's also why the original Klan will only fade away when its purpose is achieved.

So down upon the street went John Burleson. The first man whom he met ascending the steps of the hotel was Judge Denton. Extending his hand cordially, he said in a voice that all could hear, "Judge, I am ashamed to say I was in that hellish affair last night. I did not know what it was till we got to the Cross, nor did any of them but the Commanders. That made no difference, though. We were in for it, and I do not doubt would have carried it through, but for Miss Lily Servosse. She deserves a statue, judge. I've no excuse to make. I'm not a child and was not deceived. Any time you want me, I'm ready to plead guilty to anything I've done. In any event, this is the last raid I shall join, and the last that will be made, if I can prevent it."

He stalked off, leaving the astonished judge to gaze after him and wonder if he had heard aright. Burleson repeated the same language, with various *addenda*, to every group of loungers he met on the street, so that in a quarter of an hour the word had gone out that John Burleson had "gone back" on the Ku-Klux. It spread like wildfire. He had occupied a prominent place in the order, and it was known that he knew many fatal secrets connected with it. It was telegraphed in every direction and went from man to man among the members of the Klan in a dozen counties where he was well known. They knew that he could not be silenced by threats or bribes. A great fear took hold of them when they heard it, and many fled the county without further inquiry. The little town in which they were was almost deserted in an hour. Perceiving this effect and thoroughly comprehending its cause, John Burleson approached Judge Denton and Colonel Servosse, and said to them—

"Gentlemen, the train will be here in an hour. I have no right to advise with regard to your movements. But you will allow me to say that I think, after what occurred last night, that the more prudent course would be for Judge Denton to return with us to Verdenton and then spend a few days at Warrington. It will be only an exchange of hospitalities anyhow.

"On the contrary," said Denton, "I was just trying to persuade Colonel Servosse to send for his wife and make his visit, despite our *contretemps* last night."

"It is quite impossible," said Servosse. "Lily says she could never endure to cross that bridge. And in her present condition, I do not think she should be subjected to any unnecessary excitement."

"Certainly not!," said Denton. "After her heroism of last night, she is entitled to the gratification of her every wish."

"That being your feeling," said Servosse, "I am emboldened to second Mr. Burleson's view by saying that it is my daughter's especial desire that you should come home with us. She is under a terrible apprehension in regard to the future and especially in reference to you, sir. She thinks that, if you should go off into the country there, you would be sure to be assassinated. She thinks there is far less danger, if we are together, not only because there would be more hesitation in attacking two, but because, being both men of some prominence, our joint assassination would be more likely to attract the attention, and awaken the resentment of the government and the people of the North than our individual destruction. Indeed, she has an idea that the very act of my Northern birth—my prominence as a 'carpetbagger,' so to speak—is in itself a sort of protection."

"That is her very idea," said Servosse, "and there may be some truth in it. Certainly Mr. Burleson should know," he added, with a meaning glance at Denton, for the judge was too suspicious, and the new fact was too unaccountable to allow him yet to put full confidence in the professed change of that gentleman. His suspicion was increased by the next remark of Burleson.

"By the way," he said, " it never occurred to me before, but how on earth did Miss Lily get information of that raid? I don't reckon she was out riding your pet racing horse at that time of night just for fun!"

"We do not feel at liberty to speak of that at this time," said Comfort seriously.

"All right!" responded Burleson. "I only hope it is a hole that will let light in upon the thing. I have always supposed it would come and have known, that, if one ever pipped the shell, a thousand would try to be the first to get their heads out. If the idea once goes out, Judge, that any one has given the thing away, you will have your hands full taking confessions. They will be full of horrors too—more than you ever dreamed of. You'll think you've tilted off the lid of the bottomless pit, and that the devils are pouring out by brigades."

"Perhaps," said Denton, with a look of keen scrutiny, "you could tell something yourself?"

"Whether I could or not," said Burleson, "is all the same. You know me well enough, Judge, to know that I *will not* tell any thing which would compromise anybody else. I am willing to admit that I belonged to this organization, that I was the chief of a county because I think it is necessary that I should do so in order to break it up. But I do not intend to confess myself into the penitentiary nor on to the gallows. Yet I would go there sooner than to betray those who have trusted their lives and honor with me. So far as I can go without such betrayal, I am willing to act with you. That is one reason I wish you to return to Verdenton. I want it clearly understood that I have renounced the whole business. It is by no means a safe proceeding, and I may have to turn in with you, gentlemen and fight for my life. If it comes to that, I propose to make every edge cut, and, if I go down, I mean to have lots of good company. I would like to have you go in order to be convenient if the fight comes!"

Judge Denton yielded to these solicitations, and accompanied his friends, first sending word to his family to follow on the next day.

The second part of Ch. 37, "A 'Reb' View of It," in *A Fool's Errand* by Albion Tourgée.

24. A KLANSMAN CONFESSES

'Horrified and Amazed'

Michael W. Perry

If you were Lily, what would you think of this adoring Melville Gurney? On one hand he was almost a party to the murder of your father. On the other hand, having realized what that means to his ability to romance you, he is now most contrite and sad. Which do you find more appealing, a guy whose own, well-established moral standards you respect or one who seems willing to change his standards to please you? That's a most important question and one you might want to consider seriously and long.

Before the train left, Melville Gurney sent a servant to Colonel Comfort, asking a moment's interview. When Servosse came to his room, and, seeing his injury, asked the cause, he betrayed himself by asking—"And has not your daughter told you, sir?"

"My God!" said Servosse, sinking into a chair, overwhelmed with amazement. "Was it you, Mr. Gurney? Can it be that the son of one who has known me so long as your father, even though as an opponent, should have engaged in an attempt on my life? I could not have believed it." He covered his face with his hands and shuddered as he spoke.

"I assure you, Colonel Servosse," said Gurney, "I had no idea that such was the purpose of the raid, nor, indeed, did I know its purpose. I was well aware that it must be an unlawful one, however, and can not blame you for the horror you manifest. I am horrified myself and am amazed that I could ever have regarded it otherwise."

"I can not understand it—I can not understand it," said the carpet-bagger. "I always thought your father was an honest, high-minded man, and a good citizen."

"And so he is, sir," said Gurney hotly. "There is none better nor purer!"

"And you," said Servosse, rising, and looking keenly at him,—"*You* are a *murderer!*"

"I suppose," answered Gurney, with some confusion, "that I should have been, constructively at least, but for your daughter's daring interference."

"Nay, you were already," said Servosse severely. "You had started out on an unlawful errand and were ready to shed blood, if need were, to accomplish it—whether it were my blood or another's it is immaterial to consider. That is almost always the mental condition of the murderer. Murder is usually a means, not an end."

"It is a hard word, Colonel Servosse. Yet I do not know but I must submit," said Gurney. "I wish to say, however, that I did not engage in this at the wish or suggestion, nor with the knowledge, of my father. Indeed, my greatest trouble comes from the fact that I must inform him of the fact."

"Gad!" said Burleson, who had entered unperceived by both, "you needn't trouble yourself so much about that. He belongs to it himself."

"John Burleson!," cried Gurney, springing to his feet.

"Oh, you needn't mind!" said Burleson. "Colonel Servosse is too much of a gentleman to take advantage of such a statement made by me at this time." He turned, and bowed toward Servosse as he spoke.

"Certainly," said the latter. "I should not think of using a private conversation."

"It is not that!," exclaimed Gurney—"not that at all! But it is false!"

"H'st! Steady, my young friend!," said Burleson hotly. "I happen to know whereof I speak. I was present, and helped initiate him. Do you believe me now, Mel Gurney?"

"Great heavens!," exclaimed Gurney. "I did not know that! I would not have believed it but upon your assurance."

"I declare," said the Fool, "I can not understand—I can not understand!"

"Well," said Burleson, laughing, and taking Lily's hat from the bed, "here is something you can understand, I reckon."

"My daughter's hat!," said Servosse in surprise, looking from one to the other.

"For that matter," said Burleson bluffly, "I brought it here. You see, when Miss Lily rode out of the pines last night, she lost this. And so, when she charged on Gurney there, he recognized her—for it was as light as day. Our chaplain could have seen to read the burial-service—and, being a fellow that has his wits about him, Gurney quietly jogged on behind, her after she had shot him, with that broken arm flopping up and down at every step, until he was sure she had got clean off, when he came back with a cock-and-bull story about a rabbit having scared his horse, and his pistol having gone off, and busted that arm."

"Is that so?" asked Comfort in surprise.

"Lit-er-ally," said Burleson, with distinct enunciation. "Not a man in that camp had any idea that a woman had witnessed its proceedings, until we heard of your daughter having interrupted your journey. Even then it was a mere surmise, except with Gurney here."

"Then," said Servosse, extending his hand to Gurney, "it seems I have to thank you for an intent to save my daughter."

"Indeed, sir," replied Gurney, "with that horse, she had little need of my aid."

"Young Lollard is not easily matched," said Servosse, with some pride. "But that does not detract from the merit of your intention. I suppose," he added, smiling, and touching the hat, "that you wish me to relieve you of this toy."

"On the contrary," said Gurney earnestly, "my request for this interview was because I desired to ask your leave to return it to the owner myself."

"Well sir," said Servosse thoughtfully, "I do not see but you have earned the right to do so. I will see if she can receive you."

A few moments later, Melville Gurney, somewhat weak and tremulous from the loss of blood and subsequent excitement, came down stairs, leaning on the arm of his friend Burleson, and was ushered into the parlor of the hotel, where Lily Servosse leaned upon her father's arm. Pale and trembling, he presented the hat with a low bow, and withdrew without a word.

"Well, I swear!" said Burleson a minute after, "if I had thought you would show the white feather just at the last, I never would have seconded you!"

Comfort Servosse never once dreamed that the trembling creature clinging to his arm, and dropping tears upon the hat as she brushed and picked at it, was anything more than a simple child. So he said, with an amused smile, "It's not even rumpled, is it, dear?"

The third part of Ch. 37, "A 'Reb' View of It," in *A Fool's Errand* by Albion Tourgée.

25. WAITING FOR THE KLAN

Courage as a Virtue

Michael W. Perry

Notice in the opening remarks of this chapter that even those who supported the Klan and its terrible agenda still value courage highly enough to respect what Lily and later John Burleson have done. Samuel Johnson described that when he said, "Sir, you know courage is reckoned the greatest of all virtues; because unless a man has that virtue, he has no security of preserving any other." (See my *Chesterton on War and Peace*, p. 81.)

Unfortunately, respect for courage seems less common today than in the 1870s. Faced with a stand like that by Burleson, many fashionable moderns attack motives. Being brave, they say, is like "being a cowboy." Consciously or unconsciously, they're referring to the movie *High Noon*. In it, Marshal Will Kane, played by Gary Cooper, is abandoned by most of the town he was hired to defend. At noon and all alone he must face a convicted murderer and his three henchmen, who are intent on killing him. In the movie's theme song, he pleads with his new bride, played by Grace Kelly, not to abandon him.

Do not forsake me, oh, my darlin',
Wait; wait alone.
I do not know what fate awaits me.
I only know I must be brave.
For I must face a man who hates me,
Or lie a coward, a craven coward;
Or lie a coward in my grave.

In his *The Abolition of Man*, C. S. Lewis describes how cowardice spreads through a society when he writes: "In a sort of ghastly simplicity we remove the organ and demand the function. We make men without chests and expect of them virtue and enterprise. We laugh at honour and are shocked to find traitors in our midst. We castrate and bid the geldings be fruitful."

The remark about Burleson being "one of the very few private soldiers who survived the surrender of the Confederate armies" needs explaining. Many who'd been enlisted men during the war gave themselves promotions afterward, often claiming officer ranks that they'd never had. Faking a rank like general would difficult to get away with, but there were many fake captains and colonels. Burleson isn't troubled by vanity. He was and remains to that day a private. He has a strong sense of honor and honesty.

Notice why Burleson remained a private. He was too smart, too honest, too independent, and too open about his beliefs that the South would lose the war. Like most organizations, the military likes to promote those who do as they're told. Burleson wasn't that way. He was, however, so well respected that even the Klan knew it must treat him with care. Bullies do have a grudging respect for the brave and prefer to go after those easier to frighten.

The train which brought Lily and her father, Judge Denton, Burleson, and Gurney to Verdenton, did not arrive unnoted. The report of Lily's heroic ride, and of Burleson's defection from the Klan, had preceded it, and a great crowd had collected, anxious for a sight of the brave girl who had courage and wit enough to circumvent the Ku-Klux, and of the yet braver man, who, having been one of their number, had yet courage to denounce them.

What he would say, what he would do, there was the utmost anxiety to know. For once no imputation was made upon the motives of one who saw fit to stem the popular current. Men cursed and denounced him, but it was for what he had done, or was supposed to have done, and not on account of the motives which they believed to have animated him.

No one attributed either cowardice, ambition, or avariciousness to John Burleson. He was known to have disapproved from the first, at least of all the violent features of the organization, and to have done not a little to prevent their being carried into execution. He had been advanced to be the Chief of the County, both because of his known and acknowledged capacity for organization and leadership, and also because this very disinclination to promote unlawful acts had met the approval of many of the more conservative members of the order. As he had said, he went upon the raid which we have described simply to accommodate a friend, who, being required to attend, had afterward sickened.

He was recognized as bold, generous, and impulsive. He was one of the very few *private* soldiers who survived the surrender of the Confederate armies. Entering the service at the very outset of the war, he had never failed to perform his full duty and not seldom had done considerably more. Yet he had received no promotion and, since the collapse of the Rebellion, not a sign of any military title had attached itself to his name. The man who should have saluted him as "Captain" would probably have been whipped first, and invited to drink afterwards for his temerity.

The reason of this was twofold. In the first place, young Burleson, a man of unusually broad and catholic feeling, and of varied personal experience and wide observation, was as thoroughly convinced of the hopelessness of the Confederate cause in the field of battle at the outset of the war as at its close. This view he did not hesitate to declare on all occasions. And, when reproved for so doing by an upstart superior, he had the boldness and arrogance to assure the official, that, if he knew half as much as himself, he would desert to the Yankees in two days.

Besides this, it suited his humor to boast of his disinclination for a military life. When offered promotion, he curtly declined it on the ground that he did not wish to do anything that might remove his dislike for the service.

Of course such a man, though he had been of the ripest culture and most marked capacity, was only fitted for the place of a private soldier; and so a soldier he remained, always scornful of control and utterly regardless of the Pharisaical distinctions of rank, respected for his unshrinking bluntness, and feared for his terrible directness of thought, and explicitness of statement. He was perhaps the most dangerous man who could have renounced his fealty to the Klan.

Arriving at Verdenton

As HE STEPPED UPON the platform at Verdenton, a man whom he knew to be a very prominent member of the Klan touched him upon the shoulder and said, with a meaning look towards the rear of the train—"Let me see you a moment."

"Oh, go to the devil!" said Burleson, in a loud but good-natured tone of voice. "I know what you want, and I had just as lief [happily] tell you here as around the corner or in the camp. I am neither afraid nor ashamed. I am out of it and opposed to it root and branch. If any one has any thing he wants to say or do about it, he knows where to find John Burleson.

"Judge Denton!" he cried in the same tone, as that gentleman appeared on the platform, "these people are my Ku-Klux friends and neighbors who have come to see if John Burleson has the pluck to renounce what he was a fool for engaging in and knew himself to be such at the time. They don't look like Ku-Klux, do they? But they are—nearly every man you can see. I don't believe there are a dozen white men on this platform whom I don't know to be such and have not seen in their meetings more than once. They are most of them church-members, and all of them respectable. You ought to see them with their gowns and masks on! They look savage enough then. You know a good many of them, Judge, and will get acquainted with them all if Justice ever gets her dues. There's right smart of men here who to my knowledge deserve a hanging."

Such language as this increased the consternation which already prevailed. And before it was ended, nearly every white man had left the platform, and only a crowd of wondering colored men remained to grin applause to his concluding remarks. He knew that he had thrown a bomb, but he was not ignorant that its explosion might endanger himself. He knew very thoroughly the temper of the people whom he had been addressing and did not under-estimate his own danger. So when he had bidden good-by to Gurney, who went on to his home, he went and assisted his other fellow-travelers to enter their carriage. Then he took the Fool aside, and said in a low voice—

"Colonel Servosse, I dislike to ask a favor of you. But it may be that I shall be able to render you a like service before long. You know what has occurred. If I remain here tonight, the probabilities are that I shall not be troubled about getting up in the morning. I wish you would invite me to Warrington for a day or two. I do not think you will be attacked there. If you should, you would not find me entirely useless in the defense. I think we three would make a bad crowd for any force to attack. In a short time we can tell what will be the result. Either they will cry for mercy, or we must fight. I don't know which it will be as yet."

"Certainly, certainly, Mr. Burleson!," said Servosse heartily. "I have been studying for the last hour, as to whether I ought not to invite both you and your friend."

"Oh, he is all right!" said Burleson lightly. "He is not tainted with my offense. No one regards him now except as the poor fellow who had the good fortune to be shot by your daughter."

Servosse's Hospitality

"THE FACT IS," SAID Servosse apologetically, "I have become so suspicious since I have been a 'carpetbagger,' that I am never quite sure whether it is expected or desired that I should either tender or receive hospitality as a matter of course. Besides that, you will permit me to confess that I was by no means sure that you were in earnest until within the last few minutes. Of course we shall be glad to have you at Warrington and hope you may find it both safe and agreeable there, though I confess I share your apprehensions."

It was a very thoughtful company which drove to Warrington that evening. Metta, with the overwrought Lily in her arms, listened, with overflowing eyes and irrepressible sobs, to the girl's broken recital of that adventure which had been so perilous to her and so providential to her father and one of their guests, whose hearts were of course deeply affected at the thought of the barbarous death they had escaped. The other guest, realizing even more clearly than they both what they had escaped and what still impended, was deeply concerned lest he had added to the peril of those with whom he had sought shelter.

A few colored people had collected at the depot, anxious to welcome those in whom they took so deep an interest, after the great peril they had escaped. A few of them had spoken to the Fool. And all had manifested a sense of the utmost satisfaction, both at their arrival and at what had transpired at the station, but made no clamorous demonstrations of joy.

Hardly had they started for home, however, than it became evident that the excitement extended to all classes of society. From almost every house along the road they saw white faces peering at them with troubled and apprehensive looks, while the cabin of every colored man gave them looks and words of cheerful greeting. And long before they reached Warrington, it became evident that the negroes were hastening from all directions to meet Servosse. Arrived in the neighborhood of his home, the Fool found that the news of his coming had gone before, as well as the report in regard to Burleson's defection from the Klan. And a great crowd of colored people, as well as many of their white political associates, had gathered to congratulate them on their escape and to make inquiry as to the other report.

It was a most cordial welcome which the Fool and his brave daughter received from these neighbors, and the presence of Judge Denton and Mr. Burleson fully confirmed the rumor in regard to the latter. Several parties who seemed ill at ease with the company which had gathered on the lawn were cordially greeted by Burleson in his loud, careless manner. But they were rendered still more uncomfortable by this and soon slunk away, one by one, and left only the constantly increasing crowd of colored men and friendly neighbors, whose [con]gratulations could not find sufficient words.

As night came on, it became evident that these good friends, apprehensive of an attack from the Klan, had determined to stand guard about the Fool's house. This was deemed unadvisable, and, after thanking them again for their sympathy, he requested them to disperse, saying that ample precautions had been taken to secure the safety of Warrington and naming a number of their most devoted white friends who would sleep there that night. So with cheers, and overflowing wishes for their peace and happiness, the colored people dispersed, and an eventful night settled down upon Warrington.

The first part of Ch. 38, "All the World Was in a Sea," in *A Fool's Errand* by Albion Tourgée.

26. Hearty Manliness

The Jovial and the Guilt-ridden

Michael W. Perry

You'll meet two interesting new people in this chapter. The pair could not be more different, although both are on the side of the angels.

The first, Mr. Eyebright, blunt and jovial, illustrates just how complicated political alignments in the South could be. Goodness did not always fall in predictable ways. Character could trump economics and culture. Although nothing is said about whether he had ever owned slaves, we are told that he is a "well-to-do planter" and thus from the class of people who championed slavery. During the war, however, he'd been a "prominent Union man," and now he's a "Radical" and thus numbered among the Republicans. Tourgée explains why he's different from so many others in his class. His "buff and hearty manliness" is accompanied by "sincerity and kindliness." He's one of those for whom courage comes naturally. He not only denounces the Klan, he delights in upsetting its followers. He illustrates something important. The best response to intimidation and terror is often humor. Laughter vanquishes fear.

The second, Ralph Kirkwood, has been a Klansman and that now bothers him terribly. He has a conscience and is filled with guilt about what he has done. Even more important, he isn't held back by any distorted sense of honor or oaths of secrecy. He will testify and name the guilty, come what may.

It was a little after dark, and while the company at Warrington were seated at supper, that a man rode up to the gate, who, after the customary hail had been answered by a servant, made some cautious inquiries as to who was within, and then asked to see Mr. Eyebright, a prominent Union man of the neighborhood. On being informed that he was at supper, he finally consented, not without considerable hesitation and evident doubt, to enter and take a seat in the Fool's library, enjoining again and again upon the servant that only he whom he had inquired for should be informed of his presence.

Mr. Eyebright Jokes Around

MR. EYEBRIGHT WAS A portly, well-to-do planter, whose bluff and hearty manliness gave everybody the utmost confidence in his sincerity and kindliness. He had been noted for his unsparing denunciations of the Klan at all times and in all places. To hear him lavish curses upon them as he filled his pipe or puffed at the long reed stem before a glowing fire, a stranger would have imagined that nothing would have afforded him more intense and unadulterated satisfaction than the utter destruction of the Klan, and the incineration of each and every one of its individual members, unless he should note the twinkle in his soft, lazy-rolling brown eye, or mark the lurking smiles that passed over his rotund countenance, or hid away at the corners of his wide, mobile mouth.

At home he was known as the gruffest and kindliest of neighbors. Abroad he was accounted one of the most sanguinary and revengeful of the degraded Radicals. A noticeable birthmark had given him a ludicrous nickname, which had contributed not a little to confer upon one of the kindliest, and most peaceful of men a reputation for blood-thirstiness and savagery almost equal to that of the original Bluebeard [the pirate].

This quaint and humorous giant, with his assumed ferocity, abundance of unmeaning oaths, and real goodness of heart, was a special favorite of the Fool, whose devotedness he heartily returned. He had insisted upon staying as one of the sort of guard of honor that night, upon the ground that he would be of the utmost value in case of an attack, which was very true. But the Fool knew very well that the prospect of a jolly night beside the smoldering fire in the library, with abundance of good company, and now and then a sup of good peach-brandy, made at his own still and softened with honey, interspersed with pipes and politics, and stories of "the good old time when we *had* a country," had far more attractions for his fat friend than a night of actual guard-duty.

As they filed out of the dining-room, Eyebright laid one ponderous arm on the Fool's shoulder and, extending the other over his own expansive person, remarked, "After such a supper as that, Colonel, one could not help enjoying a smoke."

Servosse merely answered with a low chuckle, to which Eyebright responded, "I know what you mean, you rascal! You think I just staid [stayed] here tonight to have a good time. Suppose I did, now. It's not often we poor devils can get a dozen good fellows together, and I am for making the most of the opportunity. I tell you, you don't know how hungry I get sometimes to hear somebody else talk sense beside myself [with a laugh]!

"There's Judge Denton, I'm going to pull him out tonight. They say he's just about the best company in the State—that is, they used to say so before he became one of us 'scalawags.' I s'pose that's had a bad effect on him, as well as the rest of us.

"There's that Burleson. I like him. He'd be a good fellow if he hadn't been a Ku-Klux. Cussed if I can ever get over that! Oh, don't tell me he's out of it now and all that! It's like sheep-killing in a dog. Once they've learned how, they never forget. I wouldn't sleep in the same room with him for the State! I wouldn't, I swear! I should expect to wake up with my throat cut, at the very least."

"Hush! He'll hear you," said Servosse.

"Oh, that's nothing!," responded Eyebright. "I've been trying to devil him all the evening. He asked me at supper—you were serving the meat and didn't hear it—if I didn't think Judge Denton and himself represented the lion and the lamb very well. I told him I'd never heard before of a lion that took his lamb *roasted*."

Just then the servant who had waited on the door touched him, and whispered in his ear.

"Wants to see me, you say, Jim?" he asked in surprise. "What does the damn Ku-Klux want of me, Jim?"

"Dunno, sah," answered Jim. "Sed he want ter see you mighty per-tickeler."

"He didn't say what about?"

"No, sah."

"Well, give me a light," said he, feeling in one pocket after another for his pipe, "and let me go and see what 'tis, and send him off. We don't want no such cattle around here tonight, Jim. Heh? Where is he?"

"In de libery, sah."

"So, puffing his long reed pipe, Eyebright rolled down the steps of the porch and across the intervening space to the detached wooden building which served as the Fool's office and library. Pushing the door open with his stick, he ascended the steps and entered, exclaiming, as the door swung together behind him, "Hello, Kirkwood, is this you? What the devil are you doing here?"

The rest of the company drifted into the spacious sitting-room, and for half an hour Eyebright and his visitor were forgotten. At the end of that time his rotund face appeared at the door, and he hastily motioned to the Fool to come out into the hall. As soon as he came, and the sitting-room door was shut, Eyebright caught his hand, and said, in tones trembling with excitement, "Colonel, I'll be damned if the bottom hasn't fallen out at last! Don't ask me any questions. Bring Judge Denton over to the office. Quick! Don't let on that anything is up! I daren't show my head in there. Everybody would know something was wrong. But you Yankees—you could keep your faces straight if the world was coming to an end!"

Ralph Kirkwood Agrees to Testify

THE FOOL DID AS requested and, upon their entering the office, was surprised to find there a young man of good family in the neighborhood, whom Mr. Eyebright introduced to the judge as Ralph Kirkwood. "He says he's got something to say to you, Mr. Denton, which, judging from what he's told me, will be of interest to a good many." Eyebright spoke with a great effort at self-restraint.

"Yes," said Kirkwood absently: "there's a thing on my mind I've wanted to get off it for a long time."

"I will hear any thing you have to say, Mr. Kirkwood," said the judge with some formality, "but I must warn you that any thing you say must be purely voluntary and is given without threat or promise. I can not hear it otherwise."

"So Mr. Eyebright said," responded Kirkwood, without looking up.

"And I must further advise you," remarked the judge, "that any thing you may say here may be used against you upon trial for any crime."

"It makes no difference," said Kirkwood after a moment. "I can not keep still any longer. I haven't had a good night's rest since it occurred. I went to Texas, and it followed me there. I came home, and it came with me. It's been with me all the time and given me no rest, night nor day. I can see him now just as plain as I saw him that night!"

"See who?" asked the judge in surprise.

"Jerry Hunt," responded Kirkwood, in the same matter-of-fact, even tone, and without looking up from the smoldering fire in the grate on which his gaze had all the time rested.

If he could have seen the look of horror and amazement which his auditors exchanged, it would perhaps have surprised him almost as much as his declaration did them. Surrounded year after year by this terrible organization, whose secret blows had fallen upon every side, with no tangible clew to their source, there had grown up in the minds of these men a conviction that there would some time come a day when confidence would be lost between the perpetrators of these crimes, and they would turn upon each other and confess their evil deeds. They thought, that, when that time did come, there would be a race to be among the first to confess.

It is true there had been before some defections from this body, who had disclosed something, in a general way, of its workings, but nothing of any importance. Indeed, their disclosures had been regarded with more of ridicule than respect, because of the conspicuous ignorance which they manifested of what they pretended to disclose. They were usually attended, too, with some circumstance of suspicion antecedently or subsequently occurring, which had destroyed almost all confidence in their verity, or the good faith of the parties making them. That they should at this peculiar moment be confronted with the prospect of a revelation of one of the most noted of its crimes may well have startled them from their composure. Servosse remembered Eyebright's declaration, "The bottom has fallen out at last!"

"What do you know about Jerry Hunt?" asked the judge, as soon as he could master his emotion.

"I know a heap about his death," said Kirkwood, with a sigh—"a heap more'n I wish I did."

"Is it that you wish to tell me about?"

"Yes—that for one thing."

"Well," said the judge, "this thing must be done deliberately and in order. You remember my caution. Colonel Servosse, will you take a pen, and write down what Mr. Kirkwood says. Please lock the door, Mr. Eyebright, so that we may not be interrupted."

The first of Ch. 38, "All the World Was in a Sea," in *A Fool's Errand* by Albion Tourgée.

27. Justice Denied

A Klansman with a Conscience

Michael W. Perry

As a writer, Albion Tourgée often described a murder from several different angles. That's what he did with John Walters's murder by Democratic party leaders in a wealthy Black Belt county. That's what he also does in this chapter with the murder of Uncle Jerry by the party's zealous and violent activist arm, the Ku Klux Klan.

In Chapter 17 we read about Uncle Jerry's murder as seen through the curtains of their homes by those who lived in Verdenton—frightened people, both black and white. In this chapter we hear about what happened that terrible night from one of the Klansmen who participated in the killing. He's the Mr. Ralph Kirkwood introduced in the previous chapter. Note his reasons for being involved in the Klan:

• First, "almost all the boys" in his school were joining.
• Second, "it seemed right good fun."
• Third, men he was "accustomed to think well of" approved of the Klan's deeds.
• Fourth, for its fouler "decrees," the Klan often used people from other counties who did not know the victim and thus felt no sympathy.

The unfortunate Ralph Kirkwood has discovered too late that none of those excuses eases the guilt he now feels. To his great credit, he is willing to name names and assign blame.

Eyebright did as directed. Servosse placed himself at a table with writing materials before him, and the judge continued—"Now, Mr. Kirkwood, we will hear any thing you have to say. Speak slowly, so that it may be written down. Take your own course and your own time."

"Well," said Kirkwood, "I suppose you wish to know it all. I was a student here at Verdenton in the year 18__. I belonged to the Klan—almost all the boys in the school did. I belonged to Camp No. 4, which met at Martin's most of the time. The sheriff, Colonel Abert, was a member and was one of the officers. I think he was what they call a South Commander. My uncle was one of the officers too.

We were all sworn to obey orders. The oath was very strong, and we were all sworn to kill anybody who did not obey, or who revealed any of the secrets of the order. I was at Mr. Hoyt's school—had been there better than a year. I was preparing for the ministry then. I had been on two or three raids when people were whipped, and never thought much about it. In fact, it seemed right good fun, riding round in disguise at night, frightening niggers, and white folks too sometimes. **I didn't think much about whether it was right or not. There were plenty of old men in it who decided all such things, and men that I had always been accustomed to think well of, so I supposed it was all right.**

"One day my uncle came in and brought my horse. He put him in Mr. Crather's barn. Then he came to me, and told me that Camp No. 4 had got a decree from a Rockford camp to make a raid in Verdenton. You know that is the way they do. A camp hardly ever executes its own decree. They send it to another camp, or two or three others, and the camps that get it have to detail men to execute it.

He said our camp would send a squad which would meet another squad from Camp No. 9, at the forks of the road near the Widow Foster's, and I was ordered to meet them and act as guide for them, as I was well acquainted about Verdenton. He asked me if I knew where about half a dozen white men and about as many of the leading niggers lived. I told him I did. He said my disguise was in my saddle-bags on the colt. I was to meet the raid just above the Widow Foster's at nine o'clock.

"I thought it was all right and, when the hour came, I rode out to the Widow Foster's and met our folks. Pretty soon afterward the party came from No. 9. The East Commander of that camp was among them, and he took charge. His name is Watson. He's here in the county yet.

We went into an old pine field opposite the Widow Foster's and put on our disguises. We had just been in our own clothes before.

"Then Watson took command and organized the raid very strictly. He asked me if I knew Jerry Hunt's house. I told him I did. He said that was the man they wanted. Then he said that they had a decree from the Rockford Camp to visit the extreme penalty (that meant kill, always) on Jerry Hunt, but nothing was said as to how, so he left that to the camp then. It was voted that it should be by hanging. I don't reckon anybody voted against it.

"Then we started on. I rode beside Mr. Watson in the lead. When we came near the colored village west of the town, he ordered out pickets to stop on every corner, and some patrollers to ride up and down the streets, and prevent any interruption. They had orders to shoot anybody that gave the alarm or interfered with them at all.

Then we went to Jerry Hunt's house, and Mr. Watson tried the door, and it wasn't even locked. He opened it and thought at first there was nobody there. Then we went in, and Watson struck a match, and there was Uncle Jerry, laying there on the bed, sleeping as quiet and peaceful as a child. We waked him up, took the bed-cord out of the bed, and tied him on to the horse next to the one I rode. He never said nothing after we waked him up, only, 'Lord Jesus, have mercy!,' 'Father, forgive 'em!,' and 'Come, Lord Jesus, come quickly!' At least, I didn't understand any thing more. He was praying all the way in and never offered any resistance at all.

"When we got in there, they rode down by the trees nigh the Courthouse. I had been feeling mighty bad all the way, and when they halted, and began to make preparations, I rode out towards the Courthouse, so as not to see anything more." He stopped abruptly.

"Well, did you see anything more?"

"Yes," he responded with a sigh. "I couldn't help looking around after a while. And, just as I did so, some one drew a match and held it up, and I saw the face of Uncle Jerry as he hung there on the limb. I've been seeing it ever since, gentlemen."

"Did you recognize any of the men?" said the judge.

"Must I answer that?" asked Kirkwood.

"Just as you choose," said the judge coolly. "You have already confessed enough for your own conviction."

"Of course," said Kirkwood thoughtfully. "And they got me into this trouble and thousands of other good young men too. I'm going to make a clean breast of it, gentlemen, and tell all I know. My conscience would not be any easier, if I screened these men, than it is now. Yes, I recognized a good many."

Then he named some forty men whom he could remember having seen and said he had nothing more to say about it. What he had said was read over to him and signed by him.

"I shall have to hold you to answer a charge of murder, Mr. Kirkwood," said the judge, with a choked voice.

"I suppose so," said Kirkwood. "And I'm guilty. I don't deny the fact. But I shall sleep quiet tonight, which is what I haven't done before since that night. I've only one request to make, Judge."

"What is that?"

"Don't send me to the jail in Verdenton. I don't want to dodge or run—'twouldn't do any good to do so now—but, you know, if I were put in that jail now, I'd be hanging on the same limb they hung Jerry Hunt on before two days were over."

It was arranged that he should be held in custody without being sent to jail at that time. And then the three overwrought men turned to each other, and clasped hands solemnly, with the full conviction that "the bottom had indeed fallen out," and that thereafter it might be said of that section, that "the nights are wholesome."

There had been many knocks at the door in the mean time. It was now opened, and their friends who crowded in were briefly informed of the facts. Servosse slipped away into the house and informed his wife and daughter.

But the night was not yet ended. By some strange intuition, these facts seemed only transpired almost before they had taken place. Others came to confess other crimes and to confirm the confession of young Kirkwood. Hour by hour evidence accumulated, until, that very night, all the ramifications of the Klan in that county and much in adjacent ones were laid bare before the magistrate. It was a strange scene indeed, and the party who had assembled at Warrington in expectation of a night of vigil were kept awake by excitement, surprise, and gratitude at the marvelous turn of affairs.

The middle of Ch. 38, "All the World Was in a Sea," in *A Fool's Errand* by Albion Tourgée.

28. PUNISHING THE INNOCENT

A Moral Imagination
Michael W. Perry

We've now reached the most terrible point in our story—the one I've been warning you about. This tale does not end happily. You know enough history to understand that. It ends with many decades of unhappiness and suffering, with tired, overworked, impoverished parents and cold, hungry children crying in the night for a scrap of food. The hopes of Judge Thomas Denton and others that they could secure the "well-being of future generations" would not be realized.

Yes, the evil-doers among the planters win. That means a cruel, cotton-based economy with poverty the common lot of many blacks and whites. For generations, the region will have little to offer. Immigrants with energy and new ideas stay away, fearful bigotry would be directed at them. Factories also stay away, not wanting to deal with the complexities of a race-obsessed society. Even the planters suffered for their folly. The Union blockade created other sources for cotton. Growing it would never be as lucrative as before the Civil War.

The only attraction the Southern economy could offer was what the cotton planters had created—cheap, unskilled labor. When Southerner leaders thought outside their 'grow cotton' box, they turned to processing cotton. Eventually they would steal cotton mills away from New England by offering even lower wages.

I know. My maternal grandfather worked at one of those cotton mills for much of his life. I know little about what he did. He never talked about it. He got up about five each morning to leave for the mill and arrived back at his small hilltop farm about three in the afternoon to work the land. Even as a child I understood that his not talking about his job meant it was bad. That was the reality of life in the Old South. For millions, it was not romantic or pleasant.

The white supremacists also win, and that means racism and segregation, as well as flare-ups of Klan-like violence. Worst of all, the Democratic party wins. That brought rotten politics, with crony pay-to-play capitalism, and shoddy, segregated schools. I saw that as a kid and hated it so much that in the sixth grade I thought of immigrating to Australia, even sending off for a packet of immigration information. Other than the kangaroos, I knew nothing about the country—just than that it was as far as possible from the madness around me.

There were also losers. Black people lost the most. For some, their lives were worse than under slavery, with the sole benefit that at least now they could flee when conditions grew too terrible. The poor of both races were ill-paid agricultural laborers with no hope for a better future. Child labor and poor schools meant their children could never escape. Harper Lee has Scout describe the plight of the rural white poor in *To Kill a Mockingbird*. You might want to read it.

All that was deliberate. Generation after generation, their labor was needed to chop and pick cotton, so they had to be kept down. Because that was calculating and willful, it was hard to change. As a young boy in the 1950s, I attended a 4-H summer camp for poor rural white boys that my father helped organize. Even as a fourth-grader I could tell those boys were malnourished.

Albion Tourgée sensed all this wrongness to come and was obviously angry when he wrote this chapter. Since this is the most historically complicated chapter in his book, I'll explain what he says.

1. No Moral Imagination

FIRST, NEVER FORGET THAT powerful, highly connected, and well-educated people, both North and South, supported white supremacy. That bothered Tourgée immensely, particularly those he met when he lived in North Carolina. He knew those people and, even if they didn't regard him as a friend, they treated him politely. He had trouble believing they could be "the perpetrators, encouragers, or excusers of such acts." How could people who seemed good, he asks, do evil?

There's an answer, and it lies in the difference between *moral conformity* and *moral imagination*. **Moral conformity meant following the rules as taught by those around them.** What others regarded as wrong they see as wrong. What those others regard as right they see as right. They can be no worse or better than their culture. Since slavery had devalued the lives of black people, moral conformists devalued their lives. On the other hand, in areas where that culture taught them to be good, they were good. They could be polite and civil to fellow planters, even with a Yankee carpetbagger such as Servosse.

Moral imagination is different. It's what is meant by expressions like walking in someone else's shoes or treating people as you'd like to be treated. **When you exercise moral imagination, you are trying to understand how others feel even when they are different from you and to act on that.** That's what this book has been about. Tourgée used a variety of people to expand our imagination, so we understand how others felt and suffered. That's why he told us about John Walters and Uncle Jerry. The pictures and comments I've added do the same. I want you to see, perhaps for the first time, the poor blacks and whites who suffered under this racial madness, and to understand what life must have been like for them and their children.

I went through something similar in a different situation. In *My Nights with Leukemia: Caring for Children with Cancer*, I describe what happened to me when, through a chain of events I'd not planned, I found myself working night shift at a top children's hospital caring for kids battling leukemia. I worked alongside a nurse. She managed their drugs, while I gave hands-on care. Without treatment the cancer is always fatal, so what we were doing was extremely important.

From the start, I promised myself that I would not just go through the motions, doing only what I was told. I would do my best to understand these kids and help them in every way possible. Yes, I knew I could never really grasp what it meant to be little child fearing death, but I would do my best.

One of my patients was a slender little black girl of about eight that I've named Susie. She was dying of a tumor in her chest that had so wrapped itself around the arteries going to her heart that any attempt to cut it out would have killed her. Still worse, for reasons that were never explained, she had no family even visiting her. She wasn't just dying. She was dying all alone and terrified.

I did my best, squeezing out almost an hour from my heavy work load each night to rock her to sleep. But that wasn't enough. She would wake again and again. With six other sick children to care for, I could not rock her to sleep a second time. I was so frustrated, here's what I wrote in my book.

> The trouble began with a short sentence I'd written in the girl's flow sheets: "This girl needs someone to stay with her at night." A day nurse with a nasty bent spotted it and informed the head nurse, who was Most Unhappy with me. That wasn't the proper thing to put in nursing notes, she told me sternly.
>
> I said nothing, but I wasn't repentant. This girl did need someone to stay with her overnight. Where else was I going to write that? Should I scrawl it on the walls like graffiti?
>
> Looking back, I wish I'd made more trouble, raising such a fuss that some kind soul would have been found to befriended this lonely little girl during in her last weeks on earth. Perhaps I should have even placed a longer and more strongly worded note in her medical chart, where usually only physicians made comments. That would have been even more Not Done, but might have brought some much needed results. After all, Susie's doctors bore the ultimate responsibility for her care.

Instead, hers was one of the saddest deaths I saw. To die young is bad. To die young and completely alone is infinitely worse. The fact that some nurses on the unit had hearts of stone shouldn't have deterred me. I should have done whatever it took to get her help.

That explains, perhaps better than anything else, the difference between moral conformity and moral imagination. No, it wasn't that this children's hospital was a cruel place. As I point out in the book, it was just that abandoning children to the hospital was so uncommon that the hospital had no policies, procedures or rules for dealing with them. (Hospitals now have child life specialists trained for such situations.) As a result, these dreadful moral conformists were told nothing and therefore understood nothing. All this head nurse and day nurse understood were rules about what went into nursing flow sheets.

Fortunately, there were nurses who did have the moral imagination to know what do even when the hospital's rules were silent. In the case of little Susie, when she began to die, one of the nurses—on her own initiative and on her time—stayed over, holding her and talking with her so she would not die all alone.

That stark contrast between moral conformity and moral imagination also existed in this North Carolina community. The rules did say that they should treat Comfort Servosse tolerably well. After all he was white, educated, and from their land-owning social class even if he was a Yankee. But these seemingly nice people could not—or at least did not—imagine what is was to be one of these newly freed slaves or to be one of those impoverished 'Radical' Republicans who were demanding honest government and better schools.

For an example, think of a planter who leased part of his land to sharecroppers, both black and white. Under slavery, he'd have worried about his slaves and their health. They were, after all, a major investment much like horses and cows. That's a good business practice rule and requires no imagination. But with the end of slavery, he worried far less about them. The rules about business no longer applied. If they die, he lost nothing. He could simply hire someone else. He rents his workers rather than owns them.

If someone had forced him, this planter might have noticed that his sharecroppers looked ill-nourished on their all-corn diet and that their little tin-roofed, one-room shack might be terribly cold in winter and hot in summer. But no one forced him to think that way. All they thought about was what he thought about—the threat poor black and white voters posed to traditional planter dominance. *That* he knew had to be prevented, and *that* was why he and they supported the Democratic party, the party of the rich that—then and now—merely pretends to be the party of the poor, yelling that foul lie so loudly many believe it.

That's also why this planter didn't deplore Klan violence—merely the necessity for it. As we'll see, he was willing to see the Klan disbanded when its dreadful purpose has been achieved, but he can't imagine why anything it did deserves punishment. In fact, it's those who *fought* the Klan who draw his wrath. They made trouble, and he doesn't like that. Moral conformity does not like to be challenged. It does not like to be forced to think. That's because it does not use its imagination. For a near-perfect parallel, think about legalized abortion today. You'll find the same lack of imagination and the same hostility to critics.

2. Ridiculous Excuses

SECOND, RIDICULOUS EXCUSES WERE offered to confuse people about that evil. In a paragraph that's difficult to follow today, Tourgée (as Servosse) rejects the excuses that were being offered for the Ku Klux Klan. The violence done in its name, some were saying, were merely cases of "personal hostility, or a semi-public animosity" masking themselves as the Klan actions. By claiming that, they hoped to deflect criticism of white supremacy. If whites could behave as bad as the Klan had acted, why should they be on top? Their excuse was that those bad deeds were merely personal vendettas by a few, exceptions to the general rule.

Not so, said Tourgée. The Klan existed to terrorize and kill, as its members were now admitting under oath. In addition, he points out, nothing personal was involved. "[T]he victims were uniformly of one mode of political thought"—that meant that they were Republicans like John Walters—"or had specific relations which placed them in antagonism with the purposes of the organization"—that meant that they were either black leaders such as Uncle Jerry or whites who treated black people kindly, such as Comfort Servosse.

3. Protecting the Guilty

THIRD, TO BETTER PROTECT the guilty, the pardon was extended to include the innocent and victims. Tourgée explains that, to prevent the public from drawing the logical conclusion that "the members of the 'Ku-Klux Klan,' the 'Invisible Empire,' the 'Constitutional Union Guards,' and other organizations which had constituted orders or degrees of the Klan" must have been guilty of some terrible crimes, those legislators also pardoned "the members of the 'Union Leagues,' 'Red Strings,' and other secret societies, for all acts done in pursuance of the counsels of such societies. Strangely enough these societies were not known to have counseled any unlawful acts."

In short, state legislatures pretended to pardon the innocent and the victims of the Klan to distract attention from the fact that their real intention was to pardon the guilty. Those innocent and the victims, we have seen, were black people, along with anti-planter Unionists and Radical Republicans. Bizarre isn't it? Those who have to justify the unjustifiable often behave in strange ways. These people need to be subject to a lot more ridicule than they've gotten thus far.

4. Too-sweeping Pardons

FOURTH, THE PARDONS WERE too sweeping, extending even to those who denied their guilt. Here, Tourgée as Servosse turns his attention to the state legislatures which were by this time almost exclusively Democratic. Realizing that the Klan faced prosecution, "most of them passed immediately an act of amnesty and pardon for all who had committed acts of violence in disguise, or at the instigation of any secret organization."

He goes on to point out that this pardon was so zealous and sweeping, it even pardoned those in the Klan who were refusing to admit their guilt and those who had not yet been charged. Why? Because many of those legislators had been leaders in the Klan. Recall what John Burleson had warned in Chapter 22.

> We are advancing the power of a [Democratic] party to which we are devoted, it is true; but in so doing we are merely putting power in the hands of its worst elements, against whom we shall have to rebel sooner or later. The leaders in these cowardly raids—such men as Jake Carver and a hundred more whom I could name—will be our representatives, senators, legislators, judges, and so forth, hereafter.

5. Punish those who Protected People

FIFTH AND MOST REVEALING, these Democratic legislators "took care" not to pardon those in positions of power who had fought Klan violence. Yes, that is even more bizarre. Those were the mostly Republican judges, prosecutors, "or any one in authority" who had "the intent of repressing and punishing such acts [by the Klan], or protecting the helpless victims thereof."

In short, Klansmen in the hundreds who'd murdered innocent people would go free, but good people such as Tom Denton, who'd attempted to halt Klan violence, would receive no pardon and could be prosecuted for even the least of infractions as a judge, however petty and contrived. Such was the justice that came with Democratic party rule. Such was the supremacy that white supremacy brought. Not very impressive for Democrats or for the whites who supported them is it? Now maybe you see why, as a boy in grade school, I grew so disgusted with my state's foul politics that I wanted to move to the most distant corner of the planet.

6. Forgetting without Repentance or Reform

THE CHAPTER CLOSES BY mentioning that those who'd supported and pardoned the Klan "in a twelvemonth" wanted its very existence forgotten. A call to put a matter aside and 'move on' is common when matters are handled badly, particularly when that forgetting comes without any repentance or reform by the guilty. In this case, the Klan was disbanded but not punished because its foul purpose had been achieved. It's work done, it was best forgotten.

Notice Tourgeé's closing words about a "bloody shirt." At least as far back as the knife-stabbed toga of Julius Caesar in William Shakespeare's play, *Julius Caesar*, a bloody garment has been used to back up a political argument. In practice, after the Civil War both political parties used bloody shirts.

Republicans appealed to the bloody garments of those who'd died in the war to win the approval of Northern voters, particular war veterans. They emphasized that the war was not just to save the union or end slavery but to provide equal rights for all. That carried on what Abraham Lincoln had said in his Gettysburg Address—"that we here highly resolve that these dead shall not have died in vain."

Democrats had to be more carefully waving bloody shirts. Too much emphasis on Confederate war dead would turn a spotlight on the slave owners who'd pushed the region into that bloody, destructive and futile war. The party needed to do some fancy footwork to transform a war about slavery into one about white supremacy. When I was growing up and to my childish disgust, people were still playing the victim about the war, as if there was anything noteworthy about losing a war fought to defend something as foul as slavery.

Sadly, but for the end of slavery, which was a major accomplishment, those who die really did die in vain. Despite all the goodness and heroism we have seen, this story ends most badly. As the Rev. Martin Luther King would put it a century later, justice delayed became justice long denied. As we close out this book, we see how that happened as told by Tourgée.

T homas Denton was one of those men who believed that crime should be punished, not from resentment toward the offenders, but for what he deemed the safety of others, and especially the well-being of future generations. He therefore began the next day to issue the proper processes of law and pushed with vigor the prosecutions, sitting day by day as a committing magistrate, taking the confessions of hundreds whose awakened fears laid bare the hidden mechanism of thousands of acts of violence.

Those whose confessions related to the most trivial and unimportant of the personal outrages were released upon their own recognizances merely, or were dismissed with a sharp rebuke. Those guilty of more serious crimes were bound as witnesses. Many arrests were made, and a universal reign of terror of the law seemed impending among those who had so recently terrorized others. Already the line of examination was threatening hundreds who had been unsuspected and had involved other hundreds who were deemed equally immaculate.

1. No Moral Imagination

No ONE WAS MORE astounded or distressed at the revelations made than the Fool. He could not understand how men of the highest Christian character, of the most exalted probity, and of the keenest sense of honor, could be the perpetrators, encouragers, or excusers of such acts. He thought that the churches ought to be hung in black, that the pulpit should resound with warning, and the press teem with angry denunciation. He could not understand how the one should be silent, and the other should palliate or excuse.

2. Ridiculous Excuses

OF EXCUSE OR PALLIATION he did not deem that there could be any thing worthy of consideration. The suggestion that it was personal hostility, or a semi-public animosity against individuals, which animated these acts of violence, he deemed unworthy of a moment's thought, for three reasons—because it was negatived by the purpose and scope of the organization, because it was denied by all the confessions of repentant members, and because the victims were uniformly of one mode of political thought, or had specific relations which placed them in antagonism with the purposes of the organization.

Yet the pulpit kept silent, and the press excused. The Fool knew not what to think. There were hundreds of these men whom he knew well, and esteemed highly. Were they deliberately savage and vicious, or was he in error? Was there any absolute standard of right, or were religion and morality merely relative and incidental terms? Was that right in Georgia which was wrong in Maine? Were those ideas of liberty and of universal right, in which he had been reared, eternal principles, or merely convictions—impulses of the moment? He could not tell. He began to doubt even his own experience and reason.

3. Letting the Guilty Go Free

NEVER WAS THE HORROR which attended this secret organization so fully realized. Even those who had suffered most were moved to pity. Now that the law, stern and inexorable, was about to lay its hand upon them, the cry for charity and mercy came up from every corner. The beauty of peace and recognition was heralded throughout the land.

Fortunately, the Legislatures of the several States were in session, and most of them passed immediately an act of amnesty and pardon for all who had committed acts of violence in disguise, or at the instigation of any secret organization.

4. Too-sweeping Pardons

AND IN THE EXCESS of their zeal and lest it should be supposed that they desired to screen only their friends, they extended their mantle of forgiveness so as to cover apparently the innocent as well as the guilty—those who sought no pardon, as well as the kneeling suppliants.

In short, they pardoned not only the perpetrators of these outrages, but, in a reckless determination to forgive, they even pardoned the victims! In this act of wholesale forgiveness they included not only the members of the "Ku-Klux Klan," the "Invisible Empire," the "Constitutional Union Guards," and other organizations which had constituted orders or degrees of the Klan, but also the members of the "Union Leagues," "Red Strings," and other secret societies, for all acts done in pursuance of the counsels of such societies. Strangely enough these societies were not known to have counseled any unlawful acts. But these legislators were bound to show that "the quality of mercy is not strained."

5. Punish those who Protected

THEY TOOK CARE, HOWEVER, not to pardon any, even the least, infraction of the law, or assumption of power, committed by the Executive, or any one in authority, for the purpose and with the intent of repressing and punishing such acts, or protecting the helpless victims thereof. There are some things which can not be forgiven, even in an era of "reconciliation"!

6. Forgetting without Repentance or Reform

SO THE KU-KLUX WAS buried. And such is the influence of peace and good-will, when united with amnesty and pardon, that in a twelve-month it was forgotten, and he who chanced to refer to so old and exploded a joke was greeted with the laughter-provoking cry of the "bloody shirt."

The last part of Ch. 38, "All the World Was in a Sea," in *A Fool's Errand* by Albion Tourgée.

29. MR. RACIST ROOSTER

Michael W. Perry

The memory is so vivid, I could easily return to within a few yards of the spot. It was the fall of 1954, and I was standing on my first-grade playground looking 'catty-cornered' across a nearby intersection at several children about four or five years old who were playing in the front yard of a small white house. "Stupid," I thought, and stupid it was.

It was stupid because those children were black and, in the next year or two when they started school, they would *not* cross the street to my school. No, they'd be sent across town to the black elementary school. That made no sense even to a six-year-old me who's never been outside the South. Even then, I knew madness and folly when I saw it.

Of course I wasn't surprised. I knew about segregation. It was all around me. What mystified me was where it came from. I almost never heard adults talk about it. If you want a parallel, imagine living in a town where people stay indoors on Thursdays, never venturing out, with their doors locked and shades drawn, as if avoiding something terrible, but never explaining why. That was racism. How, asked that curious young me, could something that pervasive be so rarely mentioned?

Mr. Racist Rooster

FORTUNATELY, I ENJOYED READING despite those dull-as-dust Alice and Jerry readers that were foisted on my generation. Soon, I was reading what adults read, and that gave me the answer I sought.

In the spring of 1956, while in the second grade, I opened our local newspaper and discovered an entire page taken up with a sample ballot. State and local election primaries were approaching. In the South of that day, the Democratic primary was absolutely crucial. Its winners won the election. That's because the South was a one-party oligarchy (meaning rule by a select few). Politics was so filled with corruption and incompetence, I learned to hate it.

But what struck me most about that ballot was the logo you see on the left at the start of this chapter. Yes, a rooster crowing "White Supremacy for the Right" had been the official logo of the Alabama Democratic party since 1904. Every single candidate in the upcoming election had Mr. Racist Rooster beside his name. They really were that bad.

I'd found my smoking gun and knew who to blame. The South of my youth wasn't just a one-party oligarchy, it was a one-party oligarchy that used racism to stay in power. I'll never forget that, but quite a bit of effort has been expended to keep *you* from realizing that.

Fortunately, nothing that foul could endure the light brought by the civil rights movement of the late 1950s and early 1960s. Times were changing, and the party itself would have to change.

A decade later, near the end of January, 1966, another party primary was looming. That's when the state's Democratic party logo was changed to the one you see on the right. Two words "White Supremacy" were replaced with one word, "Democrats." Given the party's long support for bigotry, that meant little. If you think the party's leaders underwent a moral awakening, you're sadly mistaken.

Fortunately, the message in that logo was so blatant, even newspaper reporters couldn't miss its meaning or fail to be skeptical about what was happening. For once, they got the story right. News reports made clear the change was all about winning elections.

The largest newspaper in the state, *The Birmingham News*, described what happened. In a leadership meeting, the Democratic party's moderate faction, the Loyalists, had defeated the radical faction, the States Righters. The votes were by voice ballot and hence secret but for one, which was close enough, 39 to 32, to suggest that the party was still closely divided.

At this point, it helps to recall the context in which they were voting. The federal Voting Rights Act of 1965 had been in effect for over five months. No longer could black people be kept from voting. Like it or not, they would vote in the 1966 elections. A political party that did not take that into account was in big trouble.

An Associated Press story explained the change. The party's "ruling body" had "abandoned its 'white supremacy' motto Saturday rather than risk the threatened loss of Negro votes in this year's election."

Notice that the party leaders weren't motivated by guilt or showing any repentance. They had not grown warm and caring hearts. Remember, these were Democratic politicos doing what such people always do—whatever it takes to win elections. As the AP noted, the party's leaders were alarmed that, "Some Negro civil rights leaders had threatened to leave the party if the white supremacy motto stayed."

No, the AP did not explain why black people wanted to belong to a party with such a dreadful motto. That would have been an interesting story. Instead the AP said that, "in the opinion of some party leaders, the loss of a potential 150,000 to 175,000 Negro votes would mean the election of more Republican office holders in a state where the GOP has show significant signs of growth in recent years." Notice that the Republican party's low-key support for civil rights was attracting black voters, much as that party had intended during the Eisenhower years.

You see the Democratic party's real motivation in who championed that change. The chief supporter was Charles McKay. *The Birmingham News* noted that earlier he'd authored a Nullification Resolution "which sought to declare null and void the Supreme Court's school desegregation decision." Now, "McKay made it clear that the emblem change was necessary if the Democrats were to attract Negro votes this year."

Same Song, Second Verse

IN SHORT, THE DEMOCRATIC party would do what it had always done— say and do anything to win elections. It had pretended to care about poor whites while leaving them impoverished and poorly educated for generations. Soon it would pretend to care about poor blacks. No change of heart, no weeping and wailing, accompanied by sackcloth and ashes to express their guilt. Just a grim recognition that, with more black people voting, the party needed to change its rhetoric.

This being the Democratic party, we know exactly what they'd do. They would do precisely what they did in Tourgée's day when they needed to cover up their disastrous war to defend slavery and the ugly violence of the Ku Klux Klan. They'd lie, slander, and demonize.

You see that best in how the Democratic party pardoned the guilty among its ranks. These weren't poor white sharecroppers who'd merely checked a ballot box next to Mr. Racist Rooster. These were powerful Southern politicians who'd grown rich defending segregation and imposing misery on millions of people. Yet no racist Southern Democratic politician that I'm aware of ever faced party discipline for their foul deeds. As far as I know, the only Democratic who has ever apologized publicly for his racism was George Wallace after a religious conversion.

No, just as it had done during Reconstruction, the party attacked the innocent. Some blame was dumped on rural whites whose Unionist ancestors (like mine) were murdered for opposing the Civil War and later voting Radical Republican. In fact, the very group of Southerners who least liked the race-baiting, planter-dominated Democratic party were now treated as the cause of the region's woes. That wasn't fair. It wasn't intended to be fair. It was intended to win elections.

Blame was also placed on white voters who, we must admit, *had* voted for politicians who passed racist laws. But strangely, little is said—particularly in the press—about the party that had gotten their votes and actually done the evil deeds. In this morally upside-down world, they were guilty of voting for Democrats, but the Democrats they voted for were apparently not guilty of anything. Remember what I said earlier about *denialist evil*. That's what's happened here.

Nor was much made of the fact that, in the vast majority of the Southern elections, there was no alternative. The only ballot that those white voters ever saw came covered with Mr. Racist Rooster. Who else could they vote for? Their only choice was a lesser evil.

As before, the Democrats also turned to *accusatory evil*. It knew that someone must be blamed for racism so—as with the murder of John Walters—it blamed Republicans. Yes, that was stupid, but it'd worked before and might work again. That it did, particularly with the press.

Keep in mind the facts. The Republican party held only a tiny fraction of the political offices in the Deep South from the late 1870s until the 1970s. Yet the Democrats blamed Republicans for the region's racism and segregation. That was like accusing New Zealand sheep herders for the Nazi Holocaust. Much as they had done a century earlier with the murder of John Walters, the news media bought the Democratic party's argument—hook, line and sinker. No hayseed come to the big city was ever so gullible.

President Dwight Eisenhower

PERHAPS THE BIGGEST LIE you'll hear today is that during the 1960s, the Republican party developed a "Southern strategy" to attract racists. Left unmentioned is the party whose open racism they were supposedly stealing voters away from. Also, little is said about what the Republicans actually did during those years.

The truth lies in the strategy that the Republican party actually took. It began in the 1950s when Dwight Eisenhower was President. Under Eisenhower the Republican party began a quiet but effective Southern strategy to end segregation.

That's best illustrated by Frank M. Johnson, a graduate of the University of Alabama's law school, a Republican, and an ardent foe of segregation. In 1955, Eisenhower appointed him as a federal district court judge for central Alabama. Segregation had been declared constitutional in a 1896 U.S. Supreme Court decision called *Plessy v. Ferguson*. Johnson helped kill it. In 1956 he decided in favor of Rosa Parks, striking down segregated seating on Montgomery buses and ruling:

> We cannot in good conscience perform our duty as judges by blindly following the precedent of *Plessy v. Ferguson*.... In fact, we think that *Plessy v. Ferguson* has been impliedly, though not explicitly, overruled, and that, under the later decisions, there is now no rational basis upon which the separate but equal doctrine can be validly applied to public carrier transportation within the City of Montgomery and its police jurisdiction.

That wasn't all. Over his long career, Judge Johnson made over a dozen key civil rights decisions. In 1965 he ordered Governor George Wallace to permit the Rev. Martin Luther King's famous Selma March.

It's also revealing that the first attempt to pass a new civil rights law since Reconstruction did not come under FDR. The obsession New Deal liberals had with regulation never included restricting segregation. The change began under President Eisenhower. When his administration approached Congress with the Civil Rights Act of 1957, it was to fix a terrible ill. Only 20 percent of the nation's eligible blacks were registered to vote. In the South, the situation was even worse.

Unfortunately, Congress was dominated by Democrats who did not want to take any step that would weaken the party's dominance of Congress. Since nothing threatened that more than civil rights, it played a vile little game. Northern Democrats would sponsor a measure so extreme it had little chance of coming up for a vote. Southern Democrats would then block it in committee. Both would take credit for doing nothing. It was a cruel charade.

With Eisenhower and the Republicans behind this bill, if enough Democrats could be found, it was likely to pass out of committee and come up for a vote. So Lyndon Johnson (LBJ), a powerful Texas Democrat and the Senate Majority leader, sent Eisenhower's bill to James Eastland, a Mississippi Democrat who, as expected, gutted the bill of any effective enforcement before it reached the floor of Congress.

Yet even that toothless bill proved too much for many Democrats. In the House, 91 percent of the Republicans supported it versus just 52 percent of the Democrats, an almost a two-to-one ratio. In the Senate, it was supported by 100 percent of the Republicans but only 61 percent of the Democrats. Those Democrats weren't just Southerners. The Senator from Massachusetts, a less than courageous John Kennedy, voted against it. Due to those weak enforcement provisions, black voter registration only rose to about 23 percent.

Civil Rights Legislation in the 1960s

YOU MIGHT THINK CONGRESS would take up voting rights first. No, the next major step was the Civil Rights Act of 1964, which outlawed discrimination in jobs, schools, and public facilities. It was based on the Civil Rights Act of 1875—the ultimate vindication of those much-maligned Radical Republicans, although it's doubtful that any Democratic politician had the decency to say so.

Again, the act drew far more support from Republicans than Democrats. In the Senate, 82 percent of the Republicans voted for it versus 69 percent of the Democrats. In the House 80 percent of the Republicans voted for it versus 63 percent of the Democrats. Al Gore Sr., father of Bill Clinton's Vice-President, voted against it. The Republican party's real Southern strategy—eliminating race as a political issue—was slowly taking hold. Faced with a changing public, even the Democrats were coming along, although only grudgingly.

With the 1964 elections now safely behind them, Congress took up the Voting Rights Act of 1965. The numbers got better. In the Senate, it was supported by 94 percent of the Republicans versus 75 percent of the Democrats. In the House the party difference was less, 82 percent of the Republicans versus 78 percent of the Democrats.

Particularly in the South, House Democrats were scared. They'd be up for election in two years facing a much larger black vote. As we've seen, just months after this act was passed, the Alabama Democratic party removed "White Supremacy for the Right" from its official logo. Fear of political defeat accomplished what decency would never do.

The Myth of a Southern Strategy

THERE IS A MYTH abroad that perhaps you've heard. We're told that during this time the Republican party's strategy was to capture the racist Southern vote away from a mysterious party whose name is almost never mentioned. Consider how odd that is.

First, remember the Republican party was founded in 1854 to oppose slavery. For over a century it defended civil rights almost alone, although more weakly that it ought thanks to all the "n___r lover" slanders from Democrats. Why abandon that just as racism was becoming unfashionable and millions of blacks were gaining the right to vote? What sense does it make for the Republicans in Congress to cast votes as high 100% (the Senate in 1957) for black voting rights, if they intended to court white racists and ignore black voters? That'd be incredibly stupid. Only journalists and those who believe what they read in newspapers could fall for a lie that transparent.

Second, the Democrats knew their racist supporters watched their votes. That's why John Kennedy and Al Gore Sr. voted against civil rights legislation. Those who believe this myth must assume those same racists would *not* pay any attention to how Republicans had been voting. In the decade ending in 1965, over 88% of Republicans had voted for the three key civil rights bills, while only 66% of the Democrats had. Even those statistics understate party differences. Many Democrats were in states where a vote for civil rights required no courage but did require a sense of decency and fair play.

The Democrats New National Strategy

THOSE WHO UNDERSTAND THE Democratic party knew what would happen next. The party's basic tactics would remain the same—winning elections by stirring up envy, fear and hatred. That was a given. All that would change was the race they targeted. The party that pretended to care for poor whites would now pretend to care for poor blacks. In practice, that meant that their long-held Southern strategy of pitting one group against another would become a national one. No longer able to dupe Southern whites, they had to dupe other groups, north and south.

The results were predictable. It was no accident that a century of 'championing' the rights of Southern poor whites had left them abjectly poor. That was built into the party's scheming. Kept poor, badly educated, and feeling that they needed the party to protect them, they were an easily manipulated voting bloc.

The same would be true for the Democratic party's new voting blocs. There can be no worse fate that can strike an impoverished, disadvantaged group that to be subjected to the 'benefits' the Democratic party brings to it. The party will do virtually everything its power to keep them impoverished, badly educated, disadvantaged, and dependent. What it had done to poor whites, it now did to poor blacks and (more recently) to Hispanic immigrants.

Only the details changed. Cheap labor had been at the center of the party's Southern strategy. Poor Southern whites typically lived in rural areas and, like poor blacks, provided ill-paid, pliable field workers for the rich planters the party was eager to help. A similar deception lay at the center of the party's new strategy, particularly in Northern cities. The pliable votes of poor, inner-city blacks kept in power corrupt big-city governments that rewarded lucrative, pay-to-play businesses and powerful unions. (Detroit is a good example.) To keep those votes, inner-city blacks and (later) Hispanics must be kept poorly educated, with their families devastated by welfare, crime and drugs.

That's why well-meaning, good-hearted people—liberals, libertarians, and conservatives—get nowhere when they attempt to improve conditions for the inner-city poor. Providing them with good schools, stable families, ample jobs, and crime-free communities does not serve the interests of the Democratic party therefore it must not be.

In short, if you want to understand politics in America, never forget what we have seen dramatized in this book—the Democratic party's chronic indifference to suffering people, accompanied its nasty zeal to win elections by spreading anger, fear and bigotry among those it pretends to help but intentionally harms. That's the key to understanding almost all that has troubled our nation for almost two centuries.

With that I close this book. Look for more from me on this topic.

www.ingramcontent.com/pod-product-compliance
Lightning Source LLC
Chambersburg PA
CBHW051253250626
47155CB00009B/3282